TERRY LYNN THOMAS is the USA Today bestselling author of six historical mysteries. *The Betrayal* and *The Witness* are the first two books in the Olivia Sinclair series, Terry's foray into the world of domestic suspense. When she's not writing, Terry likes to spend time outdoors hiking or gardening with her husband and her dogs.

Keep up with Terry on:
Facebook: https://www.facebook.com/terrylynnthomasbooks/
X: @TLThomasbooks
Instagram: @terrylynnthomasbooks
or via her website: www.terrylynnthomas.com.

The Suspect

TERRY LYNN THOMAS

ONE PLACE. MANY STORIES

HQ
An imprint of HarperCollins*Publishers* Ltd
1 London Bridge Street
London SE1 9GF

www.harpercollins.co.uk

HarperCollins*Publishers*
Macken House, 39/40 Mayor Street Upper,
Dublin 1 D01 C9W8

This paperback edition 2024

1
First published in Great Britain by
HQ, an imprint of HarperCollins*Publishers* Ltd 2024

Copyright © Terry Lynn Thomas 2024

Terry Lynn Thomas asserts the moral right to be
identified as the author of this work.
A catalogue record for this book is
available from the British Library.

ISBN: 9780008364847

This book contains FSC™ certified paper and other controlled
sources to ensure responsible forest management.

For more information visit: www.harpercollins.co.uk/green

Printed and Bound in the UK using
100% Renewable Electricity at CPI Group (UK) Ltd

For Doug for always and ever.
XO

Prologue

Asher Ridgeland tried to wake up, but the deep sleep wouldn't let him go. Cold air whispered down his spine, continuing along the backs of his legs and his feet. Touching his leg, he realized it was bare, and that he lay naked on the cold floor. His stomach roiled as nausea threatened. He tried to open his eyes, but the effort proved too difficult, so he closed them again, letting his conscious mind swim toward the pool of darkness. His thoughts came in random waves, like an out-of-sequence film, clear thinking just out of reach. Every time his brain formed a thought – *What happened to my clothes? Where am I?* – the ability to reason would slip away. He was cold to his core, but when he tried to conjure himself awake, a curtain of fog would descend, carrying him away once again into blissful oblivion.

He dozed. Time passed. He awoke. Needed to pee. He opened his eyes, saw the flat gray light coming through the window, and realized that it was morning and the San Francisco fog had yet to burn off. The tall windows and the sheer curtains were familiar. Mikala's apartment. Grunting, Asher tried to turn on his side, but he didn't have the strength for even that simple task. Through the haze in his brain, a memory from the previous night coalesced. Mikala. Small memories floated through his brain, like pieces of an impossible jigsaw puzzle: his early return from his camping trip, meant as a surprise, Mikala dressed in the lingerie he had bought her for her birthday, two glasses on the coffee table, a cigarette butt in a crystal ashtray. The myriad emotions – shock, surprise, and finally guilt – that played over her face as he stepped into the living room, carrying a bouquet of roses and a heart full of longing. Did his heart break into a million pieces? He only remembered the anger. Yelling. Then what?

Everything after that was a blank. His eyelids became leaden. Unable to keep them open, they shuttered, leaving him in the dark. In the distance a door slammed. Still keeping his eyes closed, Asher tried to cry for help, but the words stuck in the back of his throat, which was as dry as the Mojave.

"Mikala?" His voice came out a whisper.

He recognized the purposeful footsteps as they approached. Lexy Ford, Mikala's roommate. Thank God. Lexy was level-headed, calm under pressure. Shivering from the cold now, Asher knew he needed help. He'd have to trust Lexy to get it for him.

A blood-curdling, primal scream cut through the thick fog in Asher's brain. Lexy. Shouting as though the building were on fire. The rush of adrenaline pushed Asher's eyes open as primal fear propelled him into a sitting position. When he opened his eyes, a constellation of stars burst across his field of vision.

Lexy stood in the doorway to the living room, her face white, pointing her finger. Pointing at Asher? No. Next to Asher. He turned, the effort of it causing the muscles in his neck and upper back to scream in protest. Next to him, Mikala lay on her back. She wasn't moving. Her tongue, blue and swollen, protruded, rendering her once beautiful face into a hideous caricature of itself. Lexy's screams grew louder. Just as Asher tried to cover his ears against the piercing sound, it stopped. The only sound in the room was her gasping breath.

"Oh, no." Asher's voice came out a whisper, the rush of air against the back of his throat painful. Mikala's eyes, usually

2

beautiful and blue and full of life, were now lifeless. A fly landed on the ocean-colored iris of one of them. Mikala didn't blink. Of course she didn't. She was dead.

A hot stream of vomit erupted, taking him by surprise as it puddled on Mikala's stomach and chest. Droplets of it dripped, as if in slow motion, down the side of her body and onto the floor, finally forming a puddle between them. Unable to support his weight, Asher lay back down, his naked body landing in the warm liquid, as the welcome curtain of darkness descended once again.

Chapter 1

Olivia Sinclair walked down the hill toward Magnolia Avenue on this beautiful September morning. To her right, a blanket of fog swirled over Mt. Tamalpais, halting abruptly, as though prohibited by an invisible barrier from snaking its way down Magnolia Avenue. She'd been doing this walk to her office for years, yet she had never tired of the view. As she passed the patisserie, savoring the smells of freshly baked bread and strong coffee, she noticed the figure of a woman standing in the alcove near the doorway to her office. Ava Bledsoe. It had been decades since Olivia had seen Lauren's friend, who was now – at least according to Lauren – desperately in need of a lawyer. As she drew closer to the woman, Olivia could see Ava watching her surroundings warily, as though she worried someone would find her. Olivia recognized that fear, had seen it on hundreds of women during her long career as a divorce attorney.

When the woman's eyes lit on Olivia striding purposefully toward her, she stood a little straighter, as though she were trying to be brave and put her best foot forward. Olivia recognized this behavior too. Resilience. *Good thing*, Olivia thought. If what Lauren Ridley said was true – her dear friend had a proclivity for over-exaggeration – this woman would need every ounce of strength she could muster.

"Olivia?" the woman asked, as Olivia searched her purse for her keys.

"Yes." Olivia smiled warmly. She hesitated, not sure if she should give the woman a perfunctory hug for old times' sake. "Ava? It's been a while. How long? Thirty years or so?" Olivia's office key slid smoothly into place.

"Twenty-eight and a half years to be exact," Ava said, as she scanned the street. "Can we get inside, please? I don't mean to sound paranoid, but my husband . . ."

"Understood." Olivia opened the office door and beckoned the woman to enter. Ava Bledsoe gave an audible sigh of relief when Olivia locked the door behind them. "My office is this way." The woman followed Olivia down the corridor to the office at the back of the building. "Did you want coffee? I'd have to run and get some, but I can easily do that. I'm retired and have been clearing out."

"No, thank you," Ava said, as her eyes swept around the office, taking in the lack of furniture and the pile of papers heaped next to the shredder.

Olivia watched Ava Bledsoe take off the cashmere overcoat and lay it over the chair next to her. By quick calculation, Olivia surmised Ava Bledsoe was now in her mid-fifties. Her hair, naturally dark and professionally maintained was now neglected, as a half inch of gray showed at the roots. Her eyes spoke to her ethereal beauty, blue and set wide in perfect alignment to cheekbones that most women would die for. The way she moved and the width of her shoulders suggested a life of athleticism, but her clothing was loose, likely from stress-induced weight loss. Ava's mouth had a pinched look and the lines around her eyes were deeply etched, dehydrated from lack of sleep. As she reached into her Gucci purse and took out a package of tissues, Olivia noticed the woman's bitten and bloodied cuticles, incongruous against the polish of her clothes and makeup.

Casting her mind back all those years, Olivia remembered

Ava as the fresh-faced young woman who'd turned heads in her youth and had stolen the heart of Lauren's drummer, Ricky Lee. The two had met backstage at one of Lauren's concerts, had fallen instantly in love, and had eloped to Las Vegas for a secret ceremony. Olivia remembered Ava as a naïve but beautiful young woman, in awe of the entire rock-and-roll experience. The music scene reverberated with sorrow when Ricky Lee had died in a car accident months after the wedding. After that, Ava retreated to the recesses of Olivia and Lauren's younger days.

"I've taken to random bouts of crying, thus the tissues. Not sure whether the tears are from joy or sorrow." Once Ava had dried her tears and regained her composure, she leaned back in her chair and focused on Olivia. "Thank you for agreeing to see me. Lauren told me she called in a lifetime of favors to make this happen, but I need help. And I need it fast. When my husband discovers what I've done, he'll hunt me down. If he finds me, he'll kill me."

"Why don't you tell me what you've done, and then we'll discuss what I can do for you."

"I left. I can't believe it, but I've left him, walked out. I need a divorce, but I need to do it so Mark can't find me."

"If your husband is as violent as you say he is, you might be better off with a big firm, one that can provide you with security—"

"Absolutely not," Ava said. "I've tried that. I went to an attorney from one of those so-called *big firms*." Ava made air quotes. "They failed to grasp the seriousness of the situation, especially when they found out my husband is the billionaire icon of the entire financial world, to hear him tell it. He's charming socially, adored by many. He gives to the right charities, belongs to the right club, has a soft spot for the underdog, and is a steward of the environment. This is the shiny façade my husband has cultivated and his team has curated over the years.

"I don't know how much Lauren told you, but all that moral

goodness is a veneer. At home, in private, he's an arrogant blow-hard who takes pleasure in making people – namely me – suffer," Ava said, with an admirable amount of chutzpah. Olivia liked this lady. "That man has been terrorizing me for years. I want to be free of him. I'd like to get divorced. If that cannot happen in a way that makes me feel safe, I'm just going to go home to Sweden. My father is an investment banker. He's received some threats over the past few years, and now has a security detail. My family can protect me there. I don't care about the money, don't care about getting my share. Money doesn't matter if I'm dead. Make no mistake, Mrs. Sinclair. If my husband finds me, he'll kill me."

"Aren't you afraid your husband will come to Sweden, chase you down?"

Ava shook her head. "No. My family is too well insulated."

"Then why don't you just go now?"

"I'm waiting on a new passport. My husband took mine and locked it in his safe. Once I get it, I'm on a plane."

"How are you going to get your new passport? Don't they need to mail it to you?" Olivia asked.

"I've arranged for it to be delivered to the Swedish Embassy. Again, thanks to my family and my father's connections, I'm getting help. I haven't got a cell phone, so I need to call them. Once they have my passport, I will go to the embassy, get it, and return home to Sweden. To safety. To my family."

"So basically, you just need me to keep you safe for the next forty-eight hours?" Olivia asked. "I think a security firm would be your best bet for something like—"

"And I want to start divorce proceedings, Mrs. Sinclair. I need Mark to know I'm serious about severing ties with him. All ties. I want out of this marriage."

"Okay. Got it. Why don't you give me some backstory? What made you finally leave? If his actions are provable, we could get a restraining order—"

"Are you joking?" Ava laughed, a brittle bark that conveyed her distrust. "Trust me when I tell you a restraining order wouldn't keep him away from me. Mark Bledsoe operates outside the law. And he's careful to protect himself. If he were ever to be charged with domestic violence, he would lose his job. He's being groomed to chair the Securities and Exchange Commission. Jeffers Miller – the company where he works – would fire him immediately if they got wind of what a brute he is. They have a morality clause in their employment contract. So does the television network, for that matter."

Olivia held her pen ready. "What would you like me to do for you? Tell me your ideal scenario." Over the course of her career as a family-law attorney, Olivia had dealt with dozens of women – and a handful of men – who had fled violent situations, sometimes sneaking away in the middle of the night with nothing but the clothes on their back.

"Last November, my husband broke my jaw. He sucker-punched me because he didn't like the way I loaded the dishwasher. I fell and hit my head, suffering a mild concussion. He had to take me to the hospital because a neighbor chose this time to stop by with a package that was delivered to her house by accident." The hand that dabbed her eyes with a tissue shook. "That injury and my well-intentioned neighbor in some strange way saved my life. Had the neighbor not come by, I wouldn't have gotten medical treatment. She insisted on calling an ambulance. Good thing she did. It turned out that I had a concussion.

"When the time came for me to leave the hospital, Mark didn't let me go home. He was afraid that the neighbors would check on me, realize what he had done, and try to get me away while he was at work. He made a generous donation to a private hospital in Arizona and sent me there to recuperate away from prying eyes and our neighbors' suspicions. His plan backfired. During the three months I was there, I slowly recovered myself – the self I was before I married him."

She'd been staring down at her lap while she spoke. Now she raised her eyes and met Olivia's gaze straight on. "The self I was when I first met you and Lauren all those years ago." Olivia recognized the dogged determination, a quality that Olivia not only admired but knew was necessary if Ava were to deal with the difficulties that lay ahead. Extricating herself from a man like Mark Bledsoe would not be easy. At least Olivia now knew Ava would be up to the task.

"We've been married for five years and dated for about a year before we tied the knot. Honestly, Mark was the most loving, charming, gentle man I'd ever met. He wowed me and everyone else in our circle of friends. When he proposed, I accepted immediately. When he wanted a quick wedding in Las Vegas, I accepted that too. That should have been a red flag. The controlling behavior started shortly after our honeymoon, becoming worse as time went on. We were two years in when he hit me for the first time. He backhanded me when I didn't agree with something he said."

Ava ran her hand over her face. "I don't even remember what it was. I threatened to file reports. But he always talked me around, promised he would change, cried and sobbed, and bought me expensive jewelry. I was stupid enough to believe him. I never pressed charges. The fights got worse, louder, and soon the neighbors started calling the police, so we moved to a big, beautiful house in Belvedere, far enough from the neighbors so they couldn't hear us fight.

"Once he had me isolated, his rages became more violent. When he punched me and broke my jaw, he surprised himself, had a flash of awareness of the consequences of his actions. Not out of concern for me, mind you. He just knew that he would lose his job, his prestige, and his money if his abusive ways were to become public. I know the cycle, know how it starts. I'm sure you do, too. Remorseful at first, followed by lavish gifts, bestowed with a seemingly heartfelt apology and a promise to never do it again. But they always do it again, don't they? My broken jaw got me a four-carat diamond and a brand-new Mercedes. Four years ago, he broke my clavicle."

She reached up and touched her collarbone, in the process revealing the jutting bones of her chest. Olivia imagined this woman, frightened for her life, waiting for her husband to leave the house, risking life and limb as she made arrangements to flee to safety.

"As penance for that injury, he bought me – never mind. It's a cycle. An ugly, filthy circle of events. I'm sure you've heard this more times than you care to remember.

"While I was in Arizona, I made friends with one of the nurses. She was an emergency room nurse, who was getting her master's degree in psychology. She had also schemed her way out of an abusive relationship, and in telling me her story of escape, she gave me strength. My time of rest afforded me hours and hours to concoct an escape plan. It started out as a game, planning how I could run away, but by the time I left the hospital, I decided I could be as cunning and manipulative as Mark. After all this time, I knew how to play him, and I set out to do so.

"When I got home from the hospital, I pretended the time away had rekindled my love, that I wanted our marriage to be good again, that our troubles were my fault. In hindsight, I can't believe I pulled it off, but I made him think I would do anything to get back what we had when we first met.

"I set out to convince Mark that I loved him, that he was the center of my world. My husband is so ego-driven, Mrs. Sinclair, that I had him eating out of my hand. He was so grateful, he cried in my arms and promised to do better. Although the physical contact with him sickened me, I played along. I made love to him every night. Dressed in his favorite outfits, pandered to his every whim. I was conning him, and the con job gave me the fortitude to continue. Meanwhile, I was squirreling away money, opening a bank account, and shipping a few personal possessions – some

10

linens and silver that were wedding gifts from my grandmother – home to Sweden.

"Four days ago, when Mark left for work, I packed as many of my personal belongings as I could in three suitcases. Any more wouldn't be manageable. After that, I cleaned out our joint checking account and our joint savings account, walked away, and didn't look back. In case you're wondering, Mark has plenty of money. I did not leave him destitute."

"Understood," Olivia said.

"Once I was ready to go, I called a cab, left my cell phone and my keys on the counter, and walked away from Mark Bledsoe for good."

"I wonder if he's filed a missing person's report."

"He doesn't have to. He'll hire someone private. That way he can find me – and if I'm honest, have me killed – without bringing in the police."

"And the first thing they will do is hunt down that cab driver."

"I know," Ava said. "That's why I had the taxi drop me off at the bus station. Once there, I purchased three bus tickets, one to New York, one to Chicago, and one to Milwaukee. Then I got in another taxi and got dropped off in South San Francisco at a mall. Once there, I changed clothes, put on a wig, and took Golden Gate Transit to Larkspur, where I met Lauren. And here I am, with you. I can give you power of attorney to negotiate my divorce, right? Then I can leave for Sweden once I get my passport."

"Do you anticipate a problem with your passport?" Olivia asked.

"No. I've requested an emergency passport. Once my Swedish citizenship is verified, I'll be able to leave."

"You can't use a power of attorney to have someone start court proceedings. I'm sorry, but if you want the divorce, you are going to have to file papers and have them served on your husband."

"He'll be furious."

"Yes, he will. He won't like you being in control."

Ava Bledsoe reached into her purse and fished around for a

moment. "Damn it. I quit smoking two months ago and still catch myself reaching for one in times of stress." She tossed her purse back onto the chair, leaned back, and crossed her legs.

"I do want a divorce. And I know that once I leave, there's no coming back. You're going to want to verify what I've told you," Ava said. "Please do that. But don't do it in a way that Mark's operatives can find out what you're doing. I know you work with your partner, an ex-cop who is now private. Lauren told me I could trust you both. I am. With my life. I also understand if you don't want to get involved. But the clock is ticking for me. Mark is going to find out that I've taken money. It won't take long for him to discover that I've sold jewelry over the past few months. From there, he'll figure out that I've been planning my escape. The fact that I bested him will kindle his need to get me. Everything I sold belonged to me, but still. This will not sit well with him. He's going to be enraged, and he's going to act. Will you help me?"

"I'm going to take your case, Mrs. Bledsoe. I'm supposed to be retiring, but I'm going to postpone that to help you."

"No, not Bledsoe. From now on, I'm Ava Olson. And thank you, Mrs. Sinclair. I know that you're helping me because Lauren asked you to, and I'm very grateful. I read about what happened with your ex-husband. Being arrested for the murder of his mistress? I read about the way the journalists hounded you; the cameras were camped out across the street from your house. Even though they only managed to get a couple of fleeting shots of you, you never lost your cool; you always seemed so calm, so measured. I also saw the video, where you saved that officer's life. Wasn't she the detective who arrested you for murder? I have no doubt that you know what it's like to be brave."

"By necessity," Olivia said.

Ava tucked a strand of hair behind her ear before she folded her hands on the desk.

"So, what do we do now?"

"We are going to prepare your petition for divorce."

Chapter 2

After her meeting with Ava, Olivia's promise of a short day at the office fell by the wayside. By the time she filed Ava's paperwork with the court, and sent the summons out with a process server to hand-deliver to Mark Bledsoe, it was 6:30 p.m. The smell of garlic and Brian's signature shrimp scampi greeted her as she walked inside and kicked off her shoes, leaving them near the front door. She found Brian standing in front of the stove, a glass of wine in one hand, a wooden spatula in the other. She watched for a minute as he stirred the sauce, set the spatula down and sipped his wine, his well-loved and extremely tattered San Francisco Giants T-shirt covered by her flowered apron, creating a heartwarming domestic tableau. He'd set two places at the bar in the center of the kitchen, complete with a bottle of Taittinger, which sat on ice, ready to be consumed. As she moved into the kitchen, her heart squeezed with love for him.

"Hello there. Sorry I'm late."

"You're here now, and that's all that matters." He fiddled with the buttons on the stove, covered the large skillet, and pulled Olivia into his arms. After a lingering kiss, Brian stepped away and studied her face. She leaned in and savored the warmth of him.

"How did it go with Ava Bledsoe?" Brian asked.

"As to be expected."

Brian moved away and poured them each a glass of champagne. They held their flutes in salute and sipped. Olivia sat on one of the barstools surrounding the island in the middle of the kitchen, while Brian carried the boiling pot of pasta over to the sink and emptied it into the drainer. Once the pasta was drained, he put the noodles back in the empty pan and carried them back to the stove.

"What's wrong?" Olivia could tell by the set of her beloved's shoulders that something was bothering him.

Brian picked up his champagne and sat next to Olivia. "I'm just naturally suspicious."

Olivia ran her hand along Brian's arm. "I know. That's why I love you." While Olivia and Brian sipped their champagne, Olivia gave a rundown of her meeting with Ava. When she was finished, she said, "Now you know what I know. What are your concerns?"

"I don't know, Liv. It's just too pat. Why come to you now? Why even file for divorce? If she's that afraid, it seems like getting away would be the first order of business. I understand her wanting her freedom, needing to legally sever her connection. But if she's so terrified, why not leave? Why not hide in another state until she gets her passport?"

"I didn't think to ask her." Olivia waited while Brian refilled her flute with the golden bubbles. "She's been in touch with the embassy and is awaiting her passport. Once they verify citizenship, she'll get it. If I had to guess, she wants to be around someone she trusts. She wants someone to protect her, but I'm also betting she wants potential witnesses. Mark Bledsoe seems to be about appearances – at least according to Ava. I think she'll simply feel safe if she isn't alone."

"Okay, I'll buy that. Listen, Liv, I know that you and Lauren have a *sisterness* about you. It's obvious when you two are together that your relationship is one of trust and loyalty. But Lauren's called in a big favor here. We're supposed to be retiring, selling the house, and moving near your daughter and granddaughter. Honestly, I'm looking forward to teaching Carly how to fish. And I can tell you miss Denny by the look in your eyes when you talk on the phone. Plus, she probably could use some babysitting."

"Carly's just a baby, my love. You've got a few years before she'll need fishing lessons." Olivia set her flute down. "I do miss Denny. And I'm just as ready as you are to retire. But Lauren was always there for me. When I went into labor to have Denny, Richard was in Washington D.C. trying his first high-profile case. He couldn't be there for the birth. Lauren was. After Denny was born, Lauren moved in and helped me every day, somehow managing that without making me feel like she was invading my space." Olivia gazed off, reminiscing about the past. "She's always been that totally dependable person in my life, and she's rarely asked for anything in return."

"I had no idea," Brian said. "She's a good friend. More than a good friend."

"When I got arrested, the detectives got a search warrant. They tore my house up. As in left no stone unturned. By the time I made bail and came home, Lauren had put everything away. That's the kind of friend she is. She's done favors like that for me, without me asking, the entire time I've known her."

"Don't you find it interesting that she's called in a favor for someone else and not for her?"

"No." Olivia shook her head. "When 'Love You Blind' went to the top of the charts and Lauren's career was launched, she picked up a stalker. We didn't really know what stalking was back then, and there were no laws yet to protect people from that kind of behavior, but there was a man who was really terrorizing Lauren. He'd break into her house and leave notes on her pillow, send her roses . . . I know it sounds like a cliché now, but she really was scared. The police tried to find the guy, no luck.

"Anyway, one night, Ava was at a club where the band was playing. She had just started dating Ricky and was sitting at the bar watching the show. The bartender got a tray of drinks ready for the band and set it on the bar, waiting for the cocktail waitress to deliver it. Lauren was known for ordering Scotch on the rocks back then. Ava saw a man put something in Lauren's drink. She plowed through the crowd, warned Lauren, and was able to point the man out to the police. I don't really know how everything went down, but it turns out this man was Lauren's stalker. The police searched his car and found a notebook full of photos of Lauren, along with a bunch of other evidence."

"So now Lauren owes Ava."

"I guess. But Ava drifted away. She married Ricky Lee, and shortly thereafter, Ricky Lee died. And then Lauren lost touch with her."

"Until now," Brian said.

"You find that suspicious?"

"I might." Brian smiled sheepishly at Olivia, who stood up and threw her arms around his neck.

"Good. You can be suspicious. I wouldn't have taken this case if I didn't have you to help me."

Brian kissed her. "Of course I'll help you. And when this is over, we'll chuck it all in, okay? We'll get out of here and spend the next chapters of our lives reading books, fishing in our new boat, and enjoying our new house."

"That sounds like heaven," Olivia said.

"I understand how hard this is."

"What are you talking about?"

"Selling the house where you raised Denny, moving away from the friends you've had for a lifetime; it's a tremendous step. I appreciate that. If you're not ready, I understand. You had a life in this house, and your garden – I know what your garden means to you."

As he said these words, he'd moved away from Olivia. She closed the space between them and wrapped her arms around his neck, meeting his eyes, connecting with him, so he would know how serious she was.

"I'm ready to sell this house, ready to move. We're going to be near Denny and Carly in Tahoe. I want to make a new garden, a new life, with you, Brian. Once this case is over, we're out of here."

"Okay. Let's eat dinner, drink some more champagne, and then you can tell me about the case. We can make a plan."

"Thank you." Olivia let out a long sigh of relief. "It's going to be a tough one, and I'm going to need your help for protection and investigation."

"You've got it." Brian kissed Olivia's forehead before he turned away and tossed the pasta with olive oil. "Not that I don't love a nice bottle of champagne, but what are we celebrating?" Olivia asked as she topped off their flutes.

"Our offer was accepted." He smiled and held up his glass. "We are now the proud owners of a house in Lake Tahoe."

Later, Olivia and Brian lay entwined on the sofa in front of the crackling fire, the bottle of champagne upside down in the ice bucket.

"The very act of running away speaks to her courage. He's going to hunt her, Brian. Hunt her down like prey."

"This is the Mark Bledsoe who appears on the *Financial News* at least once a week?"

"The very same."

"Have you seen that guy? He's like a Viking. Seriously, Liv. He's a hulking brute of a man, and all muscle."

"I've only seen him peripherally. Definitely got the football-jock vibe." She'd never given Mark Bledsoe more than a passing thought. In just a few short weeks, she expected she would know everything about him, including the secrets he kept. Brian, a retired homicide detective who now had a very successful one-man PI firm, was very good at his job. If Mark Bledsoe had skeletons in his closet, Brian Vickery would unearth them.

"She said he's violent?"

"Terrifyingly so. She told me of two incidents this morning, one where he broke her jaw. The other when he punched her when he didn't like the way she loaded the dishwasher. He also broke her clavicle."

"Jesus." Brian sat back down next to Olivia. "This makes me nervous, Liv. He's mean, and he's powerful."

"I know."

"Is she going to fight him for money?"

"No. She drained their joint accounts when she left."

"That's poking a wasp's nest," Brian said.

"She doesn't even want spousal support. She wants the divorce, mostly she wants to stay off her husband's radar until she can get her emergency passport and run home to Sweden."

"She thinks she'll be safe in Sweden?"

"Apparently her father is an investment banker of such importance that he has a security detail. Why? Is that strange?"

Brian got up, pulled on his sweatpants, and handed Olivia her clothes. "Yes. An investment banker with a security detail? Sounds like organized crime to me. You're so quick to take this woman at her word."

"I know. But she's truly terrified. I want to help her. If she's playing me, for whatever reason, we'll find out."

"Fair enough," Brian said. "I'll be the suspicious-minded devil's advocate."

"I would expect nothing less." Olivia stood and stretched, tired all of a sudden, and emotionally drained from her encounter with Ava.

"Is there any chance Bledsoe could track Ava to Lauren's house?"

"I don't think so. Ava and Lauren were friends – mostly through Ricky Lee – before she met Mark. As far as Ava knows, Mark doesn't know that Ava and Lauren are friends. She left her cell phone, all her electronics, and her car at home. She took a circuitous route to Lauren's too."

"Good thinking."

"She planned for every contingency."

18

Olivia sat back down, close to Brian. He put his arm around her, so they were sitting shoulder to shoulder, basking in the fire's warmth. "I'm going to put more cameras around the house."

"Okay," Olivia said.

"Wow. No pushback?" Brian looked into Olivia's eyes. "You're afraid, aren't you?"

"Let's just say I'm aware of the danger, and I know the only way to stay safe is to assume the worst. The best course of action here is to pretend he'll be coming for her, and for me, full throttle. He's going to want to get to Ava. Once I file divorce papers, he'll know that I can lead him to her. It makes me vulnerable."

"It does," Brian agreed. "He's going to hire private investigators, and he's going to hire someone really good. They'll vet Ava's history. Eventually whoever he hires to hunt Ava will discover her relationship with Lauren. When that happens, both of you will be on his radar."

"Surely he wouldn't be so stupid as to harass me?" The minute Olivia said these words, she realized how foolish they were. Of course Mark Bledsoe would come after her. As Ava had said, he doesn't operate within the law. The reality of her situation and the danger she'd brought to their lives sunk in. "Oh, Brian. What have I done?"

"Your job, Liv. You've chosen to exit with a bang," Brian said.

"Now all we have to do is gird ourselves for a fight," Olivia said.

"How are you going to manage this case? Other than getting this woman divorced, what's your end game?"

Olivia leaned into Brian, nestling close to him, letting his warmth soothe her. "I filed the petition for divorce and sent the summons out for service with Jeff Hinton. He's the only process server I trust with a case like this. He'll be able to personally serve Mark with the divorce papers and then be finished with him. He always carries a gun, and he's aware of Mark's volatile nature. The only leverage I have is Ava herself. She doesn't want half of her husband's money. She wants a divorce. If he agrees to let her go, she won't take another dime."

"Okay, so we play the game? I dig into this guy's finances, find out where he's hiding his billions, and then you make a more-than-fair offer?" Brian brushed Olivia's cheek with his fingers, his touch light and sensual.

"And make him think that he's in control and calling the shots. That's pretty much the only strategy I've got, which doesn't really matter because Ava doesn't care about the money. She wants out, and she wants to get away," Olivia said.

"I think I should speak to Lauren myself, just to make sure she knows how dangerous Mark can be. She knows about Ava's abuse, but I'm not sure if she knows the extent—"

The blaring ring of a cell phone interrupted Brian mid-sentence.

"That's mine," Olivia said, as she rummaged through her purse.

"Who's calling at this hour?" Brian asked, switching on the lamp as Olivia pulled her cell phone out of her purse.

"It's Jeff Hinton," Olivia said as she fiddled with her phone and put it on speaker.

"Jeff?"

"Olivia?"

"I'm here."

"Hold on a second."

Brian came to sit next to Olivia as they waited for Jeff to report. From the sound of traffic and Jeff's occasional cussing, Olivia surmised he was driving.

"Okay. I'm here. Sorry about that. I got your guy served. Apparently I caught him just as he was coming home from the police department to file a missing person's report about his wife."

"Was he furious?"

"Not at first," Jeff said. "Shocked, more like it. Although he could have been faking it. Said they'd been together for five years, and their relationship was solid. He thought they loved each other. She was the love of his life, blah, blah, blah. We chatted like two mates at the bar having a drink. While we were talking, he opened the back door of his car, tossed the papers in, and pulled out a baseball bat."

"Oh, no," Olivia said.

"Lucky for me, I brought my gun. I actually drew on the son of a bitch. That stopped him long enough for me to get into my car. But as I was turning around, he started swinging. Smashed in my passenger window."

Olivia felt the blood drain from her face.

"Liv, you've been giving me your business for over twenty years, and you know that I'm grateful. Always will be. But I'm charging hazard pay for this one. Seriously."

"No problem. I'll pay for the car, too. Just send me a bill."

"Thanks. You've got Brian with you then?"

Olivia put her hand on Brian's leg. "He's right here."

"And the wife, she's somewhere this lunatic can't find her?"

"Yes," Olivia said.

"Good. Be careful with this one, Olivia. Assume the worst. This guy is unstable. He's a giant. Have you seen him? You should have seen the look on his face when he came after me with that bat. Thank God I was armed. He would have killed me. Swear to God. He was crazed."

"Thanks, Jeff," Olivia said, her voice subdued. Once she hung up, she turned to Brian. "I think I've made a mistake."

"It'll be okay." He pulled her into his arms. "We can handle it."

They were in a somber mood as they walked through the house together, checking that all the doors were locked, the security cameras recording, and the alarm turned on. Once they slid under the warm duvet and lay like spoons in a drawer, Brian fell asleep almost immediately. As he snored softly, Olivia lay in bed, chastising herself for her inability to say no.

Chapter 3

Despite his assurances to Olivia the night before, Brian Vickery had his worries about the Bledsoe divorce. Logging into the software that allowed him to search for people, criminal records, court records, and assets, he downloaded and read seven domestic violence police reports prepared in response to 9-1-1 calls from Ava and the Bledsoes' neighbors. Once finished, Brian was convinced he could not protect Ava, Lauren, and Olivia by himself. As he walked toward the office, he plotted how to convince Olivia that the best course of action was to find Ava an attorney who worked for one of the big firms in San Francisco, someone who had an entire security team at their disposal.

The minute he conjured a cohesive argument in support of this, he realized the utter futility of it. Olivia was not going to walk away from this case. Although they had only known each other for a year, Brian knew Olivia's mind; she was like a dog with a bone when it came to cases like this one.

He approached the office, glad to find the door locked. Letting himself in, he once again locked the door behind him, taking a moment to study the cars and foot traffic that milled on Magnolia Avenue on this September morning. He would need to convince Olivia – along with Ava and Lauren – that extra security was needed.

If they argued, he would put his foot down. If that didn't work, he'd hire a security detail and not tell them. Olivia and Lauren would be angry with him for hiring security without their permission, but they'd have to get over that. He walked down the thickly carpeted hallway, coming to a quiet stop in Olivia's doorway.

"Liv?"

She yelped, jumped out of her seat, and wound up facing him, her hand on her heart, gasping for breath.

"Brian. God. You scared me."

He went to her, but she held up her hand.

"Please. I don't need protection." She smiled. "You've got that crusading knight look in your eyes. I love it, I really do, but right now I'm up to my ears in . . ." She pointed at her computer. "Mark Bledsoe has money hidden everywhere. I've found it all. Well, maybe not all, but enough to give me the leverage I need to usher through this divorce. We both know I'm going to unleash a monster when I confront him with my knowledge of his financial shenanigans. Judges don't take kindly to parties in a divorce hiding assets. Maybe we could figure out a way—"

"We need to talk."

She stopped mid-sentence, looked at Brian as though seeing him for the first time. "What's happened?"

"Nothing's *happened*. But I've been researching an entire library of police reports your client and the neighbors have filed on Mr. Bledsoe, Olivia. You need to get rid of this case. Mark Bledsoe is dangerous. He's powerful enough to operate outside the law, and there's not a thing we can do to stop him."

Olivia ran her eyes over Brian's blazer, noticing the holster and the gun. "That bad?"

"That bad. Mark Bledsoe is powerful. His wife has served him with divorce papers. He's no longer in control." Olivia stood up and moved to her office window. She stood with her back toward Brian as she gazed at Mt. Tamalpais, her shoulders so tense they nearly touched her ears.

She turned to face him, a look of sheer determination on her face. "I'm sorry, Brian. But I can't abandon Ava."

"Sometimes you need to say no. Surely you can see this is one of those times."

"I'm saying no now, to you. I'm going to see this through to the end. If you don't want to help me—"

"Don't be ridiculous. Of course, I'm going to help you," Brian snapped, angry now, and desperate to make Olivia see just what she would be subjecting them to.

"This woman needs my help. Ava trusts me. Any other firm that would take her case, no matter how well equipped they are to handle Mark Bledsoe and all that he entails, will treat Ava like a billable commodity. Ava needs me. I'm the only one—"

"Stop right there. Listen to yourself, for God's sake. You think you're *the only one*?" Brian shook his head and started to pace. "You need to reel your ego in here and take an objective look at what's going on."

"What did you say to me?"

He took a deep breath. "That was out of line. I'm sorry."

"Do you really think I'm taking this case to satisfy an overblown ego?"

"No. I shouldn't have said that. It was cruel and uncalled for."

"Why did you?" Olivia studied him in that inscrutable way of hers that made Brian feel as though she were looking right into his heart. Her features softened, as she cocked her head and looked at him. "You're scared, aren't you?"

Brian hesitated before he spoke, recognizing what might be his only chance to make Olivia send Ava off to another lawyer. "I am. You should be too. I'm worried for Lauren and Ava, and I am glad that Denny and Carly aren't in the area."

Olivia sat down at her desk and buried her face in her hands. Brian sat down opposite her and waited. When she looked up at him, he noticed the blossoms of purple under her eyes and the pinched look of worry there. It had only been twenty-four hours since Ava Bledsoe had stormed into their lives, and already the stress of it was wearing on Olivia's face.

"Okay. Message received. What should we do, Brian? How can we work this case in a way that keeps us safe?"

Brian had a plan; the only obstacle would be convincing Olivia to enact it. "The only way to play this is to circle the wagons. Hire outside help to keep an eye on us and on Ava and Lauren. Your client has a budget, right? Because I can't protect Ava, Lauren, and you at the same time. I'm going to need some help."

"She does."

"Okay. We put a guy on Lauren's house. We stop working here at the office and move everything home."

"That's doable," Olivia said, warming to his idea.

"And if Mark tracks us to the house, we get a security team there or go off grid."

"Go off grid?" Olivia shook her head. "Don't you think that's a bit overzealous?"

"I don't. We should plan for the worst-case scenario, and then we can be pleasantly surprised if we don't need to run for it. And before you say anything, this is not up for debate. If you don't agree to my plan, I'm going to get protection anyway without consulting you. Best if you're on board."

"Okay," Olivia said. "Consider me officially on board. Do whatever you need to do."

"Since we're communicating so freely, you should know that I'm mad at Lauren. As in really pissed off, Liv. We're supposed to be retiring, and she brings you a case with a seriously violent husband? And since I'm being so unabashedly honest, I'm pissed at you, too. I wish you hadn't taken this case. I know you feel obligated to help, but you need to draw a line in the sand. At some point you're going to have to learn to say no."

Olivia sat back down at her desk, not meeting his eyes. As she bowed her head, revealing the bony vertebrae on the back of her neck, Brian realized that Olivia didn't want to take this case either.

But now that she was in, she'd see it through, see Ava safely sorted. That was Olivia's nature. He could no more change that about her than he could stop the Earth from revolving around the sun.

She pushed away from her desk and came toward Brian. When she got close to him, he pulled her onto his lap. "I know you're not going to walk away. I get it. Promise me, Liv, once this case is finished, we're done. We walk away, move into our house in Tahoe, and get away from here."

"Promise. You can go buy your fishing boat now, you know. You don't have to wait until we move."

Brian started to say something, but Olivia wrapped her arms around his neck and kissed him deeply. He responded and had just pulled her to her feet when they were interrupted by a knock on the office door.

Olivia tensed in Brian's arms, as he instinctively moved in front of her, drew his gun, and peeked into the hallway.

"Are you expecting someone?"

"No," Olivia said. She pushed past Brian and headed for the office door, seemingly forgetting their entire conversation about the need for caution and care. "It's Dan Winters."

"Who's Dan Winters?"

"A colleague." Olivia pulled her office key out of her pocket and let Dan inside the office. Once he was in, Olivia closed the door and locked it behind him.

"Dan. What are you doing here?"

"Sorry for the drop-in, but I was in the area—" Dan's eyes traveled around the empty reception area, coming to a stop when they reached Brian, who was holstering his gun.

"Brian, this is Dan Winters. Dan, Brian Vickery." Olivia stood near Brian.

Dan stepped toward Brian with his hand out. "You're the investigator, right?"

"One and the same." Brian shook Dan's hand with a firm grip, sweeping his eyes over his Italian suit and his well-manicured hands.

"Why is the office so empty?" Dan asked.

"I'm retiring," Olivia said. "Brian had been leasing the office from me for the past year. I haven't really been taking cases, but now I've sold the building and am moving."

"I'm jealous. If I didn't have kids in college, I'd be right behind you."

"What can I do for you?" Olivia asked.

Dan spoke to Olivia as though Brian wasn't there. "Can we talk privately? I'm representing Mark Bledsoe."

"No need for privacy. Brian's working the case with me. Let's go in my office. I've got chairs in there."

Once they were seated, Dan pulled a sheaf of papers out of his briefcase and handed it to Olivia. "I've set the support hearing for Tuesday, the eighth."

"I didn't request a support hearing," Olivia said, reading through the papers Dan handed her.

"I did. Your client looted both the savings and checking accounts, as you'll see from our financial disclosures. We're asking for these funds to be used for spousal support until the divorce is finalized."

"You really want to go down this road, Dan?"

"I'm on the road, Olivia. Your client is engaging in a character assassination. During their marriage, she made a habit of accusing him of spousal abuse. Every time the police got involved, she would backpedal."

"Come on, Dan. You've heard of coercive control."

"I have evidence that she's filed police reports almost eleven times."

"Have you seen the reports?" Olivia pushed. "Checked out what damage was inflicted upon Ava?"

Dan continued, as though he hadn't heard her. "Now she's stolen Mark's money and run away. My client's reputation is very important. Did you know she staged her house to make it look like she disappeared under suspicious circumstances? My client went to the police and filed a missing person's report. He was worried that she'd been abducted and was just coming home from the police station when your guy served him with divorce papers. My client has a lot to lose if his wife continues to—"

Olivia interrupted and stood up, ready to usher Dan Winters out of her office. "Thanks for giving me the heads-up, Dan. I'll see you on Tuesday."

Dan reached into his briefcase and handed Olivia another clipped batch of documents. "Mr. Bledsoe's financial disclosures. I'll expect yours as soon as possible." Dan stood and collected his things. "Nice to meet you," he said to Brian.

After he had gone, Brian watched Olivia peruse the documents Dan had given her, resisting the urge to shout *I told you so!* "Liv, how come you didn't tell Dan about the attack on our process server?"

"I'll be disclosing that info in open court on the record, taken down by the court reporter." Olivia continued to read the papers. "Oh, this is interesting."

"Care to share?" Brian asked.

Olivia looked up and pushed the papers toward Brian. "These papers are chock-full of lies. I've got statements of bank accounts, money market accounts, investment accounts that have ten times the funds as the accounts Ava liquidated. Dan Winters is not the most thorough attorney I've been up against, but moving forward with financial inaccuracies that he knows I'll repudiate in court isn't his style. At all."

"You think he's up to something?" Brian asked, knowing what Olivia was going to say.

"I think he's letting his client be the puppet master."

"Probably afraid of him," Brian said. "I know I would be if I were in his shoes."

"I'm guessing Mark Bledsoe wants to get Ava to court, so he can see her in person. Maybe scare her?"

"Or have someone follow her after court and see where she goes.

I think we should assume the worst possible scenario," Brian said. "She'll be safe in the actual courtroom. It's the back and forth that concerns me. That's where she could be vulnerable."

"You're talking like you have a plan."

"Oh, I've got a good plan. I just need to figure out a way to bring it to fruition. The hearing's on Tuesday?"

"Yes," Olivia said.

Brian stood. "I need to make some arrangements. I'll get us lunch?"

"Thanks," Olivia said.

"I'm sorry about what I said earlier. You're not ego-driven. At all."

"I'm not?"

Brian hesitated. "Well, maybe a little. But you're sexy as hell, so you can get away with it."

Olivia laughed, trying to push Brian away as he kissed her. "You're distracting me."

"I just don't want you to get hurt."

"I know. I'll be careful."

Brian left the office, once again checking the street, the parked cars, and the foot traffic around the office for anything unusual or suspicious, the proverbial white van. As he scanned the area, he punched in a number on his cell phone.

"Scott?"

"Brian Vickery? How's it going? When are you taking me fishing?"

Brian chuckled. "I need a security team. Three people need watching. My girlfriend's one of them."

"I'm listening," Scott said.

Brian gave Scott the details. "Give me an hour, and I'll get back to you with a proposal."

Chapter 4

Asher opened his eyes. Blinking at the bright lights, he took in the industrial ceiling and the IV in his wrist. As his eyes adjusted, he realized he was in the hospital. Outside his room, a shrill and chastising voice filled him with a sense of dread.

"I will not allow you to speak to my son alone. He's not up to it. You've no right—"

The voice that responded to his mother was soft and well-modulated. "I'm going in the room now, ma'am. Inspector Lambada will stay out here with you." The door opened, blasting his hospital room with bright light and the hum of activity in the corridor beyond. His mother's voice cut through, louder now and full of her particular brand of bossiness.

"Why have you taken his clothing?"

"They are evidence, ma'am. Excuse me."

His mother. Great. Just great.

His head spun a bit when he opened his eyes and slowly sat up, but the wooziness was gone. His mother's purse, a ginormous bag that carried whatever knitting project she was working on, plus a couple of books, sat in one of two guest chairs. How long had he been here? He imagined her keeping a vigil on his behalf, planning ways to pull him back home into her cloying sphere of good intention. His mouth was dry as a desert. On a tray next to his bed, a full pitcher of water and an empty glass beckoned. As he lifted the pitcher, his hand shook so badly that he gave up and leaned back into his pillows. Maybe if he just closed his eyes for a second.

"Mr. Ridgeland?"

A woman stood in the door, the light from the hallway haloed around her.

"That's me," he croaked.

As she stepped into the room, she shut the door on Sabine, who was arguing with another man – probably this cop's partner – about being allowed in Asher's room.

"I'm Inspector Standish, SFPD. I'd just like to ask you a couple of questions, if you're up for it?" When she noticed the empty glass in Asher's hand, she said, "Here, let me get you some water." She poured a small bit of water into the glass and handed it to him. "I'd sip it slowly if I were you. If you feel nauseated, let me know, and I'll get a nurse. I'm assuming you didn't take a potentially lethal dose of Rohypnol on purpose?"

Asher nearly choked. "Rohypnol? No. I don't do drugs. Any drugs."

"Okay." The woman's tone of voice was friendly and warm. Asher sipped.

"Your mom is quite a tiger."

"Yes, she is. But you're not here to talk to me about my mom."

Ellie pulled the visitor's chair close to his bed. Asher took in the warm brown skin, the muscular arms, and the no-nonsense expression. He waited. Eventually she softened, and the look she gave him was earnest, without guile, designed to evince trust. "I know this isn't the best time, but I need to talk to you now, while things are fresh in your mind."

For a second, Asher wondered what *information* would be fresh in his mind, until the image of Mikala, lying next to him, dead, strangled, shocked him so thoroughly he spilled the glass of water down the front of his hospital gown.

31

"Crap," he said under his breath, looking for something to mop up the frigid water.

Ellie Standish stepped into the bathroom and came back with a towel. "You remember?"

"It just came back to me. God. Her face. I can't unsee it." Asher closed his eyes against the vision of Mikala lying dead next to him, but it didn't do any good.

"Do you want me to come back? If you're not able to talk to me now, I'm happy to come back later."

"No. Let's do it now."

Inspector Standish watched him for a moment, as if making sure he was up to talking.

"I'm fine," Asher reassured her. "Really."

"Okay. It looks like you were both drugged. I'm operating on the assumption that whoever gave you the Rohypnol murdered Mikala while she was passed out. There was no sign of forced entry, so we're pretty certain she knew her killer."

Asher felt Inspector Standish's subtle scrutiny as she let those words sink in, evaluating his reaction. Did she suspect him? He'd been drugged hadn't he? Alert now to the consequences of freely communicating with this police officer, Asher sat up in his bed and tried to collect his thoughts. "Are you a homicide cop?"

Her hesitation told him all he needed to know.

"Got it. I'm wondering if I should have a lawyer before I speak to you."

"That's absolutely your right. But I don't think you killed her, okay? It doesn't make sense that you would murder your girlfriend and then drug yourself with that much Rohypnol. But I have a job to do. I would appreciate your cooperation. I'm assuming you want to help. You can give a statement now, freely, or I can bring you down to the station after they discharge you and interview you in a more formal setting. How do you want to play this? It's entirely up to you."

Her tone had grown edgy. Asher, who prided himself on being

an excellent judge of character, didn't get the sense Inspector Standish was strong-arming him. "I want to help you," Asher said.

"Good." Ellie pulled out a notebook. "This isn't a formal statement. We can deal with that later. Right now, I just need you to tell me everything you remember while it's fresh in your mind. If you need me to get a nurse or you want to stop talking to me, you're free to do that, okay? I'm not trying to trick you."

"Okay. I'm reassured. Thanks." Asher took a deep breath and closed his eyes.

"Why don't you start with yesterday. Where were you? What were your plans with Mikala?"

"I took an impromptu road trip. I work in IT."

"Which company?"

"Mine. I freelance. Search engine optimization is my specialty, in case you're wondering. I've been overdoing it. My company is fairly new, so I haven't been able to turn away work, but I don't have the resources yet to hire help. I got too busy and nearly crashed and burned. Anyway, after I wrapped up my last project, I went camping. By myself."

"Where?" Ellie asked.

"Desolation Wilderness. Lake Tahoe. You know it? I didn't hike too far in. Just took my tent, my sleeping bag, and a few sandwiches."

"Did it help? Getting away?"

"Yeah," Asher said. "Being alone in nature always cures me."

"Okay. Understandable. Tell me what happened when you got back into the city."

Asher nodded at the glass of water. Ellie handed it to him and he took another sip. "Mikala and I had plans to meet at her house around 8:30 or 9:00 that evening. I arrived early and wanted to surprise her. When I got there – to her apartment – I could tell she'd been partying with someone else, that she'd had company. Whoever she had in the apartment with her remained hidden. Mikala and I had words. I realized she'd deliberately positioned

33

me with my back to the door, so she could distract me while whoever she was with snuck out. I tried to follow, bolted outside and chased for a few blocks, but I didn't get a glimpse of him."

Detective Standish stopped writing and looked up at Asher. "If you didn't see him, how do you know it was a man?"

Asher shook his head, trying to clear it. "He was tall, like a man. And Mikala had on what she jokingly called her slutty lingerie. God, I'm an idiot. I thought we were exclusive. I thought we were going somewhere . . . We got into a fight." Asher rubbed his eyes. "A big fight. Mikala grabbed her purse and left on foot. I followed her. We wound up at Elevations, the club near Mikala's apartment. We fought there, in public, for all to see. Then we made up and went back to Mikala's house for the make-up sex. That pretty much sums up our relationship. I remember a bottle of champagne – I don't like champagne, but she handed me a glass, so I took a sip. And then I woke up and saw her lying next to me . . ."

"How long had you been dating?" Ellie asked.

"One year, two months, and three days. I loved her. I didn't kill her."

"Okay," Ellie said. "That's good. I know this is tough."

Asher's exhalation came out in a slow whoosh. "I can't believe this is happening."

The door to Asher's room burst open and his mother barged in, cheeks flushed, eyes snapping, the male detective standing behind her, shaking his head. "I demand you cease this interview immediately. My son will not be talking to you without a lawyer present."

"Mom, stop it," Asher said.

"You're not thinking clearly," Sabine snapped at her son. "You need to let me handle—"

Ellie Standish moved around the bed until she was blocking Sabine. Asher's admiration for the inspector solidified as he watched his mother try to scoot around Inspector Standish to get to his bedside, while the inspector countered his mother's every move, step for step.

"You need to go back outside, ma'am." Inspector Standish's voice caused his mother to stop in her tracks.

"Your intimidation tactics will not work on me, young lady."

Inspector Standish relaxed and held up her hands in a gesture of acquiescence. "Okay. I'm sorry. I wasn't trying to intimidate you. But I am going to speak to your son alone. And there is nothing you can do about it."

"I'll report you."

"Listen, lady, I understand and have respect for your mama-bear-with-teeth schtick. If I were in your shoes, I'd probably be acting the same way. But I'm not the woman you want to pick a fight with. Okay?"

"You're going to blame my son for something he didn't do—"

"I'm the cop who's going to help you avoid the press when you leave the building."

"Press?"

"There's a mob in the lobby. Luckily, the nurses here are as efficient at keeping people away as you are. But you don't want your son to deal with the press today, correct?"

"You're right. I'm sorry. We're all just a little shaken by the whole thing." Sabine shivered and pulled her quilted jacket around her shoulders.

"I understand. Now, if you'll let me talk to Asher, I can get out of your hair."

Sabine allowed the other inspector to lead her out of the room.

"You ready to continue?"

"Yes. Sorry about that," Asher said.

"I know these questions are going to sting. But I need to ask them."

"Understood."

"Do you think this is the first time that Mikala has been with someone else?"

"Given what I saw last night, probably not. My work requires me to travel. I have clients all over California and Oregon. I just assumed when I was out of town that she was being faithful to me, that we had a normal, monogamous relationship that was leading to something more permanent. She had me fooled. Based on what happened last night, I'm betting that she's been cheating on me all along."

"But you don't have any firsthand knowledge, any suspicions about other boyfriends, or anyone who didn't like her?"

He closed his eyes, tired now, ready to leave the hospital and retreat to his studio apartment to lick his wounds, far away from his mother and the police.

"No one. Mikala liked to help people. She had a wild streak – that's for sure. And she had a way of manipulating people. But she was also kind. People gravitated toward her, if that makes sense."

"Asher, I have to ask you a favor. You can say no. But I'm ready to clear you, so I can find out who murdered your girlfriend. Will you let us search your apartment? The only people who will conduct the search are Inspector Lambada and me. We will leave your home exactly as we find it; I give you my word."

"Of course," Asher said. "I think the police probably have my backpack? There's a key in there."

"Thanks, Asher. I'll return the key to you when we're finished."

"Just find who did this to Mikala," Asher said.

"We're going to try. Okay, then. I'm just going to leave you to rest. Uniformed officers will escort you out of the hospital through the service entrance. My business card is right here on this nightstand. If you think of anything, call my cell phone anytime. I'm going to want to talk to you again."

Asher lay back and closed his eyes, tired all of a sudden. He heard the door open and shut. Sensing that he wasn't alone, he opened his eyes to find his mother standing over him, her face awash in worry and despair. He'd hurt her with his harsh comments. Closing his eyes before she noticed he was awake, Asher felt her cold dry hand as it straightened his hospital gown.

He pretended to doze, until the door opened once again, this time with more commotion. He opened his eyes and watched his mother stand up and shake the doctor's hand.

"He's sleeping," Sabine said.

Asher wanted to shout that he had not been sleeping, that he had been lying there with his eyes closed so he could avoid dealing with her.

The doctor moved over to his bed. "Asher? Can you wake up?"

"I'm awake." Asher opened his eyes and pulled himself to a sitting position. When Sabine made to move toward him, he gave her a glance that sent her scurrying back to the chair in the corner of the room.

"I'm Dr. Fisher." Asher took in the thick bushy eyebrows, the glasses hanging from a beaded chain, and the pencil behind the doctor's ear. "You gave us quite a scare, young man. You're lucky the paramedics got to you when they did."

"Officer Standish said I was given Rohypnol?"

"Yes. A sizeable dose. Do you remember anything?"

"Not really," Asher said. "When can I go home?"

"You can go home within the next couple of hours, as long as you have someone to stay with you for the next twenty-four." Dr. Fisher turned. "You're his mom?"

Sabine stood and held out her hand. "Sabine Ridgeland. Asher will come home with me."

"Good. It's best that he's not alone until the drug wears off. He'll be out of the woods by this time tomorrow." Dr. Fisher turned back to Asher. "No driving for you, no exercise either. You may have some residual drowsiness and dizziness. Be careful, use your good sense. If you have any questions, you can call my nurse. Her number will be on your discharge forms." Dr. Fisher wrote furiously. "Probably a good idea to follow up with your primary care doc in a few days too, just to be safe."

"Thanks," Asher said.

"I'll get things rolling so we can get you out of here. I'm glad you're okay," Dr. Fisher said. He nodded, looked at his watch, and hurried out of the room.

"From now on, I will not say I told you so. I will not utter one ill word against Mikala. We both know I didn't like her, that I didn't think she was good enough for you. That being said, she didn't deserve to die."

For a second, Asher considered picking a fight with his mother. Reminding her that the few times he'd brought Mikala to family functions, his mother had done her best to make her feel uncomfortable, unwanted, and out of place.

"Thanks," Asher said.

"Let's get you home. You can lie in bed, and I'll wait on you until you tire of me. How does that sound?"

"As long as home means my house, that sounds pretty good right now." Asher paused.

"Home to your house it is." Sabine smiled at him, but the smile was forced and it didn't quite reach her eyes.

Chapter 5

Carlo Lambada was new to Captain Wasniki's homicide division. After spending over ten years in vice, Inspector Lambada's daring undercover adventures had earned him quite a reputation. His reputation as a lady's man and a solid cop with good street smarts preceded him, and – at least in Ellie's view – his ego. After her previous partner, Sharon Bailey, had gone on disability, Ellie had been relegated to desk work. When Wasniki called her to work Mikala Glascott's homicide with Lambada, she'd jumped at the chance, despite her reservations about him.

She knew Lambada thought she'd gone easy on Asher Ridgeland. He'd wanted to leave two uniforms out in the corridor and come into Asher's room with her. Ellie had visions of Lambada bending over Asher's hospital bed, pointing a finger, playing hardball. He had a reputation for playing rough, and – if the rumor mill was accurate – had been disciplined for it in the past. Ellie had pushed back, told him that she would go alone for now. Lucky for her, Asher's mother had starting throwing a fit, and Lambada had pushed away from her to get things under control.

By the time they left the hospital, with permission to search Asher's apartment, Lambada was bursting with a list of things

Ellie did wrong. When he started in on her, Ellie had ignored him, grateful when two nurses had joined them in the elevator.

"He didn't do it," Ellie said, as she slipped into the driver's seat and put her seatbelt on.

"How can you know that? You haven't even investigated the guy yet. Desolation Wilderness? His alibi's a bit shaky, don't you think?"

"I trust my intuition." She pulled into traffic, ignoring Inspector Lambada's gaze, tuning it out and keeping her eyes on the traffic.

"You didn't even ask him to come down and give a formal statement. We need to ask him questions on the record, while the camera is running."

"Agreed. We will. But I don't want to alienate him out of the gate."

"You should have pushed, that's all I'm saying," Lambada said.

"In front of his mother, while he's coming off a nearly fatal dose of Rohypnol? That would be a PR nightmare, wouldn't it?" Ellie shook her head as she pulled into traffic.

"She wasn't happy Asher agreed to let us search, was she?"

"No. What's the word, *helicopter parent*? *Hover mom*?" Ellie said.

"Look, Standish, just to set the record straight, you should know if you and I are going to be partners, I have a few rules. First of all, there will be no going rogue. Anything that happens, we do it together. Got it?"

Unable to contain her anger, Ellie pulled the car over, not caring that she'd doubled parked, pointedly ignoring the blaring horns.

"What are you doing?"

"Where do you get off talking to me like that? Wasniki hasn't made you lead. And as for Sharon – Inspector Bailey – that wasn't . . . No one went rogue—" Ellie hesitated.

"What?" Carlo Lambada said.

"Never mind. That's none of your business. You're not my boss. How many homicides have you worked?"

"Seven," Carlo said. "But my ten years in vice—"

"Twenty-four here. This isn't vice, Lambada. I had the best mentor. Even you have to admit that. Sharon Bailey solved her cases. She has the highest close rate in the department."

"Yeah, but her methods were unorthodox at times."

"And yours aren't? But she solved her cases." Ellie pulled back into traffic. "And she did it in a way that didn't ruffle feathers. She did her job, quietly and thoroughly. I strive for that. You're not my boss. Deal with it."

"I would have pushed, just saying."

"Do you think he would have let you search his apartment if you pushed?" Ellie waited a beat. "Didn't think so."

"Have you spoken to Sharon Bailey since everything went down? Are you in touch with her?"

Ellie bristled, but focused on the traffic, not wanting to show Lambada her weak spot.

"I heard she can't be around water, like, at all."

Still Ellie didn't say anything.

"Okay, I get it. You're not talking."

"Her hands and feet were bound and she was thrown in the bay and left to die, Lambada. If I were her, I probably wouldn't even want to take a shower. You want us to get along, work well together, don't gossip about my ex-partner."

When Lambada gave Ellie a knowing smile, she was overcome with the feeling that she'd passed some unspoken test.

Ellie hadn't seen Sharon in a while. As far as she knew, her old partner was getting better and planning a life away from SFPD. "Just drop it, okay?"

"Fine," Lambada said.

Ever since Sharon left, Ellie's career had been in a state of uncertainty. She'd been stuck in an office, working cold cases. Although she'd cleared a few, the desk work was claustrophobic. Ellie was a think-on-her-feet kind of cop. Being stuck in an office, sitting all day, had started to take its toll. To make matters worse, she felt certain that other cops gave her the side-eye when she walked into the room. Sometimes conversations would stop, the sudden hush creating a vacuum. Cops who used to stop and chitchat over coffee would scurry by, not making eye contact. The job had become lonely for Ellie.

Lambada crossed his arms over his chest and sank back into his seat. "Listen, I didn't mean to piss you off. You're right about Inspector Bailey. I was repeating gossip. Not cool. It won't happen again. But will you at least admit you didn't treat Asher Ridgeland like a suspect."

"Because he isn't one yet," Ellie said.

"He's on my radar until he is properly cleared."

"Everyone's on the radar until they are cleared. You have your style; I have mine." Ellie stopped at a red light.

"How do you want to divvy the work?"

"Until we get phone records and the dump from the electronics, how about I take Mikala Glascott and you take Asher Ridgeland."

"What about Lexy Ford?"

"We should verify her alibi. Let's do that together. We can track down her alibi witnesses after they get off work. They all work at the same law firm, right? Wasniki won't want to be briefed until the end of the day. After we meet with him, we can find Lexy's friends."

"Yep. Sounds good."

"I wonder who paid the rent on Mikala's fancy apartment?"

"Me too," Ellie said.

Lambada pulled his phone out of his pocket and started texting, his fingers flying, his focus on them intense. Once finished, he tucked his phone away. "Is Inspector Bailey okay? Not gossiping now, I swear. I always liked her."

Ellie changed the subject. "There's a couple things you should know about Captain Wasniki. He'll do anything for his team, but he's also the first one to stress the importance of PR. Asher's mother – Sabine, right? – if I'd gone aggro in there, she would have gone straight to the top with complaints of us harassing her son while he was in the hospital."

"But the element of surprise—"

Ellie plowed on. "And you have to admit, I did gain his trust. He didn't think twice about giving us permission to search his house. He even gave us his keys."

"We could have gotten a warrant," Lambada said.

"In three hours," Ellie said. She turned onto Chestnut Street, onto Mallorca in the Marina District, just as a parking space opened up right in front of Asher's building. "In three hours, I plan on being deep into Mikala Glascott's background."

"Okay, fair enough," Lambada said.

Ellie and Lambada stepped onto the sidewalk. "What is it with you and Asher Ridgeland? You seem to have it out for him."

"I'm suspicious of people with too much privilege. Guys like Asher Ridgeland – Marin County rich boys with trust funds at their disposal – can do whatever they want."

"They can't break the law," Ellie said.

"They can. And then their people – parents, families, whoever – cough up more dough than we make in ten years for a high-priced lawyer to get them off."

"Cynical much?" Ellie said, heading into the lobby of Asher's building.

"It's reality, Standish. It's the truth. And I think on some level you know that."

Asher lived on the third floor. Ellie sighed and opted for the stairs. "Everyone is a suspect until they are cleared. That doesn't mean we have to act like bruisers." She took off up the stairs at a trot, hoping Lambada would take the elevator.

"Okay, fine. Got it."

Ellie slipped the key into the well-oiled lock and stepped into Asher's spacious studio apartment.

"I can't believe a guy lives here," Ellie said.

"Is that patchouli oil?" Lambada said at the same time.

"No," Ellie said as she stepped into the spacious apartment. "It's Nag Champa. Buddhist monks use it. The idea is to burn the incense and then open all your windows. The incense takes the bad energy away. And surprisingly it doesn't leave a residual smell."

"Where do you come by this info, Standish? You're a regular encyclopedia."

"Thank you," Ellie said.

The large apartment held a queen-sized bed, neatly made and covered in a navy-blue corduroy duvet. A large mahogany desk covered with two large monitors and a multitude of complicated-looking technology took up most of the room. Lambada walked over to it.

Lambada rifled through a stack of papers sitting under a bronze dragonfly-shaped paperweight. "Well, lookie here. A receipt for gas in Sacramento. How convenient."

Ellie ignored him and surveyed the gleaming galley kitchen. A shelf held two each of cups, bowls, and plates. The stove gleamed as though it had just been scrubbed. A tiny café table sat under the large window, a stocked retro napkin dispenser sitting smack in the middle.

A large shelving unit ran up one wall. Aside from the expected knickknacks, sports paraphernalia, and a heavy-looking bronze baseball glove mounted on a stand, most of the space was filled with books. True to form, they were organized by size. Lambada randomly pulled one off the shelf. He fanned the pages, tossed it on the floor and reached for the next one.

"No way, Lambada. I gave Asher my word we wouldn't trash his apartment."

Lambada smiled as he picked up the book and put it back exactly where he found it. "I know. I was just kidding."

Just great. I've got a joker on my hands. Ellie put on gloves and went into the surprisingly large bathroom. As expected, the room was austere and clean to the point of almost being sterile. The only cabinet was the medicine cabinet over the sink. On quick glance, Ellie saw shaving equipment, sunscreen, tooth-brush and toothpaste. She took note that there was only one toothbrush and wondered if Mikala ever spent the night in this apartment, and, if so, how she coped with Asher's fussy ways. Because even though Asher Ridgeland wasn't in the room, the way he kept his house spoke volumes. Ellie opened the medicine cabinet. Band-Aids, hydrogen peroxide, shaving cream, blade refills, not a pill in sight, not even aspirin.

"I'm finished in here," Ellie said.

Before they left, Lambada held up Asher's mattress while Ellie checked underneath for any surprise hiding places. Nothing.

"This place is clean," Ellie said.

"No shit," Lambada said. He turned a slow circle in the middle of Asher's home. "Strangely clean. This guy's a weirdo. I'm telling you."

"Maybe. We'll see." They left together, this time taking the elevator to the lobby.

Once back at the police station, Ellie couldn't get away from Inspector Lambada fast enough.

"See you up there."

"Where are you going?" Lambada asked, as he stepped in the elevator going up to the homicide division.

"Basement. Want to look at items from Mikala's apartment."

Ellie stepped up to the counter in the evidence room, signing her name and badge number on the sheet attached to a heavy metal clipboard. Soon she was greeted by a harried-looking woman who was busily logging bags of evidence behind the counter.

"How can I help?" the woman said without looking up.

"I'm wondering if I can see items taken from a murder scene this morning?"

The woman stopped what she was doing, glanced at Ellie, and moved over to her computer, where she tapped something into the keyboard. "Decedent Mikala Glascott?"

"That's the one."

"The items aren't logged yet. So you can't take them."

45

"That's fine. I just want to look at them, if you don't mind."

The woman sighed. "Follow me."

Ellie followed the woman to a windowless room filled with fluorescent lights. The buzz from them echoed off the stainless-steel countertops and the tile floor, the effect reminiscent of a swarm of insects.

"That's it." The woman pointed to a collection of evidence covered in plastic.

"Thanks." When the woman hesitated, Ellie said, "You don't have to stay with me. I'm just going to look. Maybe take a shot or two with my cell phone."

"Very well."

Waiting until the footsteps reduced to an echo and then were gone completely, Ellie cleared her mind and took a deep breath before she moved to the table and surveyed the evidence that – with luck – would lead to the capture of Mikala Glascott's killer. Taking out her phone, Ellie snapped pictures of Mikala's clothes, Asher Ridgeland's clothes, Mikala's purse and its contents. Mikala's cell phone and any computers in her possession would likely be with the computer lab for processing. She'd have to wait for that.

Circling back to Mikala's clothes, Ellie skimmed the items once again, until her eyes rested on the tie that had been used as the murder weapon. Casting a glance to the door to make sure she was still alone, Ellie turned it over. No tag. Interesting. She studied the print as best she could through the plastic. Was the tie hand-painted? Looking closely, she scanned the fabric until she found a very subtle signature. Levi Lawrence, a San Francisco designer whose flame had fizzled out along with shoulder pads. Mikala Glascott was murdered with a hand-painted tie made by Levi Lawrence. Interesting.

Chapter 6

As she had done on dozens of Saturdays before, Olivia parked her car in the small space on Lauren Ridley's cobblestoned driveway. Under normal circumstances, she would be eager for their usual walk, followed by a calorie-rich breakfast. Not today. The morning was chilly and quiet; a soft layer of fog cloaked the houses and trees in a hazy mist. She was going to miss the long walks and carb-loaded breakfasts that she and Lauren had shared over the years. Lake Tahoe was a beautiful place, but nothing beat the walk on the bike path along the bay to Sausalito. Lugging a castoff backpack that Denny had used for a bookbag in high school, Olivia headed up the walkway, redolent with fallen leaves and rich, loamy earth, and wondered what mood awaited her behind Lauren's front door.

As if she'd been waiting for her, Lauren stepped outside and closed the door behind her. She grabbed Olivia's arm and pulled her away from the house, out of earshot of Ava. This morning her mass of silver curls was twisted into a bun and held in place by two paintbrushes. The lines around her mouth were deep from exhaustion, and her eyes had a worried look in them that Olivia had never seen before. "No offense, Liv, but you look like the ghost of doom and gloom."

"That's an accurate description of how I feel." The two women huddled together outside the front door.

"How's it going?"

"She's terrified." Lauren glanced over her shoulder. "Hate to admit her terror is rubbing off on me. I thought Ava would feel safe here, but she's walking around like a field mouse being stalked by a bird of prey. Do you think we're in danger? Are you in danger?"

"I don't think so," Olivia said.

Crossing her arms over her chest, Lauren scrutinized Olivia. "Why do I get the feeling you're holding something back?"

"Brian thinks her husband will hire professionals – the best investigators money can buy, to use his words – to hunt for Ava. Eventually, they'll stumble across her connection with you."

Lauren gasped. "What should we do?"

"Brian's working on a plan. He's going to come over and speak to both of you later on today. We're being hypervigilant, just as a precaution."

"This is bad, Liv. I didn't know it would be like this when I offered help." Lauren fell into step behind Olivia as they stepped inside Lauren's living room, with its floor-to-ceiling picture windows and the sweeping view of Mt. Tamalpais.

Ava peeked around the corner. "Good morning, Olivia."

"Hello." Olivia set her backpack on the floor as a bell dinged in Lauren's kitchen.

"That's the quiche," Ava said, hurrying away, leaving Olivia and Lauren alone.

Olivia watched Lauren as she double-bolted the locks on her front door and turned on the alarm.

"New alarm?" Olivia asked.

"An upgrade to the old one. I got a serious discount on my homeowner's insurance for installing it. It's attached directly to the fire and police departments."

"Should we find Ava another place to stay? If you're uncomfortable—"

"I'm the one who brought you into this mess, so no. She can stay here. Brian will protect us. God, I can't believe I said that. So much for my righteous feminism. Anyway, Ava needs us. She's a sister in distress. This isn't going to be easy. I know that. Although I'm surprised to see you so rattled. You're as tense as I've ever seen you. Maybe we should start smoking . . ." Lauren gave Olivia a sheepish smile and they both laughed.

"Ava told you about Mark's abuse?"

"She gave me a play-by-play of her entire marriage last night." Lauren shivered. "Brian must be furious with me for bringing this into your lives right before retirement. If I'd known, I would never have – is he going to have security guards watching the house?"

"Probably."

"So don't go in front of the windows naked?"

"That'd be smart." Olivia felt her shoulders relax as she followed Lauren into her living room, where coffee, fruit, and croissants waited. Through the double doors leading into the kitchen, Olivia watched Ava as she moved around like a pro.

"Would you be willing to move to your beach house? Brian will provide security. We think you'll both be safer there."

"You're worried about him finding our connection, aren't you?" Olivia nodded.

"Whatever you think would be best. Sure. The woman can cook like a pro. She made the best scones I've ever tasted. She's been binge-cooking nonstop since she got here. My fridge is now full of so many casseroles and soups that I won't have to cook for years."

"How is she doing?"

"Not great, if I'm honest." Lauren spoke softly as she poured Olivia a cup of coffee. "She's terrified, of course. Jumpy."

"Excuse me." Ava came into the room, the front of her shirt covered with a wet stain that smelled of orange juice. "I've got slippery fingers this morning. Breakfast will be ready in a second. I'm just going to change my shirt."

Neither one of them spoke until they heard Ava's bedroom door open and shut.

"I'm not going to stay for breakfast. I just really need to talk to Ava," Olivia said.

"No problem. I figured you'd be busy today." Lauren sighed. "Congratulations on your house. I'm excited for you. Hate to see you move, but the house is gorgeous."

"You'll help with packing? I need you to help me downsize."

"Of course. I'll be ruthless."

"We'll get her through this," Olivia said.

"I can't abandon her," Lauren said at the same time.

They smiled at each other.

"When she gets back, I need to talk to her for a minute."

At the sound of Ava's bedroom door and footsteps on the flagstone hall, Olivia and Lauren stopped talking.

"I want Lauren to stay," Ava said, as she walked back into the room. "She should know what's going on. She's taking a risk by having me here. She needs to know what Mark is up to."

"Fair enough," Olivia said. "But I need to discuss some strategic issues. Discussing them in front of Lauren could be construed as a waiver of attorney – client privilege, which could harm us if we go to trial. I think it would be better—"

"Go to trial?" Ava's voice rose an octave. "I told you in our initial meeting that I will not sit in a courtroom or any room with my husband. I cannot do that. I won't."

"I'll just go in my bedroom and let you two talk." Lauren stood.

"I don't mean to sound difficult, but I want you to stay. Please," Ava said. She reminded Olivia of a frightened bird, delicate and wary, as she sat on the sofa. Her hands fluttered as she started to pick her cuticle.

Olivia bit back her irritation. When Ava noticed this reaction she said, "I'm sorry. I really am. I'm just not quite sure what's going to happen. You two are being so helpful, and I appreciate that. But I do not want to be around Mark. And I need Lauren to stay because I have the attention span of a piece of lint. It's good to have an extra set of eyes and ears." Ava sat down on the couch, tucking her legs underneath her. Lauren sat on the floor, Indian style, as Olivia grabbed her legal pad out of her backpack.

"There have been a few developments." Olivia was quick to reassure her. "Nothing we can't handle. You know we filed a complaint for divorce against your husband?"

"Right," Ava said.

"Remember that financial document, the Income and Expense Declaration you signed?" Olivia took a copy of the document and handed it to Ava. "We need to submit that to Mark. It's required by law. We need to appear before the judge to go over that, just to confirm the numbers are accurate." Olivia held up her hand in an effort to stave off questions. "This is normal, as I mentioned."

"But you told me we weren't requesting a hearing because I didn't ask for spousal support," Ava said, her face awash with confusion and fear.

"Mark asked for the hearing. And you're going to have to appear."

A look of abject terror bloomed across Ava's face. "There's no getting away from him, is there? Guys like Mark Bledsoe always win. What was I thinking trying to leave him? Maybe I should go back. Do you think I should go back?"

"No," Olivia replied.

"Absolutely not," Lauren echoed.

"What do you think he'd do to you if you went back?" Lauren asked.

"Kill me." Lauren and Olivia waited while Ava buried her head in her hands. When she finally looked up, she seemed diminished, defeated somehow.

Lauren said, "You need to get safely away, Ava. And Olivia is the only person I would trust to make that happen."

"You've done the leaving, Ava. You're safe here. But you do need to show up in court. We could get a restraining order, just to have it on file. We've got enough evidence of abuse to support it. That would give you an extra level of protection."

Ava stared at her hands. "No restraining order."

"Why not?" Lauren didn't bother keeping the surprise from her voice.

"Because he will just ignore it, and it will make him more angry. Plus, he could lose his job if it gets out that he's – that he is what he is." Ava turned resolutely to Olivia. "I'm assuming you have a plan. Tell me what it is."

"Your husband gave me his financial disclosures. They are not truthful. If we are going to fight him – notice that I'm saying *if* – I could use this misrepresentation as leverage."

"But we're not going to litigate because I'm leaving the minute my passport comes through," Ava reiterated. "Can you explain why we have to go to court?"

"It's not usual procedure," Olivia said. "Dan Winters, your husband's attorney, told me that his client wants it on the record that you took money. I think that Mr. Winters is doing whatever Mark tells him to, even though it is not customary. But we – you – have to show up for this hearing."

"I know my husband. He's trying to lure me out, isn't he?"

"That's what we think."

"I should have known something like this would happen."

"Ava, listen to me. I told you when you came to my office that things were going to get worse before they got better. We can handle this."

Ava's face had turned an alarming shade of white. For a moment, Olivia thought she was going to pass out. Lauren moved to the couch and sat down next to her.

"You need to trust Olivia. She'll keep you safe. I promise." Lauren put an arm around Ava and shot Olivia an imploring look.

"This isn't the first abusive husband I've dealt with," Olivia said. "Honestly, I'm not even worried about the hearing. Here's why. Courtrooms have armed bailiffs in them. There will be a bailiff outside the courtroom door, and Mark will have to go through security to get into the courthouse. The only time you will be vulnerable is going to and from the courthouse. Brian, my investigator, will have you well covered during that time. We'll have someone stationed by Lauren's car, just in case Mark attempts to put a tracking device on it. Brian and one of his colleagues will escort you from the car to the courthouse. They will be armed. You will never be alone. After the hearing, you'll be gone before Mark can exit the building."

"What if Mark runs Lauren's license plate and finds me that way?"

"That's a good point. We thought maybe after the hearing the two of you could move out to Lauren's beach house. It's a safe spot, owned by a third-party trustee."

"I used to escape there during the rock-and-roll days," Lauren explained. "No one will find us. We'll be safe there."

Olivia continued. "Brian will have someone with you full-time. You and Lauren will have to be hypervigilant." Olivia glanced at Lauren, happy to see her nodding her approval. "Brian is a retired cop. He knows how to deal with this."

Ava looked at Lauren. "What do you think?"

"I think it's a good plan. As I said, my beach house was my hideaway when my band was in full swing, and I needed to get away. The title is held in a shell company that Mark would be hard pressed to find. We'll be safe there."

Olivia hesitated, not sure if she should tell Ava about Mark's violent reaction to getting served papers. In the end, she decided against it. Nothing would be gained by instilling more fear into these women. Brian would keep them safe, of that Olivia had no doubt.

"I know you're afraid," Olivia said. "We just need to stay focused."

Olivia and Lauren exchanged a look while Ava sat on the sofa, her body wound tight, fists clenched, taking deep breaths.

Olivia gathered all the papers and stood to leave. Ava and Lauren followed her to the front door.

"Brian will be over this afternoon to discuss security arrangements for the hearing."

Ava nodded.

"I'm a phone call away." She heard the deadbolt latch as she walked to her car.

Olivia had just pulled away from Lauren's house when Brian called her.

"How did it go with Ava?" At the sound of his voice, the tension in her shoulders eased away.

"She's scared. As expected. Did you enlist help?"

"All taken care of," Brian said. "For the hearing. Actually, starting right now. The exterior of Lauren's house is covered. Should I arrange for a man inside?"

"That's a good idea. Do you mind working this out with Lauren? I said you'd call or visit this afternoon to work out the details."

"I'll do that right now."

"Good. I'm on my way home. I'm starving."

"How about a spinach and mushroom omelet, roasted new potatoes, and a strong pot of coffee?"

"Oh, Brian, how I love you," Olivia said.

"Would you mind stopping by my office and getting my phone charger? I left it on my desk. When you get here, I'll be plating your breakfast."

"Sure. See you soon."

On this sunny Saturday, Magnolia Avenue was populated with people strolling along looking at the shops. The outside tables at the café were full of people lingering over coffee as they read newspapers, while hikers and mountain bikers headed toward King Mountain and Mt. Tam. Olivia loved the village feel of her town.

She took in the scene before she stopped in front of her office and started to put her key into the door.

"I haven't abused my wife," said a voice behind her.

Olivia wheeled around, instinctively reaching in her purse and grabbing her mace. Mark Bledsoe. She recognized his face from the photos Ava had shown her during their first meeting. He was tall, Olivia guessed six foot two at least, with broad shoulders, a thatch of blond curly hair, and icy blue eyes. On first glance, Olivia judged Mark Bledsoe as a *man's man*, the type who was comfortable in hunting lodges, drinking Scotch neat, and bragging about what he killed that day. She saw the anger in his eyes, and knew that he was no better than a schoolyard bully come to try to intimidate her. When Mark Bledsoe saw the can of mace, he raised his hands in surrender as he took two steps back.

"That won't be necessary, Mrs. Sinclair. I've never laid a hand on my wife, nor any woman for that matter." He further broadened the gap between them as he allowed a woman pushing a stroller to pass through. When they were once again alone, he smiled at her, as though they were old friends, his perfect white teeth and the predatory expression in his eyes reminding Olivia of a hungry wolf.

"My wife stole money from me. She drained all the money out of my checking and savings accounts. She's a gold digger, Mrs. Sinclair. Has she paid you yet? Because if not, I suggest you get your money. She's not to be trusted."

"I'm not going to discuss the case with you, Mr. Bledsoe. We can go over all your allegations if your divorce goes to trial. You should know that won't happen until after I do a forensic audit of all your holdings." Still clutching her mace, she smiled at him. "You know, I've been a divorce lawyer for over twenty years. I've dealt with men who try to hide money from me." At his condescending smile, Olivia said, "Don't believe me? Ask Dan Winters. He knows what I'm capable of. Now if there's nothing else, I'm ready for you to stop bothering me." Olivia turned her back on him and unlocked her office door.

"Did she tell you that she tried to poison me? Make sure to have your boyfriend get that police report. We were having a romantic weekend in Yosemite – three years ago, that was . . . She gave me Gatorade spiked with ethylene glycol. Lucky for me, I didn't swallow much and got to the hospital just in time. Check it out."

"I don't believe you. Please leave."

"Fine. I'll go. But you're making a mistake."

"I believe Ava."

"Of course you do. You women stick together, don't you? You're a man-hater, aren't you? Make your living cheating men out of their hard-earned wages?"

"I'm calling the police."

"Don't bother. I'm leaving." By the time Olivia was safely locked in her office, Mark Bledsoe was gone.

Chapter 7

Asher woke up Sunday morning to discover his apartment bliss-fully empty. His mother had left, and for the first time since Mikala's murder, he felt clear-headed and ravenously hungry.

As he got up and made coffee in his galley kitchen, Asher let himself think about the past fourteen months since Mikala had stormed into his life. They had met serendipitously at a club when Asher had gone to a bachelor party for one of his friends. The night had gone along as expected. By eleven o'clock, all the groomsmen and friends were drunk out of their minds, thanks to shots of Jägermeister. Asher, who had only consumed one beer, was totally sober and ready to call it a night.

As plans were made to move on to another venue for live music, Asher, who doubted he would be missed, decided to slip away. He found Mikala, with her raven-black glamour goth look and her long legs, trying to stay upright on impossibly high heels while hailing a taxi in front of the club. As she started to tumble, he moved toward her without thinking. "I've got ya," Asher said, grabbing her elbow.

Asher remembered the exact second she looked at him with her unusual turquoise eyes. He'd never been so instantly attracted to a woman in his entire life. He was a goner.

When Mikala hiccupped and said, "Apologies. I've had a bit too much," he did something totally out of character and asked her to go have breakfast with him.

They went to Fog City Diner for pancakes and had ended up staying at the restaurant drinking endless cups of coffee until the sun rose.

After their early breakfast, Asher paid the bill and drove Mikala home. They made a date for dinner the next night, and – at least as far as Asher was concerned – had been a couple ever since. Asher poured himself coffee and opened his fridge, mindlessly looking for something to eat. True to her word, his mother had packed his fridge with two casseroles, and several containers full of what looked like pasta salad, chicken salad, and cut fruit. There was a note on the counter.

I've filled your fridge with your favorites.
You know I love you to the moon and back.

He'd just taken his first sip of coffee when his intercom buzzed.

"It's Lexy. I've brought bagels. Lox and cream cheese. Just how you like them. Can I come in?"

"Come on up." He buzzed Lexy in and quickly pulled the duvet over his bed and tossed some dirty laundry in the bathroom hamper.

Asher had always liked Lexy Ford. He knew her to be a hard-working, down-to-earth lawyer. She'd had a rough childhood. Through no fault of her own, she wound up in foster care, finally aging out of the system with no job and no place to go. By virtue of sheer willpower and hard work, Lexy had managed to put herself through college and law school while working two jobs. She had a ferocious kind of energy about her that made Asher feel certain she was a powerhouse in the courtroom.

"Thanks for seeing me. I hate to drop in, but we need to talk." Lexy came into the apartment, set the bag from Luther's Bagels on the kitchen counter, and did a 360 pivot, taking in the large windows, and the two chairs strategically placed to enjoy the view.

"You're the most immaculate man I've ever met," Lexy said, her voice awestruck.

Asher laughed. "Nope. My mom stayed with me all day yesterday. While I slept, she cleaned my house and filled my fridge."

Lexy wiped her eyes with the back of her sleeve. "Sorry. I've been trying to hold it together. But I can't forget finding you two – God, it was horrible."

Awkward, but obligated to do something, Asher went to Lexy and put his arms out, as if to hug her.

"Please, don't. If you try to comfort me, I'll lose it and fall apart completely." She moved into the kitchen and pointed at the plates stacked neatly on the shelf near the large kitchen window. "Do you mind?"

"Go for it. There's coffee in the pot. Mugs are right there on the shelf."

Asher sat in one of the chairs and waited for Lexy to join him. Once they were seated, they each took a bagel and spent a few minutes adding cream cheese and eating in silence. Lexy spoke first.

"I thought and thought about talking to you – you know – telling you what Mikala was up to. If I were in your shoes, I would want to know the truth. Every time I started to say something, we would get interrupted or I would lose my courage. I am sorry."

Asher turned to face Lexy, but she wouldn't look at him. Instead, she clutched her coffee mug and stared into it, as though the secrets to the world were contained there.

"Don't blame yourself. She was cheating on me. Probably for a long time. Don't feel obligated to disclose Mikala's dirty secrets, Lexy. If I'm honest, I really don't want to know."

Lexy put her coffee cup down. "I need to tell you something, but I need your assurances that you'll not tell anyone."

"Okay," Asher said.

59

"I used my law firm's PI to find out this information. I could lose my job."

"Okay," Asher said.

"Mikala is not who she says she is."

"What are you talking about?"

"The PI ran a background check on her. He couldn't find anything. She doesn't exist. There's no one in California named Mikala Glascott that meets our Mikala's physical description."

"But that's impossible. She's Mikala – everyone calls her that. She worked as a cocktail waitress at Elevations. Surely she had to fill out an application, show proof of identification to get a paycheck?"

Lexy shook her head. "You're kidding right? Mikala worked for cash."

"Well, where else did you check?"

"Nowhere," Lexy said. "Too risky. I'm not going to go near a murder investigation." She tucked a lock of hair behind her ear. "There's more. You're going to hate me after I tell you this." She put a gentle hand on Asher's arm. "But you need to know the truth about her. You need to know what I told the police."

"Just say it, Lexy."

"What do you remember about the night it happened?"

"I remember coming home, finding Mikala with another man – shocked the hell out of me, if I'm honest. We fought. Went to Elevations. Fought some more. Came back to the house. Drank champagne. After that . . . Nothing. My mind is completely blank. I don't remember anything except waking up in the morning next to Mikala's strangled—"

"There was more than one man, Asher. I'm sorry." Lexy wadded up her napkin and tossed it on her empty plate. "Mikala loved you as best she could. But she was really messed up. How do you think she paid for her apartment?"

"I don't know how she paid for her apartment," Asher said. "When I asked her about her finances, she shut me out, as in slammed the door, hard."

"And you didn't push? Didn't you wonder how Mikala paid for such an expensive apartment? I would have pushed back and asked her, if I were you."

"We'll you're not me," Asher snapped. "Sorry. I just figured she was private about finances."

Lexy stood and grabbed her purse. "I shouldn't have come. I'm sorry, Asher. Really."

"Wait. Wait. Please," Asher said. "This is hard for me to hear. Just give me a minute, okay? Can you sit down and give me a minute?"

Lexy hesitated. "Maybe we should do this later, after you've taken another day or two to rest. Then we can talk."

"No, I can talk now. Tell me what your PI found out. I'll be discreet. Am I a suspect?"

"You? God, no. You're totally in the clear. I mean, you were drugged too. You could have died." She watched him, as if to make sure he was capable of handling her revelations.

"Tell me," Asher pushed. "I can handle it."

"You realize that your relationship with her was a bit dysfunctional, right? I mean it was obvious that you loved her. Because of that, I can see why your judgment could be a bit jaded. But she used to pick fights with you. God, she used to wail on you. Don't you see that she'd work you both into a frenzy, until you got angry, and she became violent?"

"I never raised a hand to her," Asher whispered.

"Of course you didn't. I told the police that you didn't. I grew up around violence. I know in my heart, and I would swear in court, that you are not a violent man," Lexy said without rancor. "But think back. She picked fights for the make-up sex."

The make-up sex. The mind-blowing, intense, insane make-up sex. "Okay, I'll concede that."

"I told the detectives – many times – that there was no way you would have laid a finger on Mikala. I told them she had other lovers, at least two that I know of. And I think she was blackmailing them."

"What the actual hell, Lexy. Why did you tell the police that? It makes Mikala look like a – I don't know—"

"Because it's true, Asher. And because someone murdered her. Drugged you and murdered her. I'm the one who found the two of you. Remember? I'll never unsee that. I haven't slept. I can't eat. My doctor wants me to see a psychiatrist." Lexy, who had also started crying, wiped her eyes. "I want her killer found. I want to see him suffer. But she was engaged in risky behavior. You should know that. You know, I met Mikala at Elevations when she was a waitress. We became friends, probably because we have similar backgrounds. When she offered me a room at her luxury apartment for next-to-nothing rent, I jumped. By quick math, I realized that if I could live with Mikala for a year and continue to pinch pennies, I could pay off my student loans."

"Mikala was generous," Asher said, thinking of the times she'd emptied her wallet for someone who was homeless and living on the street.

"She was. Sometimes. But there was one catch to living here. Mikala had a man friend, a sugar daddy. He paid one year's rent in advance. She had to get permission from him to let me live there. The only proviso was that I had to leave when he came calling."

"How often did that happen?"

"I don't know. Every three to four months?" Lexy sipped her coffee and took a bite of her bagel, acting as though she were buying time. "She had another guy she was seeing. And I know she hit him up for money. I heard her threatening him if he didn't give her ten thousand dollars."

Blackmail. The unspoken elephant in the room. Mikala may have had a sugar daddy paying her rent, but that didn't explain Mikala's general lifestyle. She lived as though money weren't an object.

"She was messed up psychologically, Asher," Lexy said. "You need to know that."

Asher reflected on the fights, the times Mikala got violent. The little slips in manners and social decorum that his mother never hesitated to point out after Mikala had spent time with her. "I'm aware of Mikala's psychology. We dated for over a year. Are you making excuses for me?"

"I think she may have pulled the wool over your eyes."

The bluntness of Lexy's statement hit home.

"You love her, right?" Lexy shook her head. "Loved her. I could tell when the two of you were together." Lexy closed her eyes and shook her head. "Look, I'm sorry. I'm not saying that you were gullible or anything. Mikala had a certain – I don't know – way of pulling people in. Her victims probably didn't even know they were being conned."

"Point taken. But she loved me," Asher said. "I believe what you are saying about her, but I know that she also loved me."

"Agreed," Lexy says. "Honestly, I think you were the only stable thing in her life. I think she knew that you were too good for her."

"I'm going to find out the truth about her. I'm going to find out who she really is, and then I'm going to find out who killed her."

"No. You cannot do that." Lexy was serious.

"I have to do this, Lexy. It's like I'm being called to see it through."

"Listen to me. Do not involve yourself in her murder investigation. Not now. You will make nothing but trouble for yourself. Don't make me regret coming here and telling you what I've discovered. Please. I'm begging you."

"I don't want Mikala's name dragged through the mud," Asher said.

Lexy shook her head. "I don't believe this. You're still loyal to Mikala, despite what you know about her?"

"It's a character flaw."

Lexy's features softened for a moment. "No, it's not. You're one of the good guys, Asher. Don't ever change."

"Do you know who any of her—" Asher stumbled over the words "—lovers were?"

"No," Lexy said, her expression stern now. "The police will find out who they were. They'll discover she was a blackmailer. Soon they'll know everything. All you can do, the best thing you can do, is wait it out and keep your distance."

"I don't know if I can do that."

"You need to try." Lexy stood. "I really have to go."

Asher walked Lexy to the door. "Do you have a place to stay?"

"Yeah. I'm staying with friends. Looking for an apartment." She gave Asher a weak smile.

"When I was lying in that living room, naked and unable to move and you came home . . .?"

"Yeah."

"When I heard your footsteps, I knew that everything would be okay, that you would know what to do."

Lexy laughed through her tears. "And then I totally fell apart."

"You likely saved my life. I was given a nearly lethal dose of Rohypnol."

"We're a mess, aren't we?"

"You were a good friend to Mikala."

"I loved her," Lexy said. "Despite her faults."

"Me too. Despite her faults."

"Mikala's blackmail, the shady things she was up to, I made it a point to stay out of that part of her life. I didn't approve, but I didn't leave because of the cheap rent. Shameful, right?"

"No," Asher said. "I get it."

"Speak soon?" Lexy said.

Asher nodded.

Once Lexy was gone, Asher opened his laptop and sat down in his favorite chair. He started checking his email when the jarring buzzer rang. Someone was downstairs and wanted in. He stood too fast and immediately became woozy. Using his hand to steady himself against the wall, he hit the intercom button. "Hello?"

"Asher? It's Inspector Lambada. We met in the hospital?"

Asher sighed. The visit from the police, despite his cooperation, was inevitable. "What can I do for you, Inspector?"

"I have a handful of questions."

"Come on up."

Asher was waiting when the inspector stepped into the landing with his black leather jacket, tight jeans, and black boots.

"Do you always work on Sundays, Inspector?" Asher asked as he held the door and motioned Lambada into his apartment.

"No days off while investigating a murder." Once inside, the inspector stood in the middle of the studio and turned a slow circle, studying the room. For the briefest moment, the cop reminded Asher of a wolf, a predator. He felt a frisson of fear start at the base of his spine; he pushed it away, as he sat back down in one of the club chairs.

"I need to sit. Still a bit woozy."

Lambada remained standing. He pulled out his phone. "We found the gas receipt on top of your desk. But can you tell me anyone you spoke to while you were gone? Someone who actually laid eyes on you, spoke to you? A waitress in a café, someone like that?"

"No. I was alone. Can't you get CCTV from the gas station? I'd have thought you would have done that already."

"Okay. That's it for now. Thanks." The inspector tucked his phone into his jacket pocket. "Don't get up. I'll see myself out."

"Let me know what I need to do, so you can clear me," Asher said.

When Inspector Lambada met his eyes, there was no mistaking the challenge there.

"We appreciate your cooperation." The inspector moved to the door. But he didn't leave. Instead, he scrutinized the apartment, his gaze traveling up and down the walls, to Asher's desk, across his hurriedly made bed. Finally, he nodded at Asher, slipped out the door, and was gone.

Chapter 8

Much to Olivia's surprise, Ava Bledsoe arrived at the Marin County Courthouse on Tuesday ready for a fight. She strode into the courtroom, flanked by Brian and two men that Olivia had never met before, a look of steely determination on her face.

"I'm ready," Ava said.

Olivia made eye contact with Brian, who gave the subtlest nod, indicating that their plan, and all allowances made for contingencies, was in place. She turned to Ava and said, "Let's step over here for a second."

Ava followed her over to the expansive window that looked out over Highway 101, now full of traffic heading south to the Golden Gate Bridge toward San Francisco.

"This shouldn't take long," Olivia said. "The main thing for you to do is not say anything, no matter what Mark says. In fact, if I were you, I wouldn't even look at him. He's going to try to trigger you when we get in there. You're clear on what Brian and his guys are going to do after the hearing?"

"I'm clear," Ava whispered. "We rehearsed it a dozen times. Your boyfriend is nothing if not thorough."

"Okay. So when—"

"If I had your job, I'd never sleep—" Ava's eyes widened in shock as the color drained from her face.

Olivia was once again struck by Mark Bledsoe's charisma. Today he wore a bespoke suit. His curly ginger hair was slicked down with hair gel. His eyes, startling blue and bloodshot red, were full of rage, not the same knife-sharp edgy emotion she'd experienced when he confronted her at the grocery store. No. Today's anger was a direct result of loss of control. Ava was no longer under Mark's thumb. Mark resented that. This wasn't the first time Olivia had encountered a bully, so it was easy for her to remain calm. She caught Brian's eye. He gave her a weak smile before he placed himself between Ava and Mark.

"Look at me." When Ava met Olivia's gaze, she said, "Stay strong. Don't let him see your fear."

"Okay," Ava whispered.

"Ava?" Mark Bledsoe's voice, pleading and desperate, rang through the corridors.

"Take a deep breath. We've got you. You're safe."

Ava nodded as she fought for control.

Behind her, Olivia heard Brian speaking to Dan Winters, his voice a low murmur. Mark Bledsoe jumped in, his voice booming. "Are you telling me she thinks I'm going to harm her in front of all these people?"

Brian spoke again, his voice too low for Olivia to hear what he was saying.

"Fine. Fine," Bledsoe said.

When the bailiff opened the courtroom, Olivia ushered Ava inside. She smiled at Johnny Jack, a familiar bailiff who had just started his job when Olivia tried her first case. Over the years they had become friends and often joked they had grown up together.

"Johnny," Olivia said.

"Is that Mark Bledsoe?" He nodded towards Mark and Dan Winters who were whispering to each other in the hall.

Two tables were arranged in front of the elevated bench, where the presiding judge would sit. Strategically eyeing the table closest to the fire exit, Olivia said to Ava, "We'll sit at that table. You take the chair closest to the door, so Brian can whisk you out of here."

"Okay," Ava said, her voice dry and tense.

As Ava walked away, Olivia whispered to Johnny, "Please have your men be on guard. Mark Bledsoe went after my process server with a baseball bat."

His smile and affable nature grew serious, as his hand instinctively went to his Glock and lingered there.

"Is everything okay?" Ava asked as she accepted the legal pad and pen Olivia handed her.

"Fine. I just put the bailiffs on high alert. Not that I think we'll need it."

Ava shot her a look indicating she did not share Olivia's confidence. "Do I need to take notes?"

"Only if you want to, or if something comes up that you want me to ask the judge. You aren't not allowed to address the court or speak unless you are sworn in and in that witness box there." Olivia pointed to a wooden desk next to the judge with a microphone and a comfortable looking chair.

Olivia sensed Mark and Dan Winters enter the court room.

"Don't look at them," Olivia said. Out of the corner of her eye, she watched Mark and Dan Winters sit down at the table next to them. Johnny Jack was in a huddle with the three other bailiffs. When they saw Mark Bledsoe sit down, they broke rank and moved into a tactical position. Two of the bailiffs near the bench, and two others stationed in the corners near the attorneys' table.

Olivia glanced over to Mark Bledsoe. Their eyes met long enough for Olivia to sense the fury there. He wasn't the first abusive husband who thought he could intimidate Olivia with a stare. She didn't look away, instead she stared back until Mark Bledsoe averted his eyes, just as another bailiff stepped into the court via the door by the bench and called for all to rise as he announced Judge Andrews.

"Be seated," Judge Andrews said.

Olivia leaned into Ava and whispered, "You okay?"

Ava nodded.

"We're on the record in the Marriage of Bledsoe." Judge Andrews looked through the pleadings as he read the case number into the record. Olivia had a begrudging respect for Judge Andrews. Small in stature, he had a tonsure, and the shiny smooth complexion of a young man. On first glance, Judge Andrews had the look of a medieval monk, especially in his robe. Over the years she'd heard other lawyers make fun of him, but she had learned early on not to underestimate him. In reality, he had a reputation as being a thoughtful man, with a rapier intellect, and an ability to memorize case law and opinions verbatim. Now, he looked across the bench over his reading glasses, taking in Olivia and Dan Winters.

"I see the petitioner in this matter, Mrs. Bledsoe, filed her complaint for divorce, yet didn't request spousal support or a hearing." Judge Andrews directed his gaze to Dan Winters. "What's going on, Mr. Winters?"

Dan Winters stood and buttoned his jacket. "We're here because of Mrs. Bledsoe's actions. She left her home under suspicious circumstances—"

"Objection." Olivia rose. "There was nothing suspicious about her leaving. She's not obligated to report her actions—"

"Olivia, I'll give you a chance to speak." Judge Andrews addressed Dan Winters. "Why did your client request a spousal support hearing? Just answer that question. Directly, if you please."

"When Mrs. Bledsoe left the marital residence she emptied the parties' joint checking and savings accounts. My client wants the record clear, so that at the time of trial, that money can be accounted for."

"So, Mr. Winters, you filed a spousal support hearing even though neither one of you wants spousal support?"

"As I mentioned, Mrs. Bledsoe took all the money out of

the parties' joint checking and savings accounts. Without his permission."

"Did she leave her husband destitute?"

"No, Your Honor."

"Mrs. Sinclair, would you like to weigh in here?"

"Mrs. Bledsoe left her husband, and took the money out of the joint accounts because she needed money to leave. It's our position that the money she took can be dealt with at the time Your Honor deals with the equitable distribution of the marital assets. There was really no need for this hearing today. I'm honestly not quite sure why we are here, to tell you the truth."

Out of the corner of her eye, Olivia watched Dan Winters turn around to confer with his client. Mark Bledsoe took a pen, wrote something on a legal pad, threw the pen down, and sat back in his chair with a defiant grunt.

Olivia continued, "If I can just add, Your Honor, as you can see from our financial disclosures, Mrs. Bledsoe has no source of income. She doesn't have access to any of the other accounts, which we claim are assets. She was aware – is aware – that her husband has access to assets far greater than the money she took when she left. The parties' financial picture is set out in our paperwork and includes information on the parties' other accounts."

Olivia sat down. Dan Winters stood, ready to speak again. "Judge, if I could—"

"The only matter before me today is spousal support, and I've got what I need to make a ruling, Mr. Winters, thank you. Since the petitioner didn't request spousal support, none will be ordered at this time. I'm ordering you both to mediation to occur within the next sixty days. If you can't resolve this matter at mediation, I'll see you back here after that for a trial-setting conference. Let's go off the record."

"That's it?" Mark Bledsoe jumped out of his chair. His outburst caused the two bailiffs – both of them armed – to hurry toward him. "You're letting that woman get away with stealing my money?"

The bailiffs closest to the judge closed ranks, and stayed near him until he was safely out of the courtroom. Meanwhile, the other two bailiffs moved toward Mark Bledsoe. Olivia stuffed her paperwork in her briefcase and slammed it shut.

Brian appeared at Ava's side. "You okay, Liv?"

"Yep."

"Come on, Ava, you know what to do."

Ava stood and she and Brian hurried out of the courtroom, taking the side exit that led to the back parking lot.

Heart pounding, Olivia ignored the escalating chaos around her, as she grabbed her briefcase, and rushed out of the courtroom. A quick glance over her shoulder revealed Mark Bledsoe still yelling, so caught up in his own tirade Olivia doubted he even realized Ava was gone. By the time she reached her car, she was anxious and more than a little terrified. When her phone beeped, Olivia answered it. Brian.

"We're safe. Pulling out of the parking lot now. Where are you?"

"In my car. Leaving. Going home to lock myself in the house." Olivia rested her forehead against the steering wheel. "I'm wondering if it's too late to get out of this case."

"Probably," Brian said, his voice calm and professional. She heard him sigh through the phone, a deep and heavy breath that conveyed the meaning of a million words. "I'll keep you safe, Liv."

"I know. See you at home." Olivia hung up and had just started the car when a staccato rapping on the driver's side window startled her. She cried out, ready to start the car and drive away, willing to run over Mark Bledsoe if he tried to stop her. But it was only Dan Winters standing outside her car, an apologetic look on his face.

"What do you want?" Olivia snapped.

Dan motioned for her to roll down her window. "We're safe. Mark is still in the courtroom. For all I know, he's getting arrested."

Rather than look up and have Dan Winters tower over her, Olivia got out of her car and faced him. "Your client is a menace."

"Maybe," Dan said.

"He went after my process server with a baseball bat."

"A baseball bat?" Dan fidgeted with his tie. A sheen of sweat broke out on his forehead, despite the chill in the air.

"You're afraid of him, aren't you?" Olivia knew the answer without asking, but she wanted to hear Dan admit that his client was dangerous.

"I wasn't until this morning. I admit, the hearing was Mark's idea. He insisted he get an opportunity to speak to the judge. I tried to talk to him about his expectations, tried to tell him that he couldn't testify or address the judge, but he wouldn't listen." Dan set his briefcase on the ground and leaned against the car that was parked next to Olivia's. "What does your client want, Olivia? Let's make this go away."

"She wants a divorce. She wants never to be in a room with her husband again."

Dan raised his eyebrows. "You're telling me she doesn't want to go for half of his money? Come on, I don't believe that for a minute."

"If your client will come up with a lump-sum offer – and between the two of us, she's desperate and will take anything – and if he will agree to leave her alone, she'll take it."

Dan scrutinized Olivia's face. "Why are you being so forthright?"

"Why do you think? My client's terrified. And so are you." Olivia opened her car door. "Talk to your client. Tell him I'll find any assets he's got hidden, convince him the best thing to do is to settle and be done with it."

"Three days. So by Friday?"

"You can have the weekend. Make it Monday morning."

"I'll do my best to have an answer for you first thing." Dan picked up his briefcase, nodded at Olivia, and walked away.

Chapter 9

As Asher pulled into the municipal car park across from the office that Brian Vickery shared with Olivia Sinclair, he wondered if he was making a mistake. Maybe Lexy was right. Maybe he should walk away and leave the entire thing alone. *Nope.* He said the words out loud. He had to move forward. Now was not the time for second-guessing.

Being cautious by nature, Asher had done his own investigation into Brian. The Internet search hadn't revealed much information on the elusive detective, which was impressive in and of itself. Brian Vickery, or someone on his behalf, had done a respectable job at keeping the PI's digital footprint to a minimum. Asher's only hesitation in hiring Brian Vickery was his involvement with Olivia Sinclair. This angle presented a host of potential problems, the foremost being his meddlesome mother, who knew Olivia peripherally through their joint involvement in the Marin Arts Council.

And then there was Olivia herself. Olivia's daughter, Denny, had been Asher's best friend in middle school and high school. Asher never had kids over to his own house to play. His mother had been too fussy, too irritated by loud noises, especially the gleeful laughter of children. In hindsight, he wondered why his mother had allowed him to spend so much time at Olivia's, where he and Denny had made up imaginary games, often involving the moving of furniture and the repurposing of kitchen items into pretend weapons. The freedom to run rough and tumble without worrying about upsetting the resident adult had been a joyous and intoxicating thing for young Asher.

He sighed and thought of Denny: fierce, opinionated, the merciful leader, who he gladly followed on their childhood adventures. She also had a kind streak and had no qualms about sharing the last bar of chocolate. In his youth, Asher had considered Denny his best friend. But as all kids do, they'd grown apart as they aged and developed their adult likes and interests.

Asher jay-walked across Magnolia Street to a discreet office suite next to the historic Larkspur Theater. No sign was on the door. No indication of any business was etched onto the glass-fronted office. On a quick glance, he saw a man who was average height and build, hair worn a little longer than was fashionable, and a face that Asher liked to call "well seasoned" with wrinkle lines around intelligent eyes, a testament to a life well lived. It was Brian Vickery's handshake that told Asher all he needed to know. Vickery was tough, quiet, and – Asher would bet – extremely observant. When he spoke, his voice was well measured and kind. "My office is the first door on the right. Go on back."

As Asher headed down the corridor, he saw Brian step into the street and study the surroundings, like a hawk circling a field looking for mice. Asher wondered at the extra diligence.

Once he was seated across from Asher, Brian took a fresh legal pad out of a drawer.

"Okay. As I mentioned when we spoke on the phone, I am getting ready to retire and not really taking new cases. Tell me what you're looking for. If I can't help you, I can refer you to someone who can."

"First of all, thanks for agreeing to see me," Asher said.

Brian leaned back in his chair and waited, the look on his face inscrutable.

Asher took a deep breath. "Is Olivia here?"

"You know Olivia?" Brian asked.

Asher had a preternatural ability to judge people's body language, a skill he honed and used as a coping mechanism when dealing with his domineering mother and his misogynistic father. At the mention of Olivia's name, the detective's shoulders had tensed, and he had leaned forward in his chair, ever so slightly. The question had put Brian Vickery on edge. Asher wondered why.

"Through Denny. We were best friends when we were kids." At these words Brian's shoulders lost the tension that had crept into them, as he once again settled back into his chair, melding into the soft leather as though he hadn't a care in the world. Asher looked around the office, remembering when the walls were full of bookshelves, and Olivia let them play with the typewriters. "I spent many a happy hour in this office. Denny and I used to pretend we were avenging lawyers. We fought crime by taking pictures of our faces on the photocopy machine." Asher smiled at the memory. Brian Vickery waited.

"I will be sure to give Olivia and Denny your regards. Off topic, but how did you find me? I don't advertise."

"I searched for a private investigator on the Internet. Your name came up, so I dug deeper and discovered your affiliation with Olivia during her criminal issues. I'd appreciate it if you didn't tell Olivia or Denny we met. I need help, but I need it quietly." Asher launched into a precise – because he wrote it out and rehearsed it for an hour – explanation of the events surrounding Mikala's death. Lexy's allegation that Mikala was not who she said she was, and his desire to discover the truth about her. While he spoke, Brian Vickery listened intently, every now and then taking notes, his script so small and tight, there was no chance of Asher reading it across the desk. Asher finished his speech with assurances that money wasn't an issue, and that all he wanted was to find out who Mikala really was, if she had family, and if so, where they were.

"First of all," Brian said, "I'm sorry for your loss. I can tell that you loved Mikala."

"Love. Present tense. Not over it yet. But thank you."

"So are you a suspect?"

"In Mikala's murder? No. The police came to speak to me in the hospital. I gave them a complete rundown of my actions the forty-eight hours before the murder. I gave the detective my keys and let her search my apartment. They know I didn't do it. I'll cooperate until they officially clear me."

"Let me get this straight. You are here because your girlfriend, who's been murdered, was not who she seemed. As such, you want to find out who she really was?"

"That's correct."

"I'm sorry, Mr. Ridgeland, but I don't think you're being completely truthful with me. There's more to this than you're telling me. I don't take cases unless I'm satisfied that I've received the complete picture. What if I tell you that Mikala was up to criminal activity and had a slew of boyfriends?" Brian held up his hand. "Sorry. No disrespect meant to Mikala's memory. But when people want to find out something, they usually have something very specific they want to do with that information. What are your plans?"

"I don't have any," Asher said.

Brian Vickery steepled his hands on the desk. "You love her and want assurances that she loved you?"

Asher paused for a moment as he weighed Brian's words. "I would say that's accurate, yes."

"Why the worry about Olivia finding out? Don't worry. I'll respect your wishes. I'm just curious. If you know Olivia, you know that she is discretion personified. You're worried about someone finding out you're investigating Mikala. I'd like to know who."

Asher felt himself relax. He'd known Brian Vickery for less than fifteen minutes, and he already knew that calling him had been the right decision.

"My mother, Sabine Ridgeland, is a friend of Olivia's. Mikala is – was – a bit garish, wild, for lack of a better word. My mother didn't approve of her, thought she wasn't good enough for me, and took every opportunity to remind me of that fact. She thought Mikala was a gold digger. Not that I have tons of money, but my mother does. And she's neurotic about who she allows into her circle. Mother is certain Mikala had an ulterior motive as far as I was concerned. Speaking of my mother, she's a meddler, so it's best she doesn't know I'm pursuing this. It's easier that way, for me, for her, and – if you take my case – for you."

"Understood. I make a practice not to discuss my clients with anyone, Olivia included, unless she is involved in their case. I often consult her about legal issues as I investigate. I don't want to be prohibited from communicating with her."

"So you're going to tell her what I'm telling you?"

"Not necessarily. But I need to be free to conduct my investigation the way I see fit. I may need to involve Olivia. If that's a problem, I can refer you to a handful of people who aren't on the eve of retirement."

"Olivia won't talk about your investigation to anyone?"

"I can assure you, she won't. But if you're uncomfortable . . ."

"No, it's fine."

"Why don't you tell me about your activity leading up to Mikala's death."

"Okay. I spent the three days before the murder camping by myself. Mikala and I had plans for the weekend, but I headed back early. I knew she wasn't expecting me, so I brought my key and used it to let myself in.

"I stepped into the entry hall." Asher closed his eyes, replaying the scene in his head. "There were lines of cocaine on the coffee table, along with two martini glasses. I strode into the room and caught Mikala standing near the stereo dressed in sexy lingerie. Whoever was with her had slipped out of the room. There's a door that leads outside in her kitchen. Actually, it leads to exterior stairs that drop into an alley behind the building. When I heard the door in the kitchen open and shut, I ran to see who was leaving, but it was too dark. Whoever she was with slipped out. Given the two glasses, one half full, on the coffee table and her utter shock at my arrival, I drew the logical conclusions. She denied having someone there at first, but then changed her story in an effort to either tell the truth or pick a fight. I am ashamed of my behavior, but I lost my temper. Completely.

"I said horrible things. She changed. Before my eyes. Her whole face took on the look of a completely different person, someone I didn't know, at all. She laughed in my face, called me bourgeois, said she's never been exclusive with me and insinuated that I was foolish to think that she could be monogamous." Asher swiped his eyes with the back of his sleeve. "I could tell by the look in her eyes that she enjoyed hurting me, enjoyed the drama. I was shocked. Couldn't believe it. I would have sworn with my dying breath that she was a loyal, faithful girlfriend, if it weren't for the glaring evidence. Anyway, we had a pretty loud argument.

"Mikala grabbed her purse and headed out the door. I followed her. We wound up at Elevations. Do you know that club? I swear, that place is like Kryptonite to Mikala. Once she stepped into that place, everything bad about her – her desire for drugs, her desire to be the center of attention, and her greed for endless quantities of alcohol – came to the surface."

Brian spoke, pulling Asher out of his reminiscences about his murdered girlfriend. "You didn't have a drink?"

Asher shook his head. "At the club? No. I don't drink much. I don't do drugs either, in case you're wondering. Mikala had two Belvedere martinis. She guzzled one and was sipping the second when I confronted her once again about being with another man. She started yelling. I yelled back, not caring that everyone was looking at us, not caring that our argument was likely being recorded. There are security cameras all over the place inside Elevations. Mikala was spiraling, becoming unhinged. When she slapped me, I grabbed her arm and pushed her against the wall. I just wanted her to talk to me. If she didn't want to be with me, exclusively, in an adult relationship that was going somewhere, I wanted her to tell me.

"When I had her pinned against that wall, I checked my behavior, caught myself overpowering this woman who I was supposed to love. I was taught to never raise my hand to a woman, no matter what. I was so overcome with self-loathing, I didn't even recognize myself. What had I become? I started to let go and push away from her, to break the contact. It's like I saw the relationship for the toxic, dysfunctional mess that it was. Mikala said she didn't want to be exclusive. Message received, right? But before I could do that, she pulled me close and kissed me. Said me being aggressive like that turned her on. She said she loved me and asked me to forgive her."

Asher laughed sardonically. "What a joke. The fighting turned her on? It repulsed me. She provoked me every chance she got. We'd fight, intense nonsensical arguments that just went round in circles, until Mikala was ready to make up. Then we'd segue into intoxicating make-up sex. I had always thought once Mikala became more secure in our relationship she'd relax and trust me. That things would become more sedate. I don't want to be in a violent relationship. Fighting does not turn me on. At all. That night, after she finally calmed down, we left the club and went back to her apartment. I'm so naïve, my plan was to ask her to go to counseling, maybe get some help. Back at the apartment, we found a bottle of champagne in the ice bucket with a flute, like a present from someone."

Brian who had sat still and quiet throughout Asher's story leaned forward. "A present?"

"It wasn't there when I got there. Now that I think about it, the other glasses had been cleared away. Someone set it up while we were gone."

"Do you know who else had a key to Mikala's apartment?"

"Other than Lexy, no," Asher said. "But Lexy was gone. She slipped out when we were fighting. That I *did* see."

"And there was only one flute out?"

"Yes. Mikala insisted I have some champagne, so she got me another glass and I drank some, just to be polite. I wanted to talk about our relationship, get us into counseling. I took a sip of champagne. I don't remember anything after that."

"Had the champagne been previously opened?" Brian asked.

Asher hesitated, closed his eyes. "I think so. It had one of those stoppers in it, so yeah, it had been opened. I vaguely remember waking up the next morning in Mikala's apartment, naked, on the floor. I rolled over on my side. Saw Mikala lying next to me, dead. Got sick. Lexy got home. Screamed her lungs out. The paramedics came and took me to the hospital.

"After I got home from the hospital, Lexy dropped by my apartment. She told me Mikala had many lovers. She had never been exclusive with me. I thought we were in a monogamous relationship; thought we were headed somewhere. Talk about a total miscalculation on my part. I just cast her in a role, for lack of a better word, saw her as I wanted to see her, not for who she really was."

"What did Lexy say when she came to see you? Do you think she is involved?"

"No way. Lexy is solid. She's a lawyer, and is probably one of the hardest-working people I've ever met. She told me she ran a background check on Mikala and couldn't find anything. Her law firm has an in-house investigator. She called in a favor. But when he didn't find anything, she let it go. She's afraid she could lose her job if she digs any further. So if you could be discreet about that, I'd appreciate it. I don't want to make trouble for Lexy."

"No problem. I'll talk to her discreetly. No need to bring trouble."

"So you'll help me?"

"I will. As long as you understand that I won't be interfering or involving myself with the murder investigation. We'll dig into

Mikala's background, find out who she really is. Beyond that, I don't know if I can help you."

"I understand. That's fine," Asher said.

"I need to ask you some questions now, just standard background stuff. And I have a contract for you to sign."

An hour later, the two men shook hands.

"I'm going to talk to Lexy first. Maybe she'll be able to tell me more about Mikala. After that, I'm going to talk to the apartment manager and see if I can find out who paid her rent." Brian hesitated.

"What is it?"

"I'm just wondering how Mikala got someone to pay her rent for a year."

"You're thinking blackmail?"

"Could be."

"Lexy mentioned her suspicions about Mikala running a blackmail scheme. Blackmail never crossed my mind. I guess that tells you how naïve I am." Asher gathered up his backpack. "You'll let me know what you find out?"

"Yes," Brian said. "If you think of anything else, just text or call."

As Asher was leaving, Brian asked, "Asher, can I ask you one more question?"

"Sure."

"Why were you with Mikala?"

Asher gave Brian a sheepish smile. "Because it seems like we don't have anything in common? She had a way of lighting up the room. Mikala was rough around the edges, loved money and shiny things. But when I was with her – it's hard to explain – I felt alive. And she had a surprisingly good head for business, despite her lack of education. When I was setting up my company, she helped me write a business plan that got me a nice grant, enough money to pay for new equipment. She acted like she found my work fascinating. Sounds crazy, doesn't it? She was good with money, I'll give her that. She seemed to understand the financial markets. She read all the financial news and followed the stock market pretty avidly." Asher closed his eyes and took a deep breath. "She got me, if that makes sense. I loved her, still love her."

"I'm sorry for your loss," Brian said.

"I'm also a realist. I fell for someone who doesn't exist. Mikala Glascott, or whoever she is, played me. If I'm honest, I think I want to know what made me fall for her. Was she a grifter? Was I her mark? That doesn't even bear thinking about."

"I'm going to help you find out why."

"While you're doing that, I'll prepare myself for the worst-case scenario," Asher said.

"That's always a solid plan," Brian said.

Asher was just about to get in his car, when he heard his mother calling his name. Looking up, he saw her heading toward him, walking resolutely.

"Oh, no," he said out loud.

"What are you doing? I saw you go into Olivia Sinclair's office. Are you hiring an attorney? Because legal matters are best decided by the family."

"Are you following me?" Asher asked, his voice incredulous at the violation of his privacy.

At least his mother had the good grace to look embarrassed. "Not on purpose. I was coming home from the shopping when I saw—" She waved her hands in the direction of Olivia's office. "Why did you go there, Asher?"

"No," Asher said, as he turned the key in the lock and opened the door of his car.

"What do you mean *no*?"

"I mean that I'm not going to discuss this with you."

"But Asher, darling, I'm just so worried—" She lifted a hand, as if to stroke his cheek. He flicked it away.

"Stop it. I'm not telling you anything about my private life. Quit following me." And with that, he got in his car and drove away, leaving his mother looking dejected in the municipal parking lot.

Chapter 10

At 8:30 a.m. Brian Vickery sat at the kitchen island, a notepad filled with his precise and careful handwriting at his elbow. Holding his mug of coffee, he replayed his meeting with Asher Ridgeland. Something didn't quite feel right, but Brian couldn't put his finger on what bothered him. Granted, he knew the minute Asher stepped into the office that this wasn't going to be a simple background check. The kid had an agenda. Given his relentless pursuit of retirement, Brian had almost given Asher a referral to another PI. As the interview went on, Brian found himself empathizing with the affable young man who had fallen prey to a manipulator.

Not too long ago, he'd fallen victim to an unscrupulous woman. Leanne Stoddard, a seasoned con artist, had nearly stolen his life savings. In the end, Olivia had seen through the woman and accurately intuited her intentions. She'd saved him, but the idea that he could so easily fall prey still shook him. He'd spent almost three decades as a homicide detective and had seen every type of con, trick, and method of deception in the book. Predators like Leanne zeroed in on a mark and exploited their weak spot. His weak spot had been his loneliness. Brian imagined that Asher's weak spot was the same, and this sense of bonhomie made him say yes to taking a new case, despite his desire to step away from everything, move to the mountains, and start the next chapter of his life.

"Good morning." Olivia stepped into the kitchen, her hair messy from sleep, her face free of makeup. Brian loved these intimate moments, this time in their relationship that belonged just to them. He'd been living with Olivia for almost seven months now. When she leaned against his back and wrapped her arms around him, he closed his eyes and wondered what he had done to have such a woman in his life. He watched as Olivia poured herself a cup of coffee and then topped off his mug. She had dark circles under her eyes. Her mouth had a tense, pinched set to it. Last night, when he had dropped a pan, Olivia, who as a rule didn't startle easily, had jumped.

"You okay?" Brian closed his laptop, not wanting Olivia to see that he had the background data on Asher Ridgeland open.

"I didn't sleep. Tossed and turned all night," Olivia said. She sat on the barstool next to him. "Bad dreams."

Brian put an arm around her. "I know. You cried out."

"It's the Bledsoe case," Olivia said, acknowledging the elephant in the room. "This morning I'm second-guessing why I even took it on, but there's a part of me that won't let it go."

They sat together in silence for a few minutes before Brian said, "Do you want to run down where we are, or do you want to drink coffee first?"

"Let's run it down while I drink." Olivia stood, taking her mug as she stood in front of the window. "We have Ava, who looted the joint bank accounts to basically run away from her husband. She doesn't want any more money – so she says – and she doesn't care if she's divorced or not. Her primary goal is to get away.

"Her abusive husband alleges she attempted to poison him, and that she's lying to me. In other words, I'm being played. My inclination is not to believe a word that man says, but if the case proceeds, we're going to have to check his accusations. I can't go into court without knowing all the skeletons in Ava's closet."

Brian sipped his coffee. "Do you think you'll go to court? I don't."

"Right. Because my client is about to abandon the proceedings and head to Sweden. I can understand her reasoning. She wants to get away. I just wish she hadn't told me she was going to leave."

"That could be an issue for you?"

"Maybe." Olivia ran her fingers through her short gray hair. "I don't know, but I need to find out. I don't blame her for leaving. She's in danger if she stays here. After meeting Mr. Bledsoe in person, I've no doubt about that."

"Why don't we get Ava another lawyer?" Brian sensed the wheels turning in Olivia's brain.

"If we proceed to trial, I intend to. I've realized that I need to set aside my commitment to the sisterhood and be honest with myself. The truth is I'm just not willing to put myself in a situation like this. Not at this point."

"What about Dan Winters? Do you think he'll make a settlement offer?"

"I don't. I'd bet anything that Dan Winters has zero control of his client. I'm sure Mark Bledsoe wrote him a check and is now running roughshod over the entire situation. Off topic now, but I have a question for you."

"Shoot." Brian closed his laptop and started to pack away his papers.

"What was Asher Ridgeland doing in your office yesterday?"

Brian faced Olivia. "I swear to God, woman, you are a witch."

Olivia laughed. "I'm not, actually. Sabine Tremblay Ridgeland called me and asked if Asher had hired me for something. When I told her I didn't know what she was talking about, she acted like she didn't believe me. She told me that she saw Asher go into your office."

"He hired me to look into something for him. And before you ask for more details, he told me that he and Denny were great childhood friends, that he had and still has utmost respect for you, but he doesn't want his mother involved in this. At all. He was very specific that I not discuss this matter with you, just in case his mother, who apparently can be very persuasive, tried to get you to talk. Asher doesn't want you in her line of fire."

"Understood, and good on him for standing up to her." Olivia took their empty coffee cups and set them in the sink. "I can tell Sabine that I have no idea, and that I'm not comfortable asking."

"Asher's mother didn't tell you anything about Asher's situation?"

"She was about to give me an earful, but I got rid of her—" Olivia paused, picking up the seriousness in Brian's voice. "Why? Is Asher in some sort of trouble?"

"I don't think so." Brian stood and pulled his computer bag on his shoulder. "Sorry I can't say more."

"Okay. Now I'm really curious. You'll let me know if you need me? I've known Asher since he was a kid. If he's in trouble—"

"Thanks," Brian said. "He's not in trouble. I'm just looking into something for him. I'll see you tonight?"

"I'm meeting Lauren for a drink," Olivia said. "I'll text with details, in case you want to join."

Brian kissed Olivia's cheek and headed out. He had a packed itinerary today. First stop, Mikala Glascott's apartment.

Brian didn't mind sitting in commuter traffic on the way into the city. He loved the view of San Francisco Bay, especially in the morning when the wispy tendrils of fog swirled along the craggy mountain side. As he slowly approached the Robin Williams Tunnel, his phone rang. It was Ian Greely, the operative who was monitoring the electronic surveillance on Ava and Lauren. Blake Curtis, Ian Greely, and Scott Levering were the best security operatives working freelance in the San Francisco Bay Area. Blake was a computer whiz who was brilliant at surveillance techniques. Ian was a decorated Marine who spent his last four years working on counter-terrorism. He never backed away from a fight and was loyal to the core. Scott, one of Brian's closest friends, had originally started his career as a lawyer, but found himself singularly unsuited for life behind a desk. Ian and Blake were with Ava and Lauren, while Brian had asked Scott to keep an eye on Olivia.

"Ian. Good morning."

"Good morning. Are you driving?"

"On my way into the city."

"Okay. I'll make this quick. We had a little activity last night."

"Activity?" Brian's stomach flipped as his hands involuntarily clenched the steering wheel. "At the beach house?"

"No, at Lauren's house in Larkspur. Mr. Bledsoe drove by at 11:00 p.m. He ended up parking about 300 yards away and walked back and forth in front of the house for approximately thirty-nine minutes. At one point, he approached the side of the house and tried to enter through the gate. He also tried to peer in the kitchen window.

"All of the windows and doors, along with the side gate entrance to the backyard, have alarms. If anyone breaches those, or if those alarms are otherwise disabled, I'll be notified immediately. I've brought in someone from my office to help with this. We are trading twelve-hour shifts. I might need to bring in a third person and do three eight-hour shifts. Need to keep my people happy and well rested."

"Understood."

"The surveillance on Lauren's house in Larkspur and at the beach house is being monitored continuously."

"Thanks, Ian."

"No problem. The beach house is quiet. You know there are no street signs in Bolinas?"

"I know. They don't like outsiders," Brian said.

"It took us an hour to find the place. It's like a maze. Anyway, I feel confident the women are safe there. Blake and I have it covered. No need to worry. I'll check in with you tomorrow. We've got this, Brian. Rest easy, okay?"

"I'll try," Brian said. He hung up the phone, surprised at how quickly Mark Bledsoe's team had discovered Ava's involvement with Lauren. If Mark Bledsoe found Lauren's house, it was only a matter of time before he found Olivia's. Would he storm the fortress and try to intimidate her? A knot formed in his gut. Fear. *I'm too old for this.*

Mikala Glascott lived in a four-story apartment complex on Bay Street. The architecture of the building was classic 1920s San Francisco, stucco with large windows along the front. Brian felt certain that the apartments in this particular building would have high ceilings and be filled with lots of natural light. After navigating his car into a particularly tight parking place a couple blocks away, Brian headed toward Mikala's building, wondering as he walked how she was able to afford the rent in this neighborhood with no job and no reportable income.

An elderly man wearing a woolen ski cap and a bespoke cashmere blazer waited for him.

"Mr. Addelson?" Brian asked.

"Call me Ezra." The man smiled at Brian as the two men shook hands. "I'm on the second floor."

Brian followed Ezra into a spacious lobby, filled with an overstuffed couch on top of a plush Oriental rug. A brass planter held an oversized Ficus tree, giving the foyer a warm and homey look.

"This is a nice building."

"My wife and I bought this place in 1985. Best thing we ever did. Not because of the money, mind you. We enjoyed the job, taking care of our tenants, working together. I'm a banker by trade. My wife – God rest her soul – was a schoolteacher. It surprised our friends when we quit our jobs to do this, but it worked out for us. Who would have thought?"

"Thank you for agreeing to speak with me," Brian said.

"Anything I can do to help. I've already spoken to the police. Do they have any idea who did this terrible thing?"

Brian followed Ezra along a musty-smelling corridor. They came to a stop at the corner apartment. Ezra opened the door and they stepped into a living room filled with chintz furniture, antique lamps, and an abundance of natural light. "My room's this way," Ezra said. Brian followed him through glass-paned French doors that led into a study/library. This room had well-worn leather furniture that looked comfortable, a floor-to-ceiling bookcase chock-full of books, and a sideboard with several crystal decanters full of dark amber liquid. A man would sit down to read the newspapers and drink a tumbler of Scotch at the end of a hard day here. At Ezra's behest, Brian sank into one of the chairs.

"My wife passed two years ago. When we bought this place, she decorated her area," Ezra waved to the flowery living room, "and I decorated mine. I miss her every day."

"My wife passed too. Cancer."

"I'm sorry for your loss," Ezra said.

"Thank you. I'm sorry for yours."

Brian nodded, appreciating the gentle strength of this man.

"I'm sorry to hear about poor Mikala. She was a good girl, despite – you know."

"That's just it," Brian said. "I don't know anything about her. I'm hoping you can help me understand who she was."

Ezra stared at Brian.

"You can trust me, Mr. Addelson – Ezra."

"Who exactly do you work for?"

Brian normally didn't disclose information about his clients, but he knew giving Ezra Addelson a confidence would go a long way toward winning the man's trust. "Asher Ridgeland, Mikala's boyfriend."

"That poor guy. He was drugged. I caught a glimpse of him when they took him out on a stretcher. I thought he was dead. Horrible."

Brian watched as Mr. Addelson struggled through the circum-stances of Mikala's death. He took a handkerchief out of his pocket and dabbed his eyes. "I'm sorry. The whole thing has been too much. My daughter wants me to rent this apartment, hire a management company, and move to DC. I'm not doing that. Not ready."

Brian waited a beat. "What did you mean when you said '*Mikala was a good girl, despite*—'? Despite what? What was she like?"

Ezra peered at Brian over his glasses. "I'll tell you my impression. You do with it what you will. Mikala was a wild party girl. Wore those fancy clothes – my God, the short skirts, and all the paint she wore on her face – and went to the discos or whatever the young kids call them now. She was something else. Men fell over her, I tell you. And the parties . . . That girl liked people, and people liked her. The men flocked. And women too, if I'm being truthful."

"She had parties here?"

"She did."

"Didn't the neighbors complain?"

"This building is solid, so the noise didn't carry much. But whenever Mikala was having a party, she'd invite everyone in the building."

"Really?"

"There are only eight apartments here. We all know each other and get along. Mikala had a lot of friends. Yes, she was wild, but she also had a good heart. When I broke my hip last year, Mikala did my grocery shopping. She cooked meals for me and accompanied me to a couple doctor's appointments. Her kindness was genuine; of that I am certain."

"How did she pay her rent?"

Ezra hesitated. "She didn't."

"Someone else paid her rent?"

Ezra nodded, as he let out a long breath of air. "Paid a year's rent in advance, cash. Came knocking on my door, polite as you please. Last November."

"So Mikala's rent is paid through December 1?"

"It is."

"Did the guy introduce himself, tell you his name?"

"Nope. Honestly, I was so flummoxed at the cash payment that I didn't bother to ask. I've never seen that much money before. I was very nervous taking it to the bank, let me tell you."

"Can you describe the guy?"

"Tall, thin, patrician nose, athletic." Ezra hesitated. "This is an assumption on my part, but he had a mean streak."

"Care to elaborate?"

"He was impatient with me. I'm old. I don't move so fast anymore. He just wanted to drop the cash and leave, but I had to give him a receipt. He didn't take off his sunglasses, so I couldn't see his eyes. Now that I think about it, that's weird, right? He wore scrubs. Maybe he was a doctor? He didn't stay long. Basically paid the rent and then left. Couldn't get out of here fast enough."

"Do you think you would recognize this guy if you saw him again?"

"Not sure. Maybe."

"I know you liked Mikala a lot, and that she was a good friend to you. But do you think that she would have been capable of blackmail?"

"I do," Ezra said without hesitation. "She was greedy. Charming and generous, but she liked money. And if I'm honest with you, I did wonder how she paid her way in life. She said that she was a waitress on her rental application, but there was no way someone who earned their living serving food and drinks could afford this apartment. I never saw her go to a job, yet she always had plenty of cash. She was always coming home with shopping bags and things of that nature."

"You rented to her, even though she didn't have a job?"

Ezra shrugged. "After the guy paid a year's rent in advance, what did I have to lose?"

"Do you know Asher Ridgeland, her boyfriend?"

"Of course. Asher is a good kid, and I know he loved Mikala. But he was in way over his head. She wasn't faithful to him. Not ever. For a while, I thought Asher would help Mikala settle down. When they were together, she seemed to be truly in love with him. Then I'd see her smooching with another man in the elevator. All of her lovey-dovey attitude must have been an act. Asher fell for Mikala hard. She convinced Asher she loved him . . . It's a shame. Of all Mikala's boyfriends, Asher was the best."

Brian rose. "Thanks, Mr. Addelson. Do you mind if I call you again? Something may come up."

"Not one bit. I hope you find out who did this."

At 11:15 a.m. on the nose, Brian stood in line at the coffee cart in front of the Ferry Building, ordering a black coffee and a chocolate chip cookie. He recognized Lexy Ford immediately, red hair pulled back into a ponytail, minimal makeup, gray pinstriped pantsuit, a deliberate expression on her face as she sought him out, recognized him, and moved in his direction. *Purposeful, likely a powerhouse in court*, Brian thought.

"Lexy? Can I buy you a coffee?"

"No, thanks," Lexy said, as the barista poured three shots of espresso and steamed milk into a large cup, popped a lid on it, and handed it to Lexy.

"Thanks, Belle." Lexy took the proffered coffee and pointed with her free hand to a row of benches. "I have a prepaid standing order. Let's sit there. I have about seven minutes."

Brian followed Lexy to a row of benches abutting the sidewalk. All of them were empty. Once they were seated, Lexy took the lid off her coffee and sipped. "As you can probably tell, I'm a creature of habit."

"Looks like a good system," Brian said.

"The structure helps me bill the required hours while having a life outside the office," Lexy said. "You wanted to talk about Asher?"

"I would like to ask a few questions, if that's okay. Then maybe if needed, we could talk again?"

"Sure."

"Given your time constraints, I'm going to cut to the chase. Do you know who paid Mikala's rent?"

Lexy raised an eyebrow. "Well played. The answer to your question is that I don't know who paid her rent. I knew she had a sugar man, at least one. I met Mikala at Elevations, the club a few blocks from the apartment. Do you know it?"

Brian nodded.

"I used to go clubbing until I got my current job. Now all I do is work. Anyway, Mikala needed a roommate, and I am burdened with massive student loan debt. When she offered me a room for next to nothing, I jumped on it, fully expecting it to be a huge party scene. But I didn't care. If I could stay there for a year and continue to live like a student, I could pay off my loans. There was a proviso, of course."

"Isn't there always?" Brian sipped the strong black coffee.

"When Mikala was entertaining Sugar Man, I had to leave the apartment." Lexy shrugged. "I could live with that. Given the amount of money I was saving, I could either stay with a friend or get a hotel room."

"Did you have to leave often?"

"Maybe twice a month at first. Lately it's been once every month or so. I think Mikala goes to him now. Or at least she did before she—"

"Do you think Mikala was a—" Brian hesitated.

"Working girl? Sex for cash? I thought about that when I first moved in. If Mikala was a working girl who entertained her clients in her apartment, I would have left. Too close to criminal enterprise for my liking, and I wouldn't subject myself to high-risk behavior like that. No. Mikala was a party girl. She had a spark that drew men to her." Lexy turned to face Brian, looking at him with a frank, intelligent expression. "I think – correction – I know she manipulated her lovers for gifts and cash. She was my roommate, not my friend. Honestly, I didn't want to blow the deal with the cheap rent, so I kept my distance. Got a lock for my door and stayed out of her business."

"Probably the best course of action."

"And now she's dead." Lexy's eyes filled with tears. "I can't believe it."

"What about Mikala and Asher? That's an odd pairing to me."

Lexy snorted. "Tell me about it. Asher's a man-child. Don't tell him I said that. They met at Elevations. Asher is definitely not a club-type person, but he was at Elevations for a bachelor party. It surprised me to see them together, especially at first. Asher's so – I don't know – normal, for lack of a better word, and soft. I was surprised that Mikala would even give him the time of day. He's got a sweet disposition and a good job. He's really smart. Honestly, I was surprised that he was interested in Mikala. On the surface, they had nothing in common. But as time went on, I saw the attraction between them. When Mikala was around Asher, she changed. I think he made her feel more respectable, maybe even safe. Mikala's childhood wasn't the most—" Lexy hesitated, as if searching for the correct word "—wholesome, if you get my meaning. She really toned it down when she was with Asher, didn't wear her garish clothes, did more sedate things, like go to arty films and museums. Asher was good for her."

"You liked her, didn't you?"

"I did. On one hand, she was an absolute train wreck, but on the other, she struck me as a woman who had a crappy start in life and was trying to build something for herself. I respected that. And I admit I felt more than a little sorry for her." Lexy stood. "I have to go. You know Asher is on a mission, right? He's determined to unearth Mikala's secrets in order to redeem himself for falling in love with her. You need to know that he might go rogue, do his own investigation. The poor guy thought they were building a relationship. I think he was going to propose to her. Not to mention Asher's domineering mother. Have you met Sabine? No? Well, you're in for a treat. Ask Asher about Easter at his mother's house. It was horrible for Asher and even worse for Mikala. Between you and me, Sabine would be a prime suspect in Mikala's murder."

"Why is that?"

"She wasn't going to let anyone take her baby. Asher stood up to his mother to defend Mikala. Probably the first time he ever talked back to his mother in his entire life. It was a big deal. No one had ever spoken up on Mikala's behalf. Mark my words, he'll dig and interfere with the police. He's a good guy who doesn't deserve all this. Make sure he doesn't do anything stupid, okay?"

"I'll try," Brian said.

"Thanks. Call if you need to."

Brian stayed on the bench, sipping his coffee, enjoying the pulse of the Financial District. He was just about to toss his empty cup into the nearest garbage can, when he was approached by a young man with shaggy blond hair, a worn sweatshirt, and jeans with holes in the knees.

"I don't have any cash," Brian said, as the young man drew close.

"Don't want your cash. I want you to quit your investigation."

"Why?"

"If you know what's good for you, stand down."

"Not gonna happen," Brian said.

"Don't say I didn't warn you." The kid turned his back on Brian, and wove through the stopped traffic onto the sidewalk across the busy street. When the light turned green, a bus drove by. Brian turned and headed toward the parking lot. On a whim, he turned around and scanned the crowd for the blond-haired kid. He was nowhere to be seen. A wave of unease washed over Brian. He'd made someone nervous enough to threaten him. The question was who.

* * *

95

Brian felt like a stalker as he drove down the street in the Marina District where Sharon Bailey lived in her studio apartment. Brian had been in the tiny one-room apartment with a galley kitchen one time. Even though it was small, the high ceilings and the large bay window overlooking the street made it tolerable. Sharon had lived there since college and used to say the only way she'd leave that rent-controlled apartment was feet first. When a car pulled out of a parking spot that allowed him to survey the bay window that overlooked the street, he took it and settled in to wait.

Sharon and Brian had a storied past. They were partners at the SFPD until Brian's wife, Maureen, was diagnosed with terminal cancer, and Brian took early retirement. Due to his own horrid communication skills, Brian hadn't warned Sharon that he was leaving the force. He still felt guilt about this oversight. Sharon, who had been friends with Maureen, had called repeatedly. Brian had ignored Sharon's efforts to get in touch.

Now Sharon was reciprocating with her own silent treatment. Brian had heard through the SFPD grapevine that Sharon was having a difficult time after a known killer had bound her hands and feet and thrown her off a sailboat into the San Francisco Bay. She'd been off work for over a year, and, as far as Brian knew, had completely walked away from her friends and colleagues. Brian didn't begrudge her that. He'd done the same thing. But he still felt responsible for her, felt duty-bound to keep an eye on her and make sure she was safe.

Keeping his eyes riveted to the bay window, Brian dialed Sharon's cell phone and was surprised when she answered on the first ring.

"Brian?" Her voice held a question.

"I'm out front of your apartment," Brian said.

"Are you stalking me?" her voice teased.

"Yes, ma'am." There was a moment of silence for a few seconds. "I'm just worried. So is Olivia. I understand if you don't want—"

"You don't have to explain yourself, Brian. Not to me. I owe you and Olivia an explanation. It's just the words have been hard to come by. It's hard to explain something I don't understand myself."

Sensing Sharon did not need to hear them, Brian bit back the reassurances.

"You and Olivia have been so kind. All the food you've sent, the flowers, everything." Sharon stepped in front of the window. Brian felt her eyes on him through the glass and the glare. "Knowing that you two were in the background, at the ready, made things easier for me. I don't know if that makes sense."

"It does, actually."

"I'm just not ready – I don't know how to say this. It's not personal, not directed toward Olivia as a person, but the idea of seeing her face to face terrorizes me. I know she saved my life; I get it. But seeing her reminds me, and I am singularly unable to cope with any reminder of what happened."

"I understand," Brian said.

Sharon put her hand on the glass, palm out, a gesture of connection. "This won't be forever. I don't know if you've heard that I can't even walk by the bay? Jesus."

Brian watched, helpless to do anything, as Sharon wiped her eyes with the back of her hand.

"Can I just say something to you? You can take it or leave it, and we don't have to discuss it?"

"Of course."

"When you're ready, I think you should face your demon. I don't know what that looks like, but I do know this. You're one of the toughest, most resilient women I've ever known. You've experienced a terrifying nightmare. But you're alive. You're smart, and you're strong. When you're ready, you'll be able to fix this. I'm certain of it."

They didn't speak. Seconds went by.

"You'll give Olivia my love? Explain to her that I'm a total train wreck?"

"I'll give your love and leave out the train wreck part if you don't mind. You're not a train wreck, Sharon."

"Thanks for calling, Brian."

Sharon Bailey would never be the same. Who would be after what she went through? But Brian knew deep down that eventually she would recover from her ordeal. When she did, he and Olivia would be there for her.

Elevations was housed in one of the many old-timey theaters in San Francisco. Severely damaged after the Loma Prieta earthquake in 1989, the building was purchased for next to nothing by an investment group in Chicago, remodeled and retrofitted, and had recently become one of the hottest night clubs in San Francisco. All this information was courtesy of the Internet. As directed by the manager, Brian opened the unlocked side door and swept into what amounted to a hollowed-out building, with several small bars tucked into the corners and one bar along the entire back wall, the bandstand on the wall opposite. With the bright lights on, Brian noticed the sticky-looking concrete floor and the litter strewn among the tables that were scattered about.

"It looks better with the lights out," said a cadaverous young man who towered over Brian. He ground out a cigarette in an ashtray he carried in his free hand. "The lighting is really magical at night. The mirrors in the bars are backlit and there are actually lights in the floor." The man looked around the room and sighed. "I love this place, but she's definitely prettier in the dark." He held out his hand. "Hugo."

"Brian Vickery." The two men shook hands.

"I've pulled Mikala's personnel file and the video footage from the night she was here. It's in my office. This way."

Brian followed Hugo into an alcove behind the big bar and down a surprisingly long corridor into a modern office. The desk held two large monitors.

"You can sit at the desk," Hugo said. "Mikala's file is right there. Is there anything else you need?"

"Could I ask you a couple questions?"

Hugo looked at his watch.

"It won't take long."

He shrugged and stood before Brian. When he crossed his arms over his chest, the sleeve of his *I love San Francisco* T-shirt rode up to reveal a Rolex watch. *Not fake.* Brian noted.

"I'm trying to get a feel for who Mikala really was. My client wants to find her family."

"Your client is Asher Ridgeland, Mr. Vickery. Sorry. Didn't mean to sound sardonic. Can't help myself. It's part of working in a nightclub, I think." Hugo sat at the edge of the desk. "I don't know Asher very well, but I know Ken, Asher's father. He used to hang out here, flashing money, buying expensive champagne, chasing girls young enough to be his daughter. Mikala – whose real name is Bernadette Mickleson – got her clutches in Dr. Ridgeland almost immediately. Anyway, you asked about Mikala's family. All I know is that she came from a crappy home, ran away young, and somehow transformed herself into a glamour girl who can manipulate men – and women for that matter – with the best of them.

"I liked Mikala. For all her flamboyance, she worked hard here. Always outsold the other waitresses by a landslide, wasn't afraid to pitch in and do the grunt work when she worked the closing shift, tipped out the bartenders generously."

"I take it she was well liked?"

"Yeah, she was. More important, I trusted her. Granted, she was extremely intractable. God help anyone who tried to tell her what to do. The male customers loved her smartass attitude." Hugo smiled. "I remember one guy whistled at her. She paused in her tracks, turned around, and said, 'Are you whistling at me? Are you kidding?' The poor guy was so embarrassed. I offered her a management role, generous salary, benefits, all of that. She didn't think twice about turning the job down."

"Did she make enough money waitressing—"

"To support her frighteningly extravagant lifestyle? No."

"Any idea where she got her money?"

"Don't know, don't care, and don't want to get involved. I can tell you with absolute certainty that nothing untoward was going on in my club." Hugo hesitated. "I'll tell you this, but it's totally off the record, okay?"

Brian nodded.

"For a while there, Mikala ran with some rough types. Scary men. I don't know why, but they stopped coming in here when Mikala quit waitressing. That's all I know, but she did have that seedy element in her life."

Brian tucked this information away to think about later. "So, you know Asher?"

"The boyfriend? Yes I do. I have no idea how those two wound up together."

Brian waited for Hugo to continue.

"You want my two cents on Asher Ridgeland?"

"Sure."

"He's a weirdo. I have no idea why a guy like that would be of interest to Mikala." Hugo held up his hands. "I could be wrong. But I was surprised when they got together, surprised that he hung around as long as he did. She cheated on him all the time." He came around the back of the desk and manipulated the mouse. One of the large monitors sprang to life, revealing an image of Mikala and Asher, a freeze frame of them in motion. Mikala walking away. Asher following her, arm outstretched, a desperate look on his face. "Just watch this video and you'll get a feel for their relationship. When you're done with that, you can peruse the file." Hugo looked at his watch. "I need to get back out there. Don't take anything. If you do, I know where to find you."

"Fair enough," Brian said.

After Hugo was gone, Brian hit play, and the figures on the monitor sprang to life. Asher grabbed Mikala, spun her around and said something. Mikala wrenched out of Asher's grip and fled away from the crowd, Asher on her heels. The angle changed, revealing the two of them in a corridor. Based on the barback who scurried by with two big buckets of ice, and two waitresses who walked by with their cocktail trays tucked under their arms, Brian surmised he was looking at the employee area. He watched as Asher and Mikala stopped walking, faced each other, and—based on body language—stridently argued, their respective gestures a testament to their anger. Mikala slapped Asher hard across the face. Asher didn't respond, didn't flinch. Mikala leaned close and said something to Asher that catapulted him into action. When he pushed her up against the wall, she softened, wrapped her arms around his neck and tried to kiss him. Asher pushed away, hands up, as though in surrender. There was no denying the disgust on his face. He shook his head, wiped his eyes with the back of his sleeve and left.

Mikala stood for a few seconds, chest heaving, before she adjusted her clothes and took off after Asher.

The video stopped.

Brian sat for a couple of minutes, taking in all that he had seen. He pulled out his notebook to write down the events of the video, but changed his mind. There was nothing to be gleaned from a re-watch. Asher's telling of the events was spot on.

He pushed away and headed out to the main area of the club. It was deserted now. His footsteps echoed in the emptiness. Hugo was nowhere to be seen, nor were any of the other employees who had been milling about in the background when he arrived. Hurrying to a door with an exit sign, Brian stepped into the fresh air and took a deep breath.

"Mr. Vickery?" a female voice called to him. He turned around to find Inspectors Lambada and Standish walking toward him, their stride purposeful, the look on their faces irritated. He waited until they reached him.

"What are you doing here?" Lambada asked.

"Working. And don't worry. I'm not interfering with your murder investigation in Mikala Glascott's death. Hugo, the club manager, showed me the video of Asher and Mikala the night they fought. He gave me a glimpse of her personnel file. That's it."

"Stay in your lane, Vickery," Lambada warned.

Brian had never liked Carlo Lambada. Handsome, sure of himself, and a bit reckless, Lambada alienated his male colleagues with his confidence. As for his female colleagues, they either loved him – captivated by his good looks and over-the-top charm – or they thought he was a chauvinist in desperate need of some feminist training.

"Got it," Brian said.

"Come on, Standish. Let's go." Lambada turned and headed toward the entrance to the club.

"Inspector Standish, can I talk to you for a second?"

Lambada stopped, turned around, and was about to say something, but Inspector Standish didn't give him the chance.

"I don't need your permission, Lambada." She turned her back on him and stepped close to Brian.

Once the two of them were alone, Ellie Standish took charge. "I can't talk to you about the murder investigation. Did Asher hire you?"

"I am not going to interfere, Inspector. If I find anything that will help you, I'll let you know, okay? I wanted to ask about Sharon. Have you heard from her?"

Ellie relaxed. "I do see her."

Brian nodded. "Good. She needs support, but won't ask for it."

"I think we're all like that. The job makes us think we're tougher than we are."

"Can I ask a question?"

"You can. I might not answer it."

"Is he still a suspect?"

Ellie smiled at him. "Have a good day, Mr. Vickery. I better not find out you or your client are interfering with my investigation."

Chapter 11

It was 6:30 p.m. by the time Ellie stepped out of the elevator and headed toward Captain Wasniki's office carrying three large coffees in a cardboard tray. She and Lambada had been on the clock with no break for twelve hours. It was five days since Mikala's murder, and Lambada and Standish had been clocking long hours. Despite that, their list of suspects seemed to grow larger by the hour. As she approached Wasniki's office, she saw Lambada and the captain deep in conversation.

"I've come bearing coffee," she said by way of announcing herself.

The way the two men stopped talking at her approach put Ellie on guard. She watched as Captain Wasniki leaned back in his chair, while Lambada stood and took his backpack off the other empty chair. For a brief second, Ellie felt like an intruder and wondered if she had interrupted a conversation about her, only to dismiss the sentiments as paranoia derived from not having a regular partner.

"The nectar of the gods," Lambada said.

"Lambada, I've got yours loaded up with milk and sugar." Ellie handed a cup to Captain Wasniki. "Black with an extra shot of espresso."

Once the coffee was handed round, Ellie grabbed her note-book – while Lambada took notes on his phone, Ellie preferred to work the old-fashioned way – and took a seat.

"Thanks for this," Captain Wasniki said. "Before you got here, Inspector Lambada was telling me that Brian Vickery showed up today."

"He did," Ellie said. "He hasn't overstepped. He won't interfere."

"You believe that?" Lambada said.

"I do," Ellie said. "Vickery's a pro. He's not going to get in our way. Who knows, he might find something that will help us."

Wasniki said, "Good. Let's move on. Lambada wants to get a digital surveillance warrant for Asher Ridgeland."

"I think we should check out his emails and finances, just to make sure he wasn't involved in any blackmail scheme," Lambada said.

"Agreed," Ellie said. "And we should probably swear out a warrant for his social media accounts too."

Captain Wasniki sipped his coffee. "So, we're all on the same page with that. Take it from the top and tell me what you've got so far."

Lambada went first. "I've been deep-diving Asher Ridgeland. He works in IT, freelance. New company."

He scrolled through this phone, reading his electronic notes as he continued. "Standish and I went to Elevations, the club where Asher and Mikala headed after Asher caught Mikala *in flagrante delicto* with another man. Asher's story checks out. I saw the video of the two of them fighting. It spoke volumes, even without sound. By their body language, I could tell they were shouting at each other. It seemed to me that Mikala was the aggressor. Asher did push Mikala up against the wall, but that was after she took a swing at him. He put his hands up and moved away from her. She tried to kiss him, and he shrugged her off and walked away. She chased after him. They exited through a back door, so that's the only video I could see. I've got uniforms trying to get any video from other businesses in the area, maybe try to see if anyone followed them back to Mikala's apartment. Still waiting on that.

"I also spoke to Ezra Addelson, Mikala's landlord. Her rent was paid in cash, by a tallish man wearing scrubs."

"A doc?" Wasniki asked.

Lambada shrugged. "Maybe. He paid an entire year in advance. I was hoping he could shine some light on whoever paid Mikala's rent. He's supposed to be working with a sketch artist, but I haven't heard anything on that yet."

"Mr. Addelson really wasn't sure that he could remember the guy. He's older and admits that his eyesight is not good, that he often forgets his glasses. He can't remember if he had them on when the guy paid the rent."

"All right. Thanks for the factual rundown. Set those aside now and tell me your perceptions about Asher Ridgeland."

Lambada didn't hesitate. "Spoiled, trust-fund type. Definitely a mama's boy, and boy does that mama run a tight ship. When we were at the hospital, it took all I had to keep her away from her baby while Ellie spoke to him. I think she's a little nuts, personally. But Asher? He's soft almost to the point of being feminine. Probably hasn't worked a day in his life. There's no doubt he was cooperative. Standish had him eating out of her hand."

"What else?" Captain Wasniki gave Lambada his trademark inscrutable look. "You're holding something back."

Lambada shrugged. "I can't substantiate any of this with facts, but there's something about Asher Ridgeland that doesn't sit right with me. I don't know what it is."

"So noted."

"Sabine Ridgeland isn't nuts," Ellie piped in. "She's got an old-world vibe. Reminds me of an Edwardian lady. Her clothes are almost Victorian. I'll bet money that she's a European aristocrat."

Carlo laughed. "I think Inspector Standish has been reading too many romance novels."

105

"He asked for perceptions, Lambada," Ellie couldn't keep the sarcasm from her voice. "I think she's a mama bear with teeth. I think that she's the type of woman would do anything to protect her son."

"Agreed," Lambada said. "Sorry, Standish. Didn't mean to insult. There's nothing wrong with romance novels. And I agree with all that."

Surprised, Ellie bit back the snarky comment. "Thank you."

Captain Wasniki continued. "Fair enough. Standish? What've you got on the decedent?"

"Turns out Mikala Glascott's real name is Bernadette Mickelson. Born in small-town Indiana, comes from a broken home, ran away when her mom remarried. Both parents deceased. Bernadette was in and out of foster care for a bit before she disappeared completely at age seventeen. I'm assuming that's when she reinvented herself. We interviewed her roommate, a lawyer named Lexy Ford. Lexy doesn't know how Mikala earned her money. When pushed, she stopped talking. They were roommates only, and my sense is that Lexy purposefully kept her distance."

"You believe her?" Wasniki asked.

"I do," Ellie said. "She had massive student loans and Mikala offered her cheap rent. That's why she stayed. She's the one who found Asher lying next to Mikala's body. If she hadn't come home when she did, Asher might not have made it." Ellie scrolled through her notes. "I'm waiting for cell phone records and financials. We've got them coming for Asher and Mikala. I'd like to find out if Mikala was running a blackmail scheme. If so, was she working alone? Hopefully, there will be a money trail."

"Asher Ridgeland might have been involved. It could be a criminal enterprise gone bad," Lambada said.

"Agreed," Ellie said.

"How are you two going to proceed?"

"We'll get financials and the digital data dump from Asher and Mikala this afternoon, hopefully," Ellie said.

"How about I continue with Asher and you take Mikala?" Lambada said.

"Sounds good." Ellie stood and resisted the urge to stretch her back and crack her neck. "Should we see if the uniforms turned up any CCTV footage?"

"Okay," Carlo said.

"No. Both of you call it a day. You can get back to it tomorrow after you've had a good night's sleep." Wasniki finished the rest of his coffee and tossed the empty cup into the garbage can. "Inspector Standish, do you mind staying?"

Ellie's heart thumped as a feeling of dread dropped over her. Just when she thought her work slump was over.

"See you tomorrow, Standish," Lambada said.

Captain Wasniki waited until Lambada had stepped into the elevator before he spoke. "How's it going? Are you and Lambada gelling?"

"I think so," Ellie said without hesitation. Captain Wasniki had a reputation of being loyal to his team. He didn't play games and did not condone political maneuvering. Sharon Bailey told Ellie early on the best way to deal with Captain Wasniki was to be forthright. "He thought I didn't push Asher hard enough in the hospital."

"I bet. You two have different styles for sure."

"True."

"Your method worked though, didn't it? Asher Ridgeland handed over his house keys and let you search his apartment without a warrant. Lambada told me. Good work on that front."

"Thanks."

"I'm just making sure you're okay. I know it's been hard for you since Sharon left. Believe it or not, I understand how difficult it is for a woman to make her way up the ranks."

Overcome with a wave of emotion and immediately embarrassed by it, Ellie swallowed the lump that had formed in the back of her throat.

"I just want you to know that my door is always open. I think Lambada is a good fit for you. He's a bit rough around the edges, but you can deal with that. Maybe you can smooth him out a bit."

"We certainly balance each other out," Ellie said.

Wasniki stood. "That you do."

"Good night, Captain. Thank you."

"See you tomorrow."

It was 8:45 p.m. by the time Ellie got out of the taxi in North Beach. She'd done her best to shower the day away, but the Glascott murder had snaked its way under her skin. Tomorrow she would spend the day at her desk, digging for clues among the pages and pages of phone records and financial documents. Weaving through the crowded sidewalk, Ellie was greeted with the smell of garlic and tomato when she reached Bricks Magic Oven. Her stomach growled as she stepped into the restaurant.

Ellie scanned the room, looking for Sharon Bailey, her ex-partner. Sharon had been on disability leave for almost a year, and although Ellie had made an effort to be supportive with frequent visits and coffee dates, work and life had gotten in the way. The two women hadn't seen each other in almost four months.

"Ellie," a willowy blonde in the corner table near the window called out to her.

"Sharon?"

"That's me," Sharon said.

Ellie approached the table as Sharon stood to greet her. When the two women hugged, Ellie was shocked at how thin Sharon was – the word *insubstantial* popped into her mind. Sharon had lost too much weight too fast.

"It's good to see you," Ellie said, as she hung her coat over the back of her chair and sat down.

"I know I look like hell," Sharon said.

Ellie started to say, *No, you look great.* She and Sharon didn't have that kind of relationship.

"You look tired," Ellie said.

"It's more than tired, I'm afraid." Sharon reached for a napkin and dabbed at her eyes. They were interrupted when the waitress came for their order.

"What's going on?" Ellie said, once they were alone again.

"I'm in the throes of some sort of breakdown, it seems."

"When did this start?" Ellie cast her mind back to the last time she and Sharon had hung out. They'd gone for a run at Ocean Beach. Sharon had seemed fine. Or maybe Ellie was too clueless to notice her friend was in distress. She remembered the conversation with Lambada, who seemed to know about Sharon's issues. How did he know?

"It's been percolating for a long time. I've been stuffing my troubles, pushing them under the rug." Sharon tore her napkin into tiny pieces. "A couple of weeks ago I totally lost it. It was horrible. I took myself to the emergency room via taxi. God, Ellie, it was so embarrassing."

"At least you were able to get yourself to the ER," Ellie said.

"I can't handle water anymore." Sharon's tone was an attempt at self-deprecation. Ellie recognized the fear.

"Like you can't go swimming?"

"More than that. I can't walk by the bay, can't go on the Marina Green. The idea of going to the beach makes me want to lock myself in my apartment and sit in the corner with the lights out." Sharon picked up her beer but set it down again when her hand shook. "See?"

Ellie thought of her own downtown apartment, far away from the beach or water. "Is being here making you anxious? We can get our pizza to go and head to my apartment, if that helps?"

"No, that's fine. I'll be okay. Honestly, I'm heavily medicated right now." Sharon spoke with her trademark dogged determination. "I need to deal with this. Need to fix it."

"How are you going to do that?" Ellie asked.

"I'm taking meds, doing therapy. Pretty soon my therapist is going to help me confront this. I don't know if we're going to have therapy at the beach or what she's got planned. I've decided to trust her. Anyway, that's enough about me." Sharon's eyes swept over Ellie. "You look happy. How's work?"

"I'm partnered with Carlo Lambada. We're working the Glascott murder."

"Carlo Lambada?" Sharon smiled and shook her head. "He's got quite an ego, if I recall. The romantic lover who would sleep with all the women if regulations allowed."

"Seriously?"

"Seriously. Did he tell you that he has rules for being his partner?"

"He did. And I shut him down."

"Good. Honestly, I don't think those rules are even real. I think that's his test to see if his partner will stand up to him."

"I stood up to him."

"I'll bet you did," Sharon said.

"I'd still be working, but Wasniki sent us home."

"He's good that way."

"Do you miss work?" Ellie asked.

"Sometimes. Now that I've been away for eleven months, I realize how the job was my life. Work-life balance doesn't come easy in our job. It's a lonely profession, really, especially for women. It takes a toll." Sharon gave Ellie a wistful glance. "I've been thinking about what I didn't get to do because of the job – like have a family, have a child. But then I've seen my share of familial dysfunction on the job, so at least I've spared myself that."

"It's not too late," Ellie said. "You might meet someone and fall in love."

Sharon laughed. "I think I need to get better before I think about that."

"Do you think you'll come back?"

"I don't know if I'm going to be able to."

"You need to give yourself time," Ellie said.

"I know. I will. To answer your question, as I sit here right now, I don't see myself coming back."

The conversation paused as the waitress brought their pizza, red pepper flakes, and a small dish of fresh grated parmesan cheese.

Once they were alone again, Sharon leaned forward. "The truth is, Ellie, that I've lost that brave part of myself. And the more I try to bring it back, the more elusive it becomes."

"So what are you going to do?" Ellie knew the answer.

"I'm putting in my disability retirement," Sharon said. "I need to move forward, and that seems like the only way."

Ellie felt her heart sink.

"You look so desolate. Is it that bad at work?"

"It's been tough," Ellie said. "I saw myself working with you for a few years. I've been doing desk work, cold cases, for the past few months. I've closed a few, but it's not the same as being involved in current cases. I like the thrill of the chase."

Sharon smiled. "You're a good cop, Ellie. Just stay focused on the job. Don't spend time worrying about the other stuff." She pulled off a piece of pizza and set it on her plate. "Otherwise, you'll wind up like me."

"I crossed paths with Brian Vickery today. He asked about you. He's worried. Wanted me to tell you that he wouldn't push, but he was there if you needed him. Should I not have said anything? His concern seemed genuine."

"No. No, it's okay. He and Olivia have reached out over and over. I just wasn't able to talk to him. And the idea of seeing Olivia sends my knees knocking. But he called today. We chatted for a minute. He was very understanding."

"You two were tight?"

"We were partners. So yeah, we were tight." Sharon reached for her beer and took a sip. "You'll be okay, Ellie. You and Lambada might actually be good together. Give it a chance. Try not to let him get under your skin."

Ellie nodded, and the two women finished their meal in silence.

After they parted, Ellie headed home. The idea that Sharon – a talented officer, with a promising career ahead of her – was retiring shook her. If only she could do something to help the woman she now considered a friend.

Chapter 12

Lauren was waiting for Olivia at the Left Bank, a half-consumed martini on the bar in front of her. Her curly, silver, Medusa-like hair was pushed into a messy bun on top of her head and held in place by two pencils. She had on a turquoise velvet jacket, the back of which had a half-moon embroidered in white silken thread. Turquoise and silver bracelets dangled from her arms, jangling as she moved. When she saw Olivia, she downed the rest of the martini and signaled the bartender for another.

"Tough day?" Olivia took off her coat and flung it on the back of the barstool before she attached her purse to the hook nestled under the bar.

"I couldn't take the energy at the beach house anymore. Ava's on tenterhooks, bless her, and she's driving me batshit crazy." The bartender set two fresh martinis down before them. Lauren and Olivia clinked their glasses and sipped. "I had no idea what that man had done to her, Olivia. The abuse was so routine that she normalized it. Like a fool, I offered an ear so she could talk about it, hoping it would take away her underlying anxiety. Her anxiety has rubbed off on me. I couldn't take it anymore. Now I plan to get hammered. If I'm too drunk to drive, I'll either take a taxi or sleep on your couch."

"Honestly, I'll be glad when she's safely on the plane," Olivia said.

"Hate to say it, but me too," Lauren said.

"Let's talk about something different. I'm ready to forget my troubles," Olivia said.

Lauren gave her a sideways look.

"What?" Olivia prodded. Lauren knew something. Olivia could tell by the sly-fox look in her eyes.

"I've heard some gossip. Word on the street is that Asher Ridgeland's girlfriend was murdered and that he's hired Brian to find out who did it. Is that true?" Lauren paused a beat before she plowed on. "And, typical Sabine, I heard she ambushed him in the parking lot, demanding to know why he got a lawyer without her permission."

"How in the world did you find that out? I swear, Lauren, you have this uncanny ability to put yourself right in the middle of it."

"I know. It's a gift." Lauren smiled to take the sting out of her sarcasm. "These things get out, especially when the conversation between mother and son takes place in the downtown municipal parking lot. She was following Asher. Can you believe that? She's always been so overprotective of that child. I'm surprised he's not – never mind."

"She followed Asher? Actually, I'm not surprised. You're right. She's the type of mother who will smother a child without mercy. And before you ask, I don't know anything about it," Olivia said.

"I know you can't discuss anything with me. I understand you keep your secrets close. That's why I love you so much. But I've got gossip. I'll do the talking and you can do whatever you want with the information," Lauren said.

Olivia skipped the second martini, opting instead for a glass of ice water. "Go on," she prompted Lauren, once the icy cold drink was placed before her.

"First of all, Ken Ridgeland and Sabine are over. They don't sleep together anymore. Rumor has it that Ken doesn't even live at home anymore. There are hints he got fired from his job at the hospital for sexually harassing a resident. Guess who that resident was?" Lauren didn't wait for Olivia to answer. "Nancy St. Cere, who used to work in your office during the summers."

At this, Olivia perked up.

"I see I've got your attention."

"You do," Olivia said.

"I don't really know anything else. If I were you, I'd call Nancy. She's got an office in Marin now, over by the hospital. Call her, Liv. See what she has to say."

Nancy St. Cere spent her summers working in Olivia's law firm until she graduated from college and started medical school. Whip-smart, quietly mannered, and compassionate, Nancy had dreamed of being a doctor since she was a child. Olivia wasn't surprised when Nancy made her dream a reality. Now Olivia needed to decide whether she should put herself in the middle of Brian's investigation. Surely there wouldn't be any harm in talking to Nancy? They'd always been close . . .

"You need to talk to her. Brian doesn't have to know."

Olivia nodded. "I'm going to talk to her, but I'm not keeping the conversation a secret from Brian."

"Good," Lauren said. "I've never liked Ken Ridgeland. Did you know that he once pinned me against the wall at one of Sabine's parties? When he tried to kiss me, I bit his lip so hard it bled." Lauren gave Olivia a sly smile. "He never much liked me after that. Anyway, if I stop drinking now and eat some food, I'll be able to drive myself home. Are you hungry?"

"Starved," Olivia said.

"I'm buying." Lauren signaled the waiter for menus.

Olivia was sitting in her dimly lit living room, finishing up an email to Nancy St. Cere, when Brian returned. Despite the low lighting, she could see the exhaustion in his rigid shoulders and the deep lines around his mouth.

"Rough day?"

"Unsettling." He set the beat-up canvas bag that held his laptop on the table in the hall and came toward her. "I spoke to Sharon."

She shut her computer and looked up at him. "Talked to her?"

"I called her while parked in front of her apartment. She stood in her window."

"And?"

"She's still terrified, but she is glad for our contact."

Olivia shivered at the memory of her desperation to swim to Sharon and pull her out of the water, while the police waited on the shore. "I told her we'd be there for her, when she was ready."

"Good. That's good." Olivia picked up a mug that sat on the coffee table and took a sip. "My tea is cold. Maybe we could—"

"I need to give you some information."

"Something's happened? Is it Mark Bledsoe?" Cold all of a sudden, Olivia prepared for the worst as Brian sat down next to her.

"It's not that big of a deal because we had measures in place," Brian said. "But Mark Bledsoe went to Lauren's house last night."

"The beach house?"

"No. No. The house in Larkspur. We've got electronic surveillance there. All his activity was caught on Ian Greely's camera. He's a genius when it comes to this sort of thing. He put cameras up around Lauren's house. They are everywhere – on the street, front yard, windows, doors, you name it – and he can watch it from a remote location."

"So what did Mark do?"

Brian hesitated.

"Don't edit, Brian. Just tell me what happened. Please."

"Mark parked down the street and walked up to Lauren's house. He tried to peer in the kitchen window and then tried to get into the backyard through the side gate. A neighbor's dog started barking, lights in the neighborhood came on, and he left." Brian scooted close to Olivia and put his arm around her.

"If anyone goes on the property, the cameras will pick it up. If anyone disables the cameras or breaks into the house, the police will be notified immediately."

"I need to tell Ava."

"Agreed. She needs to know that Mark is sniffing around. We don't want her to become complacent because she's hidden away."

"I met with Lauren for drinks today. There's no complacency going on. Lauren said the tension is nearly unbearable. Ava is terrified. Who do you have watching me?"

"Scott."

Olivia's shoulders dropped as the tension eased.

"Good. At least I'm being watched by a friend."

Brian wrapped both of his arms around Olivia and pulled her toward him. She leaned in, allowing herself a few seconds of peace before she added more stress to his day. Olivia pulled away from him and met his eyes, taking the worry she saw there. "When I was having drinks with Lauren today, she told me she knew Asher hired you. She also told me about his girlfriend being murdered. Is he a suspect?"

"Can anything happen in this town without Lauren Ridley knowing about it?"

"She gave me an earful."

"Do I want to hear this?"

"You do. It's important." Olivia waited while Brian took his shoes off and leaned back on the couch. "Ken hit on Nancy St. Cere, a young woman who worked summers for me during high school and college during her residency. It was bad. Something tells me I should speak to her."

Brian stood. "I am getting a beer. Want something?"

"No, thanks. I had a couple martinis with Lauren." Brian came back with his beer and sat down next to Olivia.

"Between Asher's overbearing mother and his licentious reprobate of a father, it's remarkable that he's turned out so solid. I've never liked Ken Ridgeland."

"You didn't—"

"I sent Nancy an email, telling her I'd like to catch up with her. Don't worry, I didn't mention anything about the case. I won't talk to her if you don't want me to."

"I need to get Asher's permission for you to get involved. He specifically said he didn't want his mother—"

"I don't have to get involved. Don't want to, truth be told. But Nancy St. Cere is a very private person. She won't talk to you. I think I might be able to break the ice, maybe find out what happened. If she gives me something useful, it might help you. It's worth a try, don't you think?"

"Okay. Go ahead and talk to her. I haven't told you anything about the case, so just proceed as you see fit."

"I may not even hear from her," Olivia said.

Brian stood and held out his hand to Olivia. "I need food. Keep me company while I eat something?"

Chapter 13

Olivia woke up Thursday morning with the inchoate throbbing of a headache forming at the base of her skull. Brian's spot next to her in the bed was empty, but the smell of freshly brewed coffee caused her stomach to rumble. Reaching for the grubby but much-loved cardigan that rested on the shopworn chair tucked into the corner of her room, she headed into the kitchen, where she discovered a note from Brian next to the coffee maker. *Running errands. Back early afternoon. Call when you wake up.* Unplugging her mobile from the wall, Olivia was just about to dial Brian when it rang. Lauren. Taking three seconds to shift her brain into gear, Olivia answered the phone.

"Good morning," Ava said. "I apologize for the early call. I'm using Lauren's phone."

"No, it's fine. I was just about to call you," Olivia lied, pouring herself a large mug of coffee. "I wanted to report on what's been happening and see how you're getting on with Lauren."

"Mark found us, didn't he? Found Lauren's house? Do we need to move again?"

"He found you, but Brian—"

"Didn't I tell you he would do this? Did he hurt anyone? Tell me he didn't hurt anyone. Oh, God. Olivia, what happened?"

"He didn't hurt anyone."

"I'm sorry." Ava's voice broke. "I'm losing my mind not knowing. I feel like I want to jump out of my skin. Tell me what happened. Please."

"Night before last, Mark went to Lauren's house in Larkspur. He parked down the street, probably so his car wouldn't show up on cameras, and walked around a bit. He didn't do anything, but he tried to look in the kitchen window, tried to get in the side gate."

"Oh, no."

"The gates were locked. He didn't do any damage, Ava. And that house is so rigged with surveillance cameras and alarms that had he tried to break in, not only would the police be summoned, but Brian would also have been alerted immediately."

"If I had been there, it would have been bad."

"I realize that. But you weren't there. You're safe where you are. There's no way that Mark can find Lauren's house in Stinson Beach. First of all, it's not in her name. Never underestimate a rock star who wants privacy. He won't find it. And," Olivia plowed on, trying to reassure Ava, "even if he did find it, there's no way he would get past Blake and Ian. I can assure you of that."

"You're right. I'm sorry. I know I'm safe, but I can't stop looking over my shoulder, can't shake the idea that Mark is going to jump out of a closet and drag me away." Ava took a deep, measured breath. "Good news. My passport came through. I'm in the process of arranging my flight, which should happen within the next couple of days."

"There's something I need to discuss with you. It probably doesn't matter, now that you're leaving, but you need to know that Mark has made an allegation."

"What sort of allegation?"

"He's saying that you put antifreeze in his drink in an attempt to poison him. He told me there was a police report."

Ava laughed, a dry croak reminiscent of an injured animal. "He's lying. The police didn't believe him. They conducted an investigation into all of this."

"Okay. I believe you. But I need to advise you that if we go to court, that accusation may come out. If it does, I can deal with it."

"You will most certainly not deal with it because I am leaving. We are not going to court. He can allege anything he wants. And I'm sorry if this causes you difficulty with the judge. You've been very good to me, and I appreciate that. I've been honest about this from the beginning, Olivia. Please don't think for one minute that I will stay here in order to have some courtroom showdown with Mark."

"Of course not. But I would like to hear your response to the poisoning allegation. I feel as though I should know your side of the story."

"Why?"

"Because Mark could dredge this up after you leave, and you won't be here to defend yourself. That in itself might look suspicious. I'm going to have to explain to the judge that you have left in the middle of your divorce."

Olivia waited. Soon she heard a big, long sigh before Ava started to speak. "This was before Mark broke my jaw, the time I like to think of as the quiet before the storm. Things seemed to have settled between us. Mark wasn't as angry, and I actually started to feel like we could save our marriage. I should have been suspicious at the sudden change in Mark's attitude, the sudden kindness and attentiveness. Stupid of me.

"Anyway, one afternoon, Mark got really sick, nauseated. He became so ill that he took to his bed and was rather ill for about twenty-four hours. The next day, he called the police and accused me of trying to poison him. He gave them the bottle of sweet iced tea that I served with our lunch. I drank it too, but nothing happened to me. Sure enough, the police took the tea to the lab and discovered that it was laced with small amounts of ethylene glycol – antifreeze. At Mark's insistence, they did an investigation, which included bringing me in for questioning. They hammered away at me for four hours, until I volunteered to take a polygraph test. Apparently I passed that, because they let me go.

"I thought the matter was dropped, until one day when Mark was at work, when the lead detective called me and asked me to come speak to him. I wondered if they were going to arrest me. You know what? I didn't even care. The idea of prison seemed better than staying in that house with an abusive husband who took pleasure in terrorizing me. Anyway, they gave me the results of their investigation. Showed me video of Mark purchasing the antifreeze and told me about Mark's various Internet searches on how to murder your wife. Apparently they'd heard about my various visits to the hospital. They were onto Mark. They offered to help, promised to take me to a shelter for battered women and helped me get a restraining order. I knew I couldn't get away from Mark. I feared the detectives would just exacerbate things.

"Two days after the detective came to visit, Mark put me in the hospital with a broken jaw. I went away to rehab, met the nurse who saved my life, and the rest is history. So you see, Olivia, I'm not being overly dramatic. If I stay here, Mark will surely find me. If he finds me, he'll kill me."

Olivia sat for a second, her nearly untouched coffee now stone cold, unsure what to do with herself. An abundance of tomatoes from her garden sat in her freezer waiting to be used. The idea of filling her house with the smell of garlic and herbs, some therapeutic cooking, was just what she needed. Ten minutes later, armed with her shopping bags and a grocery list, Olivia approached Scott Levering's nondescript gray Ford Taurus. As she drew near, he rolled down his window.

"Good morning. I wanted to let you know that I'm going shopping."

"Thanks. Where?"

"Mollie Stone's, Greenbrae. You know it?"

"You know, you don't have to wait in your car while you're watching me. You're welcome to come into my house."

"Thanks, Olivia. I'll keep that in mind. For now, I think it's best if I stay outside so I can keep an eye on foot traffic."

"Fair enough. The offer stands. Brian won't mind."

"I know. I'll see you at Mollie Stone's."

"At least have dinner with us tonight. I'm making spaghetti."

"Can't. Can I take a rain check?"

"You can." Olivia started to walk away but turned around at the last minute. "I just want to thank you, Scott. Having you watching me helps. A lot."

"No problem. We're going to keep you and everyone else in this mess safe."

Forty-five minutes later, Olivia stood in line at the grocery store, her shopping cart filled with all the things she would need for spaghetti, Caesar salad, and garlic bread, plus a bottle of red wine and a half-dozen double chocolate chip cookies. As Olivia started to unload her purchases onto the conveyor belt, she noticed Scott walk into the store, moving along the front passing each register, a look of urgency on his face as he scanned the people who were going through the checkout lines. When his eyes lit on her, he rushed to where she stood in line. Olivia was focused on Scott, when a voice behind her said, "You have a daughter, don't you, Mrs. Sinclair?"

Olivia whipped around, the bottle of wine in her hand, to discover Mark Bledsoe standing behind her, a little too close, an innocuous smile on his face, as though he were discussing the weather.

"And she has a little girl, doesn't she? She's a cute little thing. And doesn't she manage The Gables? One of my favorite bed and breakfasts. I might go this weekend. Get away."

Olivia looked for Scott, who was now running toward them, unbuttoning his jacket, ready to reach for the gun that was holstered underneath it.

"Are you actually threatening my daughter? And don't stand

so close to me." Olivia spoke loud enough to draw the attention of the people around her. If Mark Bledsoe was going to threaten her in public, she wanted as many witnesses as possible. The cashier stopped ringing up the purchases of the woman in front of her. The woman who was standing behind Mark scrolling on her phone, looked up, eyes wide with shock.

"Where's Ava?" Mark Bledsoe asked.

"You think I'm stupid enough to tell you that? Why do you want to know, so you can intimidate her?"

"I've never hurt my wife." Scott was now standing behind Olivia. He pulled away from Mark and tried to place himself in front of her.

"I don't believe you," Olivia said.

"I'll sue you for slander," Mark threatened.

"I don't care," Olivia said.

"I want to speak to my wife."

"She doesn't want to talk to you. Can you blame her? My God, you put her in the hospital when you broke her jaw. No wonder she wants to get away from you." Bledsoe's face flushed crimson. Fury sparked in his eyes. His hands clenched into ham-sized fists. Scott pushed Olivia out of the way, as the woman standing behind her held up her cell phone, openly recording the incident as it unfolded.

Olivia continued to speak, ignoring Scott, who was trying to pull her out of the line. "You're used to bullying women, Mr. Bledsoe, I get it. You get some sick pleasure watching your wife cower." Olivia shook loose from Scott and stepped closer to Mark Bledsoe. "You've clearly never crossed a mama bear. I'm not afraid of you. Threaten my daughter again, and not only will I get a restraining order, I will make sure your employer knows just what kind of man you are. After that, I will make it my bestowed mission to see you prosecuted for the abuse you've inflicted on your wife over the years."

"You can't stop me, Mrs. Sinclair. I plan to hound you until you tell me where my wife is. What do you think the police can do? I haven't done anything wrong."

"That's enough," Scott said, arranging his blazer so Mark Bledsoe could see the firearm. "I heard your threats, Mr. Bledsoe."

"And who are you?"

"One of the many people who are watching you and tracking your every move." Scott stepped close. "Store security will be here in a second. You need to leave."

"Fine."

Olivia was surprised that Bledsoe had capitulated so quickly. Her heart hammered in her chest as she watched him stroll out of the store, remarkably graceful despite his bulk. Scott Levering trailed behind him. Once they were out of sight, Olivia breathed a sigh of relief. The people who had gathered around carried on paying for their groceries, with the exception of the harried-looking woman with a shopping cart filled to the rim, who had pulled out her cell phone and filmed the entire incident.

"Are you all right? I can't believe the way you stood up to that guy."

"I'm fine."

"I recorded the whole thing, the threats, all of it. Do you want me to send it to you?"

"Would you mind?" The woman handed Olivia her phone, so Olivia could put her number in.

Olivia thanked the woman, paid for her groceries, and hurried out to her car. Scott had moved his car next to hers. When Olivia approached, he loaded Olivia's groceries for her, all the while watching the surrounding area, an avid look on his face, while Olivia dialed Denny.

"Mom?"

"Hello, sweetie. How are you and Carly?"

"We're great. On our way to Sun Valley to house-sit for a couple of weeks. The Gables is being deep-cleaned, so I get a bit of a vacation. What's wrong?"

"Is it that obvious?"

"I could tell by the way you said *Hello, sweetie.*"

"I'm working on a case for Lauren's friend."

"So you couldn't walk away, couldn't just say no?"

Olivia could hear the smile in Denny's voice.

"You know how it is, favor for a friend and all that. The husband of Lauren's friend is violent, Den. He just tracked me down at the grocery store and mentioned you and Carly and Lake Tahoe in the same sentence."

"Do you think he was serious, or just being a bully?"

"I think we should treat it as serious. I haven't told Brian yet. He'll probably want to alert law enforcement. Meanwhile, I'm glad you're not at home."

"Okay. I'm going to tell Lyndsay to be aware of anyone coming around and asking for me. I'll lay low in Sun Valley. The place I'm staying is loaded with security. I'll make sure to use it. I could even stay here another week or two if I needed to. The Gables might not be open until the middle of October."

"Perfect," Olivia said.

"Maybe Brian could call me later and tell me the best way to proceed?" Denny's voice was full of concern.

"We'll both call you tonight."

"I need to focus on driving. I'm hitting traffic. But before I go, I think I saw Asher Ridgeland on the news. He was on a stretcher. Have you heard anything?"

Olivia quickly tried to figure out what to say without alarming Denny. The last thing she needed was Denny coming home to help her friend. "Not really. I—"

"Can you let me know if you hear anything? I've called him, but he won't call me back," Denny said. "I need to go, Mom. Love you."

"Love you too. Take care of that precious cargo."

The minute Olivia disconnected from her call with Denny, her phone rang. The number looked familiar, but she couldn't place it.

"Hello?"

"Olivia? This is Nancy. Nancy St. Cere. I just had a patient cancel. If you come to my office, we can chat. I'll have about fifteen minutes."

At Nancy's direction, Olivia pulled her car around the back of the doctor's offices, parking in the out-of-the-way entrance the staff used to access the building, while Scott parked a discreet distance away. By the time she stepped out of her car, Nancy stood in the doorway, a big smile on her face. The two women hugged, and Olivia followed Nancy into a tiny office.

"It's really good to see you, Olivia." Nancy sat behind her desk, which was covered by neat stacks of charts, a dictation machine, and a computer. "I'm just trying to update all my chart notes before I head out."

"Paperwork never ends, does it?" Olivia said.

"I don't have a lot of time, so let's promise a proper dinner when I get back from vacation, okay?" Nancy looked at her watch. "You wanted to talk about Ken Ridgeland? What's he done now?"

"Nothing that I know of. This is just a reconnaissance mission. My boyfriend is a private investigator who is actually looking into the murder of a young woman who was one of Ken's—" Olivia searched for the word.

"One of Ken's women? He had an amazing number of them, despite being such an utter jackass. I don't know how his wife can bear to stay married to him."

"I'd like to hear about your time working for him, if you're willing to tell me."

Nancy gave Olivia a frank and open look. "I'll tell you anything you want to know, within reason. There was a lawsuit, and I signed a non-disclosure agreement. So when we bump up against that, I'll stop talking."

"That would be great," Olivia said.

"Do you want me to narrate or do you want to ask questions?"

Olivia smiled. Nancy had always been concise and no-nonsense with her words. "You should have been a lawyer."

"My parents would have disowned me. Family tradition and all that."

"Agreed. Go ahead and narrate."

"When I started my residency, it was a bit of a free-for-all. We worked hard, long hours, no sleep, nothing you haven't heard before. Some of the male doctors were total pigs. No one challenged it; it was just an accepted thing. Despite these modern times, there was this unspoken *if you can't take the heat get out of the kitchen* vibe. I didn't care. I was going to keep my head down and do the work. Most of the senior doctors were professional, but Ken Ridgeland—" Nancy shook her head. "I haven't thought about this in a long time. It still infuriates me.

"Ken Ridgeland was a predator. You should have seen the way he harassed nurses. I know a handful of complaints were lodged against him. I watched him grope, grasp, harass, and stalk many a young nurse. The minute they complained, they were fired. It was a nightmare. My plan was to avoid him at all costs. If he didn't see me, maybe I wouldn't fall victim – God, I hate that word – to him.

"Well, that didn't last. At first he was nice enough, asking me to dinner, things like that. When I refused, he seemed fine, seemed to move on to another unsuspecting young lady who was wowed by the idea that she was being pursued by a doctor, never mind that said doctor was not only married but also open about his numerous affairs. What I didn't realize, was that my refusal only egged Ken on. He locked on to me and became relentless in his pursuit. He would single me out at the hospital. One time he locked us in the linen closet together. I started to scream. Lucky for me, someone immediately let us out. Ken said it was an accident, but I knew better. And since I know you're going to ask, I reported every incident to human resources. Every time. They did nothing. Not. One. Thing. One night, I didn't leave the hospital until 2:30 in the morning. Had I not been so exhausted, I would have known better than to be alone in the parking garage at that hour.

"All I can tell you is that Ken assaulted me. Groped me, and from the way he was trying to tear off my scrubs, would have likely raped me, had I not hit the panic button on my car alarm and attracted the attention of the usually sleeping security officer.

"I turned in my resignation the next day. Moved home to my parents' house, grappled with depression for a year, somehow managed to pull my career together, finish my residency in a different department, and wound up here.

"Lucky for me, as the litigation moved forward, things came out about Ken that would shock you, Olivia. Lucky for me, the entire encounter in the parking lot was caught on video, CCTV, whatever they call it. The hospital tried to hide it, but the vid was leaked to my attorney anonymously just as we were about to exchange discovery. The hospital was under a court order to provide Ken's HR file and information with regard to any other sexual harassment complaints against him. My attorneys discovered that he allegedly sexually assaulted a patient after he slipped her Rohypnol on a date. The police were called, and the incident was reported, but somehow the report was lost before it got forwarded to the DA's office, so nothing came of it. Once Ken's attorneys got wind of that information, my case settled quickly. I didn't want the money, so I donated it to an abused women's shelter, and tried to get on with my life.

"A couple of years after everything was resolved, Ken tracked me down at my apartment and gave me the *look at what you did to me* speech. Unbeknownst to Ken, my dad was helping me hang some shelves." Nancy gave Olivia a sly smile. Her father was ferociously protective. "Suffice it to say that Ken Ridgeland hurried away with a black eye and his tail between his legs."

"Nancy, that's terrible. I'm sorry you had to go through that."

"There's more. That murdered girl, the one on the news? Asher Ridgeland's girlfriend? She and Ken knew each other. I saw them together on more than one occasion at the dim sum restaurant near the hospital. They were a couple."

"How do you know?"

"Ken kissed her rather comprehensively, if you get my meaning. And she didn't push him away."

Olivia now had two sources confirming that Ken Ridgeland was involved with Mikala. She only knew Ken Ridgeland during her marriage to Richard. They had been golfing buddies, and when they were together, it was all ego, the relationship between the two men a continual dance of one-upmanship. Eventually the competition between them became so fierce, Olivia went out of her way to avoid Ken at every turn. Now she looked at Nancy and said, "I'm glad you've found a sustainable way to practice medicine. You seem happy, and I'm glad."

"Thanks. I'm grateful for the work-life balance. I've met a really nice guy, and I'm dating."

"Thanks for talking to me, Nancy." Olivia stood. The two women hugged.

Nancy gave Olivia an appraising look. "Forgive me if this comment oversteps, but you look like you're about to jump out of your skin. Are you okay?"

"I'm fine. Just tired," Olivia lied. "Can we have lunch when you get back from vacation?"

"Absolutely. I'll call." Nancy gave Olivia's shoulder a gentle squeeze and met her gaze. "Take care of yourself, Liv. Stress won't serve you. But you know that, don't you?"

"I do and I'll try," Olivia said.

Olivia waved at Scott and made a twirling motion with her finger, hoping he'd get the message that she was headed home to Brian. And safety.

Chapter 14

In the nine months since Brian had moved in with Olivia, he'd come to enjoy the early mornings spent in the kitchen with his laptop open, getting a start on the day, as he sipped his coffee. Brian shivered in the morning chill, reached for his favorite sweatshirt and slipped it over his head before he did a quick check-in with Scott Levering, Blake Curtis, and Ian Greely. He sent a flurry of text messages, discussing assignments for the day and making sure Lauren and Ava were safe. Once that was handled, he opened the software he used to conduct deep background checks, typed in Ken Ridgeland's name, and prepared to slip down the rabbit hole.

It didn't take long for Brian to discover that Dr. Ridgeland was floating in a morass of legal issues. His medical license had been suspended. He had no reportable source of income, and likely wouldn't get hired anywhere once his future employer called for a reference. Despite this, he'd managed to rent an apartment in the Avenues right near the beach and lease a new Mercedes. *Where was this guy getting his money? From his wife?*

"Good morning," Olivia said in a sleepy voice.

Brian shut his computer just as she came up behind him and kissed the back of his neck. "Why did you let me sleep so late?" Grabbing a mug, Olivia poured herself a cup of coffee.

"I thought you'd be glad for the rest. Did you sleep well?"

"No nightmares." Olivia sat next to him. "What are you doing?"

"Digging into Ken Ridgeland," Brian said.

"What have you found out?"

"He's got troubles, as you can imagine. Tell me about his wife."

"How much would you like to know?" Olivia asked. "Sabine Trembley Ridgeland is an eccentric woman. She's all about appearances, and what other people think matters to her. You know who she reminds me of? Gloria Swanson in *Sunset Boulevard*. I don't think she's psycho or anything, but she's just – I don't know – odd."

"What do you think she'd do if she found out about Ken's issues?"

"Such as flagrantly cheating, losing his medical license, and being accused of sexual assault?" Olivia hesitated. "I don't know. I do know that she is imperious and not quite living in the real world, if that makes sense. She's an odd duck, but I doubt she'd ever do anything to invite scandal. Her devotion to Asher is a little much."

"Hover mom?"

"To the nth. But Asher seems to deal with it."

"Off topic, but after what happened yesterday, are you sure you don't want to file a restraining order against Mark Bledsoe?"

"Not yet. He hasn't really threatened me. If he approaches again, we'll revisit the issue. We've got the video the woman took at the grocery store. I'm hoping that once Ava's gone, Mark will be gone too." Olivia hesitated, as though she wanted to say more.

"What is it?" Brian asked.

"I might reach out to Dan Winters, maybe mention what happened."

"I think that's a good idea."

Olivia stood by the kitchen sink on tiptoes, craning her neck as she searched the street. "Where's Scott? He really shouldn't have to stay in his car all day."

"He has another case to work, so I'll be taking care of you personally for a couple days."

Olivia smiled. "I get to go to work with you?"

"Yes. It's bring-your-love-to-work day."

"What's on the docket, boss?"

"We're going to the city to see Ezra Addelson, Mikala's landlord. I've been culling photos from Ken Ridgeland's social media pages. I thought I'd show them to Ezra and see if he recognizes anyone. I'm trying to find out who paid her rent. After that, I thought I would take you somewhere for a nice meal."

"Before you bring me home and lock me in the fortress?"

"Something like that."

After a leisurely breakfast, Brian and Olivia set out for the city, driving south on 101, through the Robin Williams Tunnel and over the Golden Gate Bridge, enjoying the subdued autumn light as it danced across the San Francisco Bay.

"There's something about Saturdays in the city," Olivia said as they crossed the bridge. "I'm going to miss this view."

"We'll come back and visit."

Olivia reached over and grabbed Brian's hand. "Lucy Waynesbarrow is coming within the next couple of days to finalize the listing. She's been busy, so I told her to reach out when she's free," Olivia said.

Things almost seemed normal as they discussed selling Olivia's house and the logistics of relocating to their new house in Lake Tahoe. By the time Brian parked in front of Ezra's apartment building, Olivia's cheeks had their usual glow and the cloak of nervous energy that had surrounded her earlier had dissipated.

Ezra was waiting for them. He stood behind the glass-paneled door that led into the lobby. When his eyes lit on Brian's car, he came out to meet them.

"What a charming building," Olivia said, getting out of the car and stretching her legs. Brian came around to join her as Ezra approached.

"Ezra, I'd like you to meet my—" Brian caught himself before he called Olivia his wife. "This is Olivia Sinclair."

133

"I know who you are, young lady. I followed your case last October. Knew that you were innocent from the moment I saw you on the television." Ezra took Olivia's outstretched hand in both of his. "Forgive me for being too forward, but you are a brave, intelligent woman, my dear. We need more people like you in the world."

Brian watched Olivia as she smiled at Mr. Addelson and placed a gentle hand on his elbow as he struggled up the step that led back into his building. "Thank you for your kind words, Mr. Addelson."

"I imagine it was hell for you, being accused and arrested."

"I'll never forget it," Olivia said, as they stepped into the elevator. "Every morning, I'm grateful for—" Olivia met Brian's eyes "—everything."

"That's a good thing. Now you come into my apartment. We'll sit down and have some tea."

Soon they were seated in what Brian now thought of as Mrs. Addelson's part of the house, waiting while Mr. Addelson poured out tea into large flowery mugs. Brian didn't like tea, but he didn't have the heart to tell his host.

"So what can I do for you today, Mr. Vickery? What news of Mikala's case?"

"I'm still tracking Mikala's boyfriends. I'm trying to pinpoint the identity of the man who paid her rent." Brian reached into his pocket and pulled out his iPad. Once he had the photos on the screen, he handed it to Mr. Addelson, who acted as though he didn't want to touch it.

"I've got no idea what to do with these things," Mr. Addelson said.

"Here, I'll help." Olivia set her tea down and gestured to the vacant spot next to Mr. Addelson on the sofa. "May I?"

The old man's face softened. Brian wondered what his life must be like, living alone in this apartment, full of memories of the wife who he still held in his heart.

"Thank you, young lady."

Olivia took the iPad from him. "So, here's the first photo."

Brian watched as Olivia scrolled through the dozens of random photos he pulled from Ken Ridgeland's social media. Most of them were of groups of men on the golf course, on fishing boats, and sitting together in bars and restaurants, raising their glasses in salutation.

"I know him." Mr. Addelson pointed to the screen. "There he is again."

Brian stood and moved over behind Olivia and Mr. Addelson, who was pointing to Ken Ridgeland. "He looks like the guy who paid the rent?"

Olivia scrolled to a single photo of Ken Ridgeland, a shot of his face that looked like a selfie. "Here, I'll enlarge this."

"That's him!" Ezra said. "That's the man who paid her rent. I'm sure of it."

Olivia, in her trademark level of thoroughness, said, "Let's look at the others and see if you recognize anyone else."

Two photos later, Ezra said, "That guy right there. That's Harry George. He's a doctor. I rented an apartment to him when he was in medical school. Brilliant young man. What's he doing with that chump?" Ezra pointed at Ken Ridgeland. The photo had been taken on a fishing trip and depicted Ken Ridgeland and – according to Ezra – Harry George. The two men stood next to each other, holding up a beer, while another man held up a huge fish, a prideful grin on his face.

"Do you know the third man?" Brian asked.

Ezra took the iPad from Olivia and stared at it for a few seconds. "I don't."

"What can you tell us about Harry George?" When Ezra hesitated, Olivia said, "It's important, Ezra."

"My kids don't think I should be talking to you." Ezra looked at Brian, but his gaze settled on Olivia and lingered there. "But I've always trusted my instincts, young lady. I can tell that you're a woman of substance. Plus, I don't like my kids thinking they can tell me what to do."

"We're discreet," Brian said. "We have to be in our line of work."

"Of course you are. Okay. Here's what I know. When Mikala moved in, she had boyfriends. That girl knew how to make men dance to her tune. Every day she had different men doing favors for her. They'd move furniture, bring groceries." Ezra chuckled. "One guy even rented her a Mercedes for a weekend. She took the keys from him, hopped in the car and drove away. Left the poor schmuck standing there looking like a lovesick fool."

"Do you think she was romantic with all of them?" Olivia asked.

"Wouldn't surprise me. But Mikala and Harry were different. They seemed to like each other, or at least Harry liked her. I loved my wife, God rest her soul. Still love her after all these years. I know what a man who is in love looks like. Harry was in love with Mikala. They were together all the time. He was good for her, I think. So was Asher. Mikala seemed like a wild child, but Harry was a doctor and he was a good kid when he lived here during college. I was willing to suspend judgment on Mikala, solely based on her involvement with Harry.

"The guy who paid the rent – this Ken Ridgeland guy – once he was on the scene, things got sketchy. Mikala changed. They'd fight. Yelling, sometimes hitting. They did something to Harry that caused him some trouble." Ezra looked embarrassed. "They were fighting in the foyer when I happened to be taking my garbage out. I'm embarrassed to say that I eavesdropped for a minute. Harry said, '*How could you do this to me?*' Mikala mumbled something back. I couldn't hear what she said, but her words pushed Harry over the edge. He became furious with her. I've never seen a man so angry. I heard him say, '*It's over. I'm not giving you another dime. You want to push this? Go for it. Do your best.*' And then he walked away." Ezra gazed out the window. "You know what I'll never forget about that scene?"

Olivia and Brian waited.

"Harry George looked heartbroken. He was angry, no doubt about that, but he had the look of someone who had been deeply betrayed, wounded, if you will." Ezra squared his shoulders and shook his head. "Does that help?"

"Immensely," Brian said.

Once Olivia and Brian were back in the car, Olivia said, "We need to talk to Harry George."

Brian smiled over at her. "*I* do. But not today. I'm going to buy you lunch, and then we're going home."

"How about The Cliff House?" The Cliff House was a San Francisco institution, known for its phenomenal seafood and sweeping view of the San Francisco Bay and the Farallon Islands.

"The Cliff House it is," Brian said. "I'm enjoying working with you, Liv."

Olivia's cell phone rang. "It's Sabine Ridgeland. Why is she calling me . . .? Hello? Sabine?"

Brian waited, wishing Olivia would put the call on speaker. "Tomorrow afternoon? I'll double-check with Brian and get back to you. Okay. Bye."

"She wants us to meet with Ken and her tomorrow afternoon. Says they have something to discuss with us. Rather fortuitous, don't you think?"

"I do," Brian said.

"You seem worried."

"We're looking under rocks for Asher and finding things that have the potential to destroy his family."

"I know. But he needs the truth – deserves the truth."

"He does. But I will not be telling his mother anything. And since Sabine is your friend, this puts you right in the hot seat."

"I don't mind the hot seat."

"Then make the call."

Chapter 15

"Maybe we should stay out here and watch the sunset."

"Come on, Brian, avoidance isn't your style," Olivia teased. "I don't want to deal with Sabine and Ken Ridgeland either. Let's get this over with. Don't forget our dinner plans." She winced a little as she spoke. There were no dinner plans. Lying didn't come naturally to Olivia, but Sabine could be so annoyingly tenacious, especially where Asher was concerned. They needed an escape plan. Olivia had always felt sorry for Sabine, probably because she was once married to a guy like Ken Ridgeland, an egomaniacal gasbag, who loved the sound of his own voice and the look of his image in a mirror. Olivia had several memories of Sabine and Ken at social functions. Handsome and charismatic, young women flocked to Ken right under Sabine's nose, much as they had done to Richard, Olivia's ex. Always socially appropriate, Sabine stood by, a wry smile on her face. She had heard Ken call these interactions with other women – all of them beautiful, most of them young – harmless flirting. But Olivia recognized the hurt she had seen in Sabine's eyes.

"You seem nervous," Brian said, grabbing Olivia's hand as they walked along the paved walkway toward the front door.

"I fear this won't go well," Olivia said. "When Sabine finds out we're not going to be forthcoming with information, she's going to be furious with us."

"Are you afraid of her?"

"No. Just don't want to be here. Don't want to be doing this."

"At least you've got me to protect you." Brian gave Olivia a sardonic grin. "Not that you can't take care of yourself."

"Thanks for the vote of confidence."

Brian pulled Olivia close to him and was just about to kiss her when Sabine Ridgeland opened the door.

"You two are like teenagers." She gave them a raised-eyebrow glance before she stepped aside and smiled. "You're lucky to have found each other. Come in. Ken's in the living room. Olivia knows the way. I've thrown together a nosh. You two can go on through while I grab the tray."

Brian followed Olivia down the corridor into a room that looked like a movie set, with high-backed Victorian sofas, lots of dark wood, an Aubusson rug, and an abundance of William Morris wallpaper for good measure. Ken Ridgeland was nowhere to be seen.

"Did we just time-travel to the early 1900s?"

"Nope," Olivia whispered. "But it sure feels like it."

"How do you know Sabine again?"

"Arts council. Don't be misled by her understated elegance and her penchant for old-world living. She doesn't do technology – she doesn't even own a television – but she's a ferocious fund-raiser. And she's so elegant that even the most pretentious of the patrons dial it back when she's around. Although she doesn't brag about it, she comes from a very noble French family. She has an eye for artistic talent and has launched many a career with her international connections in the art world."

"You don't say? I was thinking you could drop her right into a Henry James novel. She wouldn't even need a wardrobe change."

Brian, an avid reader and book lover, migrated to Sabine's vast library. He was perusing the shelves when Ken Ridgeland stepped into the room. Asher Ridgeland was tall and thin, with intelligent eyes and a patrician nose. His father had the same features, but where Asher came across as soft and youthful, Ken Ridgeland's face was angular, his eyes keen and edgy. Where Asher wore glasses and had the pallor of someone who spent his days in front of a computer, Ken's face was tan and weather-beaten, as though he spent his spare time sailing or playing tennis. *I don't trust this guy.* Brian took this first impression for what it was, an intuitive hit with no factual basis. But still. The guy was irritating. Brian thought for a brief second what would happen if he walked up to Ken Ridgeland and messed up his hair.

"Olivia? Good to see you."

As Ken moved toward Olivia, she scooted next to Brian. Rather than shake Ken's hand, Olivia wound her arm through Brian's, and said, "Ken, meet Brian Vickery, my investigator."

"Ah, the boyfriend. I've heard about you," Ken said, shaking Brian's hand.

I'll bet you have, Brian thought. Given that Ken Ridgeland and Richard – Olivia's SOB ex-husband – were golfing buddies, Brian could only imagine what Ken had heard. Brian was hired by Olivia's defense attorney after Olivia's arrest for the murder of her husband's mistress. There had been a spark between them from the beginning. Although there had been no love lost between Olivia and Richard, when Richard had discovered Brian in the home he and Olivia shared, he hadn't responded well. Even though Brian was there as part of the legal team, Richard had immediately become jealous and tried to throw his weight around. When he'd actually tried to engage Brian in a physical fight, things didn't go Richard's way. In the end, he scarpered away with a chip on his shoulder.

"I do not know why my wife called this little get-together," Ken said. He gestured toward the couches. "Let's sit."

Soon Sabine came into the room, pushing an old-fashioned tea trolley, which held a crystal decanter of brandy, a soda spritzer, an ice bucket, and a silver tray of canapés.

"Jesus," Ken said under his breath.

"What's the matter, darling? I can't *not* offer food and drink to our guests."

"We don't even know why we've been summoned, Sabine." Ken looked at his watch. "I need to leave in twenty minutes. I'm usually off nights, but our hospital is terribly understaffed right now," he said apologetically to Olivia and Brian.

Brian didn't look at Olivia, but he knew she didn't miss the blatant lie.

"What can I make for you? Brandy and soda?"

"Nothing for me," Brian said.

"No, thank you," Olivia said at the same time.

"Very well." Sabine took a seat on the sofa, sitting as far away from Ken as she could.

"I called you all here because Brian and Olivia are working for Asher."

At these words, Ken Ridgeland became alert. His eyes darted from Sabine to Olivia until they rested on Brian. "What? Is that true?"

"Yes," Brian said.

"Why am I just finding this out now?" Ken didn't bother to hide his irritation.

"I've been trying to talk to you, but you keep ignoring me."

"Sabine—"

Ignoring her husband, Sabine continued. "As Asher's parents, Ken and I need to know what you are doing for him. Are you trying to discover who murdered Mikala?"

"Of course they aren't. Olivia's a lawyer, an officer of the court. She wouldn't interfere with a police investigation. She knows better than that." The tone of Ken's voice carried a veiled threat that caused Brian's hackles to rise.

"We can't discuss this with either of you," Brian said.

"That is not an acceptable answer," Sabine snapped. "We are his parents. We are trying to protect our son, whose girlfriend has been brutally murdered. Olivia, we have been friends for a long time. Can't you make an exception for me? Surely you can understand our position. What would you do if Denny—"

"Please don't bring Olivia's daughter into this," Brian said. "This situation has nothing to do with Denny. We are both duty-bound to protect Asher's confidence. I'm afraid there's no getting around it."

"I can't believe this." Sabine dabbed at her eyes with a linen handkerchief.

"I can't believe you dragged Olivia and Brian over here to railroad them into betraying a client confidentiality. What did you expect to do? Strong-arm them? It's time you let Asher deal with his life on his own. You continually coddle him. It's got to stop." Ken stood and checked his watch. "I need to go. This meeting is over. Olivia, Brian, I'll walk you out."

Left with little choice, Olivia and Brian followed Ken out of the living room and out the front door. Brian wasn't surprised when Olivia squeezed Sabine's shoulder on the way out, a gesture of solidarity and friendship, so typical of Olivia. In response, Sabine pushed Olivia's hand away and wouldn't meet her eyes.

Once outside, Ken followed Olivia and Brian to their car. Checking over his shoulder, as if to make sure Sabine wasn't watching, Ken said, "Sabine's not in her right mind. She hasn't been for a while. I honestly don't know what to do about it. If you need anything from me, please let me know, okay? I care about my son. He knows that if he needs my help, all he has to do is ask. I'm sorry about all that." Ken nodded at the house. "I'm running late." With a wave, he took off, hurrying to a black Mercedes parked under a carport.

It wasn't until Brian turned from the Ridgelands' driveway onto the twisty road that Olivia said, "Ken Ridgeland's a filthy liar."

"He is." Brian put the car in gear and pulled away from Sabine's house. "I'd like to know a little more about the good doctor."

"I'll bet his colleague, Harry George, could give us an earful."

"Agreed. Should we make an appointment to see Dr. George, or drop in?"

"I think a drop-in is warranted," Olivia said.

"Drop-in it is."

Chapter 16

Brian watched Asher Ridgeland as he put his backpack on the floor and took a seat across the desk. *He's a man-child.* The words – the judgment – came to Brian unbidden. He tucked this feeling away for later, when he could take it out and pick it apart.

"I think the time has come to let all of this go," Brian said.

"Why?" Asher's voice rose an octave.

"I've discovered Mikala's real name, and I've discovered a few unscrupulous things about her and your father." Brian waited, gauging his client's reaction to this news, watching the emotions play across Asher's face.

"My father?"

"Sugarcoating isn't my style, Asher. The only thing I know how to do in situations like this is deliver the results of my investigation the way I would want to receive them if I were in your shoes. I've discovered a connection between your father and Mikala."

Asher's face went crimson; the snake-like vein that ran along his temples started to throb. Brian waited for Asher to jump up, rage, storm, and react. Instead, the young man took a deep breath, and in a surprising show of self-control, sat back, crossed his legs and waited for Brian to continue. "When I hired you, I prepared myself for the worst-case scenario. I just need to know, Brian. Have you found Mikala's family?"

"I don't believe she has any surviving family. Olivia uncovered information that your father has some issues."

"Olivia?"

"Apparently your mother ambushed you in the parking lot after you came to see me."

A look of angry disgust washed over Asher's face and was gone just as quickly. Brian continued. "The rumor mill did its job, as you can imagine. The information Olivia gleaned fell into her lap. She didn't do any questioning or speak to anyone out of turn. I trust her without question. She cares for you and will be loyal to her dying breath. Her information has helped me."

"I'm not worried about Olivia gossiping. It's fine, Brian. Tell me about my father and Mikala."

Brian cringed internally as he delivered his findings to a surprisingly stoic Asher. "I'm also pretty sure your father and Mikala were running a blackmail scheme."

"Blackmail? Why would my father need to resort to blackmail? He's a doctor, for crying out loud. My mother is an heiress. She's got millions."

"He's not."

"Not what?"

"A doctor. Not anymore. He was fired when he sexually harassed a woman at the hospital." Brian hesitated. "She sued him and settled her lawsuit. Your father was terminated as a result of this. Later, it was alleged that he sexually assaulted a patient, too. Your father claimed they were having an affair, and the relationship was consensual. But the woman claimed your father put something in her drink and raped her while she was unconscious."

"Oh, my God." Asher couldn't catch his breath. He felt his heart clench and thought for a minute that he was having a heart attack. "How did you find this out?"

"I can't tell you that. I'm sorry. Olivia assures me the source is reputable."

"Why isn't my father in jail?"

"As far as I could find out, they discovered the woman – the patient – to be a bit of a grifter. Your father wasn't the first doctor she'd slept with and accused. I could keep digging on why no charges were filed, but I think – as I just said – that you should let this go.

"That brings me to my next section of the narrative. Your mother summoned Olivia and me to her house last night to find out what you had hired us to do. Of course, we didn't say anything. But your father was there. He claimed he had to leave early because he was working at the hospital."

"So he's been lying and my mother doesn't know," Asher said.

"Apparently."

"That's just great. Wonderful. Can you tell me more about his involvement with Mikala?"

Brian hesitated.

"Tell me, Brian. I paid you to find out this information, so just tell me. Please."

"I'm going to tell you everything I know, okay? But your involvement with this matter needs to end. We are in jeopardy of bumping into the murder investigation into Mikala's death. I was warned off by the police, okay? So we're going to have to rein the investigation in."

"Fair enough. Tell me what you know."

"It seems that your dad and Mikala have known each other for about—" Brian thumbed through a pad of handwritten notes on his desk "—three years."

"So long before I met her," Asher said. He ran his hands over his face.

"Apparently."

Resigned, he met Brian's steady gaze. "I was her mark, wasn't I?"

"I'm not sure." Brian shook his head. "What have you given her? She hasn't taken money from you. She hasn't conned you into giving her your inheritance. If she was going to con you, she'd be after something."

"Maybe she and my father were going to murder my mother. Then I'd be rich. Mikala and I would get married, then they would kill me, and – you get my meaning."

"Maybe," Brian said. "But that just doesn't feel right. In order for two people to engage in a long-con like that, they would have to trust each other. I seriously doubt Mikala would trust your father. I've met your father. I was only around him for about fifteen minutes. No offense, but I wouldn't trust him. Even though I've never met Mikala, given her successful blackmail scheme, I'm certain she's got solid instincts. Given that your father paid her rent for a year, I'm guessing she actually had the upper hand in their relationship."

"What's her real name? Is her real name even Mikala?" Asher asked.

"Bernadette Mickleson," Brian said. "I can read the despair on your face, Asher. While every side of your current situation is horrible, I can assure you – and I hope you can take some comfort in knowing – that this will all pass. The pain leaves a scar, but it will go away. There ends the sermon."

"Do you think my father was the man she was partying with the night of her murder?"

"I don't know. Possibly. Given this is an ongoing murder investigation, I am not comfortable trying to find out. I wouldn't be surprised if the police have already discovered the blackmail scheme and the connection between them. You can't engage in a blackmail scheme and not leave a trail of wreckage in your wake. Have you heard from the police?"

"No. Why? Should I have?"

"I just think it's strange that they haven't asked you to come to 850 Bryant and make a formal statement."

"I guess they didn't need me to give a statement yet."

"Strange," Brian said.

"Do you know where my dad lives?"

"He rents an apartment out in the Avenues, close to the beach." Brian took a Post-it Note and wrote out an address. "Are you sure you want to talk to him?"

"You don't think I should?"

"No, I don't. He's likely a suspect in Mikala's death. I find it concerning that a patient accused him of giving her a drug before raping her, especially in light of the fact that Mikala and you were both drugged."

"You think my father murdered Mikala?"

"If I were working this case, and I discovered your father's history, he would jump to the top of my list of suspects." Brian's cell phone rang. He put it on silent and turned it face down on the desk. "I'm going to speak to you as a friend, okay? Giving this kind of advice isn't in my job description."

"Okay."

"Stay away from your father, if you are able. He's a criminal – at the very least a blackmailer and maybe a murderer – who is about to be backed into a corner. We can be sure the police have likely discovered your father's activities. You've been cleared in the case. I would stay away. There's always fallout from situations like this. You don't want to get sucked back in."

"Point taken. But I need to talk to him. Just once."

"I understand. Want my advice about the way to approach him?"

"No," Asher said sheepishly. "But you better tell me, anyway."

"Get clear about what you're going to say to him and what your expectations of the conversation are going to be. Say your piece and then get away. Don't let him bait you, taunt you, or suck you into an argument. Don't believe a thing he says. Don't let your emotions control your intellect. It's time to let this go."

"Easier said than done. But okay. I'll try."

"Just step back and let the police do their job."

"I don't want to interfere with the police. I just want to know if I was Mikala's mark. I need to know. Was I stupid? I thought

148

she loved me. Can you keep investigating, just to see if you can find out if she targeted me?"

"With the proviso that I share what I find with the police, should I discover anything relevant to their investigation."

"No problem. Whatever you think is best."

"And Olivia will be helping me."

"Agreed," Asher said.

"Don't make me regret this. Stay away from the investigation, got it?"

"Got it." Asher stood and held out his hand.

Brian watched from the doorway of his office as Asher crossed the street, jumped in his car, and drove away, his shoulders hunched over as though he carried the weight of the world. He was just about to lock up, when there was a knock on the door. Given the Bledsoe case, Brian didn't go anywhere without his gun. Now he drew it and stepped into the corridor, surprised to see the blond man who confronted him after his meeting with Lexy Ford standing outside. Only this time, instead of wearing jeans and a worn sweatshirt, he was dressed in a navy-blue suit and a red tie. Brian holstered his gun. "How can I help you?" he asked through the glass door.

"Sorry to catch you unaware," the man said through the glass door. He held up a badge that identified him as an FBI agent. "Dennis Culligan, FBI. We need to talk. Can I come in?"

Brian unlocked the door and let the man in. Rather than lead him back to his office, the two men remained standing in the empty foyer.

"You moving?"

"Retiring. What did you want to say?"

"I did some digging into you. Heard you're all right, level-headed."

"Are you here to tell me to stop digging into the Glascott murder?"

"No. I'm asking you to stay away from the Ridgelands. All of them. I'm asking as a professional courtesy. I've checked you out,

149

know you're legit, you have a solid rep as a good cop. Honest, in possession of all the required virtues. But you are standing on an active volcano right now. We're asking you nicely to stand down. If you don't, we will cease playing nice."

"And I'm assuming more information will not be forth-coming?"

"Your assumption is correct. Just do it, okay?"

"I won't step on any toes."

"See that you don't." With a nod, Dennis Culligan walked out. It wasn't so long ago that a warning from the FBI would have driven Brian to keep digging. Now all he wanted to do was go home to Olivia.

Chapter 17

Brian and Olivia rode in silence as they navigated traffic over the Golden Gate Bridge. They were on their way back to the city once again, this time to interview Dr. Harry George.

"So why are we continuing to investigate when you told Asher to back off?"

The corner of Brian's mouth turned up as Olivia pulled down the passenger mirror and fiddled with her lipstick.

"I don't know."

She put the mirror back up and looked at him. "Something's bothering you about this situation. What is it? And why are you smiling like that?"

"Smiling because I'm with you." Brian kept his eyes on the road. "And you're right. Something's bugging me, but I don't know what."

"Liar," Olivia whispered.

Brian started to protest, but Olivia interrupted him. "It's okay, Brian. I don't expect you to divulge your every thought. And I understand how your mind works. You're a processor."

"A processor?"

"You get an inchoate idea, and you work on it, *process* it from every angle."

"Interesting," Brian said.

"You have good instincts. If something's bothering you, you'll soon know what it is."

"I appreciate your confidence in me."

"Changing the subject now, but it will destroy Sabine when she finds out about Ken. Never mind that he's been having an affair with Mikala. The fact that her husband got fired from his job and has been lying about working will throw Sabine into a spin."

"That kind of news would throw any woman into a spin," Brian said.

"I feel sorry for her."

"I feel sorry for Asher," Brian said. "I kept asking myself how much more that kid could take, as I heaped betrayal after betrayal onto his shoulders. His girlfriend, his father – I felt like I was the executioner."

"I can't imagine. He was always such a wonderful child. Very artistic from an early age. I think Ken imagined he'd given birth to a man's man – an image of himself – to suit his ego. For a long time, Ken forced Asher to play sports, soccer and baseball, among others. He never took to it. I think the other kids bullied him because he wasn't terribly athletic. Kids can be so cruel. Denny liked him though. She always had a soft spot for the kids who were bullied. I always had a pack of children at our house. When all the kids – I think there were at least five or six of them – would play outside at my house, Asher would always stay in the background. Granted, Denny liked to play rough, so I hardly blamed him. One year, Sabine signed Asher up for art camp, and I swear, he blossomed before our eyes. It was great to watch." Brian's hand rested on the console. Olivia put hers on top of it and said, "How are we going to play this interview with Harry George?"

Brian raised an eyebrow at her.

"What? I'm just asking."

"We're going to park by his car and wait."

"Are we going to ambush him?"

"Something like that. I'm going to ask him about Mikala and Ken and see how he responds."

"Asher's entire family's falling apart, and he's clinging to the idea that the woman who cheated on him, lied to him, and likely was setting him up for a con, harbored some love for him."

"Love motivates people to do strange things," Brian said.

"Dysfunctional, desperate love motivates people to do bad things," Olivia countered.

They slowed as traffic bottlenecked when they reached the tollbooth on the south side of the Golden Gate Bridge.

"What are you thinking?"

"When this mess is said and done, I'm going to make an effort with Asher. I'll ask Denny to help. He's going to need friends after this."

Brian rested a hand on Olivia's thigh. She lifted it to her lips and placed a kiss there. They rode in silence as Brian navigated traffic, both of them lost in their own thoughts, neither of them inclined toward filling the space between them with unnecessary chitchat. Brian turned into the parking structure at UCSF, the preeminent medical teaching hospital in San Francisco, driving up the twisty ramp until he found the rows of reserved doctors' parking.

"There's Doctor George's car." Brian pointed to a silver Honda Accord with the license plate DOCHRY.

Brian circled the lot until he found an empty slot a lane over that allowed them to observe Dr. George's car unseen.

"Lots of waiting in your job, I imagine." Olivia sunk into the seat and pulled her knees to her chest.

"Yes. Hours."

"We could make out," Olivia teased.

Brian laughed. "That wouldn't be terribly professional, would it?"

Minutes passed. Olivia leaned back and closed her eyes, savoring the feeling of not being tied to a litigation calendar, a daunting list of appointments, and frantic phone calls from frightened clients. All the while the Bledsoe divorce and Mark's menacing attitude lingered in the back of her mind.

"Off topic, but Mark Bledsoe has been suspiciously quiet today," Olivia said. She sat up and straightened her legs as far as she could. "I don't know if I should be relieved or worried."

"I'd stick with worried. I'm surprised you haven't at least heard from his lawyer."

"Oh, I'm not surprised. That entire hearing was a sham. Dan Winters knew it. His promise of a settlement proposal was for show."

"I've been concerned about the lack of activity as well. At least we can be assured that Ava and Lauren are tucked away in the beach house, safe, sound, and well protected."

Olivia sighed. "I know. Thanks for that, Brian. Having you in charge of security has made the entire process easier. I'll be glad when Ava's safely out of the country. I'll have to deal with the fallout of a client fleeing, but it's better than—"

"There he is," Brian whispered. They watched as Harry George, dressed in scrubs, a backpack slung over his shoulder, talked on his cell as he headed toward his car. "Stay behind me, okay? At least until we know how he's going to react to being questioned."

"Okay."

When Dr. George disengaged his car alarm, Brian said, "Let's go." He whispered in Olivia's ear, "Just play it casual." He took Olivia's hand. The two of them sauntered toward Harry George as though they were an innocent couple heading into the hospital.

When they got close, Brian let go of Olivia's hand. "Dr. George?"

Harry George was just about to get in his car. Startled, he straightened and faced Brian. His eyes swept over Olivia, hesitating for a second, as though he recognized her and was trying to place her.

"Sorry," Brian said. "Didn't mean to startle you. I'm Brian Vickery and this—"

"I already spoke to the police. They kept me at 850 Bryant for three hours. I told them everything, signed a statement, the whole nine yards."

"I'm not a cop," Brian said. "I'm not with the police, and you are under no obligation to talk to me."

"Good." Dr. George turned back to his car. "Get out of my way."

Olivia stepped around Brian, ignoring his look of surprise. "Dr. George? I'm Olivia Sinclair. We just want to ask you a couple of questions. We're trying to help Asher—"

At the mention of Asher's name, Dr. George turned away from the car toward Olivia.

"Asher Ridgeland?"

With a quick nod from Brian, Olivia continued. "His girlfriend was murdered. He was with her. They were both drugged – we want to talk to you. Off the record."

Eyes narrowed, Dr. George gave Olivia the once-over. "You're Olivia Sinclair?"

"Yep. I've known Asher since he was a kid. He had no idea about Mikala's schemes." Ignoring Brian's cue to not spill too much information, she plowed on. "He's struggling. He loved her. We're only gathering information for Asher's peace of mind. Everything you say will be treated with the utmost discretion."

"Asher and Mikala – now that's an odd pairing. How in the world did those two get together? Never mind. I've always liked Asher," Dr. George said. "And Sabine, even though she was a bit . . ."

"Otherworldly?"

"Good word for it. Yes. I picture her in a Jane Austen novel." Dr. George crossed his arms over his chest and leaned against his car.

"Ask your questions. Make it quick."

Olivia turned to Brian, who stepped forward with his hand out. "Brian Vickery."

"You're sure you're not a cop?" Dr. George said as he shook Brian's hand.

155

"Retired. Now I'm private. Here's my question: Was Mikala blackmailing you?"

Dr. George shook his head and stared at his well-worn running shoes. When he met Brian's gaze, the look in his eyes was guileless. "Yeah. She and Ken both. I had an affair with Mikala. Met her at a bar – I'm pretty sure they targeted me. Ken and I used to be friends until I witnessed him harassing a nurse. I stood up for her. He flipped. I think he wanted revenge."

Olivia watched the emotions play over George's face before he spoke. "I'm sorry Mikala's dead. God, she was beautiful. And charming and surprisingly intelligent, considering she had so little education. She actually lived in the same apartment building I lived in while I was in medical school. But you're not interested in that."

"We're interested in the blackmail," Brian said.

"When I met Mikala, my marriage was in shambles. My wife and I had kids during my residency and we were both overworked, exhausted, and struggling financially. To make matters worse, I was working long hours and wasn't there when she needed me. I was selfishly pursuing my career and it almost cost me everything. Want to know how they got me?"

"Anything you'd care to tell," Olivia said. "We won't tell anyone."

"Ken filmed Mikala and me having sex. They shook me down for $50,000. I paid that, somehow managed to keep the whole thing a secret from my wife. I had to get the money from my parents. They were so pissed at me. Once I paid, I thought it was finished. But they came back for more – $100,000 this time. The time had come for me to sit down and have a conversation with my wife. She confessed to me she'd gone to a psychiatrist to treat her chronic depression. I was so wrapped up in myself, I didn't even notice. Shameful. I told her the truth, told her what I'd done. She forgave me. We've been in counseling and are working on our marriage."

Dr. George met Olivia's gaze. *He's starting to get angry*, she thought. They needed to tread gently with him.

"When Ken and Mikala came back for more money, I played along. Told them I didn't have $100,000 lying around, but with time, I could figure something out. Ken called me on the phone, told me I had two weeks to get the money together. He gave me instructions on where to send the money. He wanted it wired to his personal checking account this time. I told him my wife knew about the affair and that his little scheme was over. After that, I played him the recording of our conversation. It gave me great pleasure to tell him that if he contacted me again, I'd go to the police. Shortly after that, a patient made an accusation that Ken was inappropriate. Of course, the hospital put him on leave before they officially terminated him."

"What a horrible ordeal," Olivia said.

Dr. George pushed away from his car. "My screw-up nearly cost me my job, my marriage, my mental health." He opened his car door. "And I'm certain that I wasn't their only victim."

"You're okay with us telling Asher about this?" Brian asked.

"I am. If he was involved with Mikala, he was probably a mark, just like I was."

"One question," Olivia said. "Who do you think was in charge of the operation? Ken or Mikala?"

Dr. George didn't hesitate. "Mikala. She had Ken Ridgeland dancing like a trained pony. Truly. She was a master manipulator."

"So you don't think she was under Ken Ridgeland's coercive control?"

Dr. George laughed. "Not even a little."

"Thanks, Dr. George," Brian said.

Dr. George nodded, got into his car, and drove away.

Chapter 18

They came for him, knocking loudly on his door, just as the sun was rising over the city, Inspector Standish tired and worried, Inspector Lambada righteous and enjoying Asher's discomfort.

"We need you to come down to 850 Bryant to answer some questions," Inspector Lambada said, all testosterone as he barged into Asher's apartment, finally coming to rest in the middle of the room. Once stopped, he circled slowly, taking everything in, surveying, scrutinizing, making Asher want to scream. But he didn't. Somehow he managed to bite back the fear and maintain his composure.

"It's just routine," said Inspector Standish, who still stood out in the hallway, guilt etched into tiny lines around her eyes. Asher reckoned it wasn't Inspector Standish's idea to personally retrieve Asher. "Can I come in?"

As if I have a choice. Asher didn't say these words out loud. Instead he stepped aside, closing the door behind Inspector Standish.

"What's going on? Am I under arrest?"

"We've come to take you in for questioning." Inspector Lambada didn't bother to hide his glee. He moved over to a stack of papers on the corner of Asher's desk, reaching out, as if he wanted to thumb through them.

Angry now, Asher took the papers out of Lambada's hand. "No you don't. Not without a warrant. Touch my things again, and I'll make you wait outside. I've been cooperating with you. That will stop, and I'll get a lawyer if you don't back down."

Lambada raised his hands, as if in surrender. "Fine. Fine. Whatever."

"You've had it out for me from the beginning, Mr. Lambada. You both know I would have come in voluntarily."

"Right, but then we wouldn't be able to perp-walk you in front—" Lambada said. "And it's Inspector Lambada, if you don't mind."

"That's enough, Lambada." Inspector Standish turned to face Asher. "I apologize for my rude partner. Can you please get dressed? We'll take you down for questioning, and bring you back, okay?"

Asher nodded, relieved that Inspector Standish, the obvious voice of reason, was on his side. He grabbed his jeans and a clean T-shirt. Lambada tried to follow him into the bathroom, but Asher somehow managed to slam the door in Lambada's face.

Once at the station, he was led to an interrogation room. They didn't lock him in. He made a mental note. If they didn't come into the room and get things moving within ten minutes, he was leaving. Just as he finished this thought, Lambada came into the room, slammed a notebook onto the table, dragged the chair as he sat down, and started asking questions, firing them as though they were missiles. He hammered Asher for four hours, asking the same dozen or so questions over and over again. *What time did you get to Mikala's? Did anyone see you enter her apartment? What were your movements on the day of her murder? Did anyone see you leave Mikala's house? Why didn't you have your cell phone with you?* Asher answered the questions, never changing his story, always keeping his cool.

Finally, Ellie Standish had come into the room.

"Stop, Lambada." She sat down across from Asher and gave him an embarrassed smile. Asher recognized her arrival for what it was: good cop, bad cop. The ubiquitous cliché from every mystery or thriller ever written.

"We know you've hired Brian Vickery, so I'm assuming he told you about your father and Mikala's affair. I don't have to tell you that nugget of info gives you motive."

"Standish," Lambada interrupted.

Inspector Standish held up her hand. "I'm playing straight with him. Deal with it." Turning her attention back to Asher, she said, "We have to ask you these questions, so we can clear you."

"Okay," Asher said, all of his senses on alert.

Inspector Standish pulled a photograph out of a notebook she carried, pushing it across the table to Asher. "Do you know this man?"

"I haven't seen him in a long time – since I was a kid – but he's a colleague of my dad's. They used to socialize together."

"You haven't seen him recently."

"No," Asher said immediately and without hesitation. "Why? Did he have something to do with Mikala's murder?"

Inspector Standish looked to Lambada, who nodded.

"Okay. Here's the deal. We think your father murdered Mikala."

Asher balled his hands into fists, as a wave of rage washed over him, as it always did when he thought of his father and Mikala together. Careful to keep his emotions under wraps, he tucked his hands under his legs, afraid that if he didn't sit on them, he'd slam them on the table.

"Do you think your dad is capable of murder?" Ellie asked.

"He's capable of anything where money is concerned," Asher said. "He's got a terrible temper."

"Does he ever hit your mother?" Lambada, who was now leaning against the wall, his arms crossed over his chest, asked.

"Not that I recall. She controls the money and doesn't see that he doesn't love her, that she's being used. Or if she does, she doesn't care." Asher rubbed his hand over his face. "Honestly, I cannot stand to be around them. And I'm tired. Can I please go?"

Inspector Standish met Asher's gaze and held it. "Asher, you want to help us find out who killed Mikala?"

"Of course," he said, irritated.

"There's a way you can do just that," Lambada said.

It was just after 5 p.m. and surprisingly warm outside when Asher headed out of his apartment in search of his father. He walked with purpose toward Chestnut Street, which was hopping with a happy-hour crowd. The restaurants and bars had their doors open, and the drinkers had filtered out into the street. Busy conversation with occasional bursts of laughter greeted Asher, but he ignored it, his mind full of other things far removed from casual connections and cocktails after work.

Known for its premium burgers and homemade French fries, Sudsy Sam's also had over twenty artisan beers on tap. The major draw for Asher was the cavernous atmosphere, dim lighting, and the dark wood paneling, perfect for a single guy to sip a beer and remain anonymous. A seat opened up at the bar. Asher grabbed it. He didn't have to wait long until Dave, the long-suffering bartender, came sauntering over.

"The usual?"

"Anything new and interesting I should try?"

"I have a new IPA from a new brewery in Yountville. I think you'll like it."

"Sure."

"Your dad's here. Just saying. I know you two don't get along. Do you want a table on the patio?"

"That's okay." Asher forced a smile. "Thanks, though."

"Sorry, Asher." Dave put the IPA down in front of Asher. "This one's on the house."

Asher raised his beer to Dave, who was now down the bar, taking a drink order from another customer. A long mirror ran behind the bar. Asher scanned the crowd. His eyes landed on a young, fresh-faced woman, probably in her early twenties. Petite, and dressed in the understated, expensive clothes that were fashionable now, she had her blond hair pulled back into a thick ponytail, as though she had just finished work. Sitting next to this young woman was his father, sipping a martini. He was dressed in scrubs. When his father leaned close to the woman and brushed his lips against her cheek, Asher downed his beer, ordered another, and ambled down the bar.

"Dad," Asher said.

Ken raised an eyebrow. When he spoke, his tone was condescending. "Asher? What are you doing here?"

"I live around the corner. Remember? The last three times you've been here, you've run into me. Why so surprised? I'm just getting dinner." Asher turned to the young woman sitting next to his father and held out his hand. "I'm Asher, Ken's son."

The woman, who looked unsure of the situation, gave Asher a forced smile and held out her hand. "Monica."

"Did you just meet my dad? Did he just approach you out of the blue, offer to buy you dinner?"

"Asher, shut up."

"He's married," Asher plowed on. "And he's a rogue. He actually slept with my girlfriend before someone murdered her. Who knows? He might even be a suspect in her death."

Fear and uncertainty flittered across Monica's face as her eyes went from Ken to Asher and back to Ken again.

"I'm out of here." She gave Ken a look of disgust as she grabbed her purse and, without another word, hurried out of the bar.

"Monica, wait," Ken called out. When he got up and followed her, Asher blocked his way. "Sit down."

"Listen, you little shit. If you think you're going to come in here and intimidate me, you'd do well to rethink your strategy. You're kicking way outside your coverage area."

Two men sat next to Ken at the bar. Asher spoke loud enough for them to hear. "The police came to my house. They told me you knew Mikala. Is that true?"

Ken hesitated.

"So you did know her." Not bothering to keep his voice down, Asher said, "Were you involved in the blackmail scheme she was running?"

"What are you talking about? There was no blackmail scheme."

A table for two in the back corner of the restaurant opened up. "Grab that table. I'm going to get my beer."

"Asher—"

"Get the table."

Once Asher returned with a fresh beer in hand, Ken said, "Asher, whatever you're hearing from the police is a lie. They go on fishing expeditions. They try to get you to say things they will turn around and use against you. Just keep your mouth shut, okay?"

"Don't tell me what to do," Asher said. "I want you to tell me about Mikala."

"No, you don't." Ken motioned for the waitress to bring him another martini.

"I know you were sleeping with her. I know you were working a blackmail scheme with her."

"Did the police tell you that?" Ken shook his head. "Doesn't matter. Yes, it's true. Mikala and I were lovers for about three years before she met you. I'm the person who paid the rent on her apartment. So what?"

"And when you visited Mikala, Lexy Ford would have to leave?"

Ken gave Asher a quizzical look. "Lexy Ford? Oh, the lawyer? Yeah. I didn't want anyone else to see me with Mikala."

"Because of the blackmail?"

His father drained his martini glass. Asher plowed on.

"Did you sleep with her while we were together?"

"Yes, but only once. She was falling for you. Saw herself living a legitimate life." The waitress arrived with fresh martini. "But that didn't last long. Mikala liked money. She liked the game, enjoyed the cat and mouse of it."

"The police know everything. They think you killed her. Did you?"

"Don't be ridiculous. Of course I didn't kill her. What motive did I have to kill Mikala? She was my golden ticket. You, on the other hand . . ." Ken let the accusation hang between them. "I didn't kill her. She had plenty of enemies, plenty of men who stood to gain with her out of the way. The police can't prove anything. Neither can you. And if you testified, it would be your word against mine. That's not proof."

"You're right," Asher said.

"Do you ever wonder what Mikala saw in you?"

"Maybe she was attracted to my integrity."

Ken tipped his head back and laughed out loud. "That's good. On the other hand, you are a perfect patsy. Naïve and easily manipulated."

"Mikala was herself with me. We spent many happy hours together. We didn't drink, snort coke, or do anything other than enjoy each other's company." Ken started to speak. "Shut up, Dad. I'm talking. You'd do best to listen. I know what you did, you and Mikala. I wanted to confront you, so I could see your lying face. I also know about the intern you harassed and the patient you allegedly assaulted. I'm going to tell Mom what I know, and then I'm going to the police."

Asher was ready when Ken stood up, sending the chair he was sitting on crashing over. Asher stood too, and when Ken moved close and tried to tower over him, like he had done many times in the past, Asher didn't back down. The two men stood, nose to nose. Ken radiated fury, whereas Asher seemed calm and in complete control. Out of the corner of his eye, Asher noticed the people around them watching.

Years of pent-up rage and hatred overtook Asher. Without thinking, he pushed his father. Eyes flashing, Ken charged, pushing Asher backwards until he finally came to rest against the wall, his father towering over him, his hands around his throat. Asher didn't know where the calm came from. He felt suspended, held still in time. He met his father's eyes, not bothering to dial back the loathing he felt for him. When Ken stared back, something in Asher's expression unsettled him. As Ken looked around, he saw the crowd that had gathered, took in the silence as everyone watched the two of them. When Ken realized he still had his hands around Asher's throat, he held them up, as if in surrender, and stepped away.

"Is strangling your preferred murder method?" Asher asked, his voice calm and clear.

Dave ducked under the bar and came strolling over, a nervous smile on his face.

"Asher? You want me to call the police."

"No," Asher said, putting his hands on his throat.

"I should call the police. I won't have this in my bar. But as a favor to you, Asher, I won't. This is a final warning," Dave said, giving Ken the side-eye. "Dial it back. Got it?"

Ken had collected himself. When he spoke, his voice dripped with condescension. "Go ahead. Tell your mother. You think she'll take your side over mine? You didn't think this through, son. I'm her husband, and I'm a doctor. You know how important appearances are to Sabine. Say you go to the police, say I get arrested. Your mother will get me the best lawyer money can buy. Then she'll use her money to influence the media, maybe drop some cash and get the entire situation resolved without it seeing the light of day. Any suspicion that falls on me will have the significance of a piece of lint. And I should tell you I've already been interviewed by the detectives investigating Mikala's death. I've been cleared—"

"But you're no longer a doctor, are you?"

Asher's words struck home. The color drained from his father's suntanned face, as shock and fear played across the planes of his face.

"You're a washed-up has-been who can't get a job. Where are you getting your money, Dad? Blackmail, right? Did you kill her? Were you the man who was at her house the night she was murdered?"

Without a word, Ken turned and walked away, the light from the street throwing him in stark relief.

Five minutes later, Asher knocked on the door of the white police van that was parked in the alley behind Sudsy Sam's. It was crowded inside the van. Most of the space was taken up by electrical equipment, consisting of video monitors and recording devices, along one wall. On the opposite side was a long bench.

"Did that help?" Asher asked.

"Everything helps. Have a seat." Inspector Standish pointed to the bench. Asher sat while Ellie lifted up his shirt and started to pull off the adhesive that held the wire in place.

Inspector Lambada sat with his back toward Asher, wearing a set of sophisticated headphones.

"You did the right thing, bringing us the photo of your father wearing the tie," Ellie said, her tone sympathetic.

"Did I?"

"The tie isn't really evidence." Lambada took off his headphones as he interjected. When Ellie gave him a scathing look, he said, "I'm not saying it's not helpful, but the picture is old."

"Now I have to go tell my mother what's happening."

Ellie gave him a sympathetic look as she tore off the last bit of adhesive and pulled the wire out from under his shirt.

"Thanks for your help." Ellie opened the sliding door on the van.

"You'll let me know what's next?" Asher asked, his voice imploring and more than a little desperate.

"You know I can't promise that," Ellie said. She gave him a weak smile and shut the door, leaving Asher alone in the alley.

The sun set in the western sky just as Asher rolled to a stop in front of his mother's house. Still running on adrenaline from the confrontation with his father, Asher felt his stomach rumble.

He'd not eaten in hours, but he had no appetite. From the street, he watched Sabine move around inside, turning on the lights in the living room and kitchen, a nightly ritual that she had completed for as long as he could remember. His mother was a creature of habit. Her mannerisms, her ideas about relationships, and her world view were decades out of step. Asher knew that Sabine's friends recognized his mother's quirks and found them charming. A twinge of guilt washed over Asher, as he acknowledged that his mother irritated him more often than not. Still, she didn't deserve the pain that Asher was about to inflict on her. No one did. Asher was about to turn Sabine Tremblay Ridgeland's world completely upside down.

When Sabine opened the door and saw it was Asher who had come calling, her whole face broke into a smile.

"Asher," she cried out as she opened her arms and pulled him into them. He hugged her, surprised at how tiny and frail she felt in his arms.

"I'm sorry, Mom."

When he choked out the words, his mother stepped away from him. Head tipped back, she stared up into his eyes. "What's wrong? You look utterly distraught."

Asher sighed. "We need to talk."

"Okay, let me just put the kettle—"

"No. No tray. No kettle. No fancy napkins. Let's go into the living room."

Asher waited while Sabine arranged herself at the far end.

"I've come to tell you what Brian Vickery has discovered about Dad."

Sabine put her hand on her chest. "Oh, Asher, I already know."

"What?" Asher couldn't believe it.

"I'm not stupid. Your father's been secretly transferring money out of our account since he lost his medical license."

"You just let him steal from you?"

"I protected myself against your father's greed a long time

ago, Asher. I'm not *letting* him do anything." Sabine turned to face Asher. "I realized after you were born that Ken married me for my money. He tricked me, and I fell for it. I thought we were in love."

"You knew Mikala and Dad were blackmailing people? Did you know they were sleeping together?"

She didn't have to answer.

"My dad and my girlfriend were running a blackmail scheme and sleeping together? Did you not think that maybe you should have told me about this?"

Sabine looked at him with sad eyes. "Would you have believed me?"

Asher sat down, defeated. He shook his head, embarrassed. "Maybe not. It would have sounded so farfetched."

"That's why I didn't tell you. I was more focused on protecting you. I figured I could manage the affair and keep you safe. Then you fell in love."

"Did you know he allegedly raped a patient? How did you make that go away?"

"I hired an investigator who discovered the woman who was accusing your father had a history of sleeping with doctors and suing them. She was a common grifter, working her way across the country, pandering to the male ego for her own personal gain. I offered her money to drop the charges. Then I took the information my investigator discovered to the DA. I don't know what happened after."

Asher couldn't quite believe what his mother was telling him. He'd always thought of her as dreamy, not quite with it, even befuddled. The idea that she could manage Ken and his landslide of personal and legal issues boggled the mind. His mother had cast herself in an entirely new light.

"Does Dad know you're aware of what he's been up to?"

"Your father is a megalomaniac. All he cares about is himself. And money. He's a drug addict who cannot be trusted."

"And you let him just carry on?" Asher couldn't hide the incredulity.

Sabine hesitated. "Your father is on a path of destruction. I figured if I left him alone, he'd destroy himself. My only focus was not to let him drag us down as well. Now I'm seeing that isn't going to work. I haven't wanted to pursue a divorce, but I see that circumstances have changed . . . Oh, Asher. People talk. If I file for divorce, things will change—"

"I cannot believe this!" Asher shouted. "Listen to yourself."

"What would you have me do?"

"Go to the police! What do you think? Dad is a blackmailer. You're not grasping the seriousness of this situation. Do you realize that Dad could have murdered Mikala?"

"I do," Sabine said. "And if he gets arrested for it, your life will never be the same."

"My life already will never be the same. I'm going to the police."

Sabine shook her head. "Please don't, Asher. You'll regret it. If you don't believe me, ask Olivia what she went through with the police and the press when her husband's mistress wound up dead." Sabine scooted closer to Asher. "Let the police do their job. If your father murdered that woman, they'll find out. If your investigator has found information that implicates your father, let him turn it over. You stay out of it. Trust me. That's the best way to go.

"I had no business keeping you in the dark about your father and Mikala. My only regret is that I wasn't straightforward with you. That was a grave miscalculation on my part. I would do anything to spare you this heartache. I hope you can forgive me." When Asher didn't say anything, Sabine said, "I'm going to bed." She stood and without saying a word, walked out of the room.

Chapter 19

Olivia awoke on Saturday from a deep sleep, snuggled under the duvet, not wanting to get up. She'd slept through the night with no nightmares for the second time since she'd taken on Ava Bledsoe as a client.

"Good morning." Brian came into the room carrying a tray with a pot of coffee and two cups.

"What time is it?" Olivia sat up, aware suddenly of the bright morning light, the sound of her neighbor's lawnmower next door.

"It's 9:30." Brian poured Olivia coffee. "You've been asleep for thirteen hours."

"That's a first for me." Olivia sipped, feasting her eyes on Brian's broad shoulders, loving the way his long hair curled around the collar of his T-shirt as he poured himself coffee.

"I almost woke you up at 8:00, but then I realized that we both need a day away from our jobs. So I made some calls, and I can tell you with certainty that Ava and Lauren are well taken care of, and Denny is content with a pile of novels and her daughter in Sun Valley." He sat down next to Olivia on the bed. "I thought today, we could just – I don't know – stay home."

Olivia sighed. "A Saturday at home."

"It's the simple pleasures," Brian said. "And you know how

I aim to please. I need to get caught up on paperwork. You're meeting with Lucy Waynesbarrow this afternoon?"

"Not until two o'clock." Olivia thought of her neglected garden, the veggies that needed harvesting, and a dozen other domestic chores that would keep her occupied for the morning.

"You can garden. I can get caught up on paperwork. This evening, I will cook you dinner. After we eat, we'll sit down and watch hours of television, like we don't have a care in the world."

"Sounds like heaven," Olivia said.

"Meanwhile, how about some scrambled eggs and toast?"

Olivia sipped her coffee. "I'm ready, Brian."

"For breakfast?"

"Yes, but I'm also ready for this type of life. These lazy mornings, the potential to have this sense of peace every day." Brian dealt with the coffee cups and took Olivia into his arms.

When Brian snickered, Olivia pushed away. "What's so funny?"

"Not funny exactly, but when you sell this house, we're going to have a lot to do to get you packed and moved."

"I know. We'll make it fun. Lauren can be a tyrant when it comes to minimalism and getting rid of excess baggage. I'll let her manage it."

Brian picked up the coffee tray. "I'll start the eggs."

"You're spoiling me."

"That's the plan."

The morning passed quickly. Olivia harvested what veggies were left in her garden, a handful of tomatoes and enough zucchini to make a half-dozen loaves of the zucchini bread Denny loved as a child. She picked parsley and basil before she moved to her rose garden, where she snipped enough for a generous bouquet.

Grabbing a large vase, Olivia took extra care in arranging the roses. Once that task was complete, she put half the zucchini and most of the herbs in a wicker basket, setting aside enough for Brian's spaghetti. Later she'd take the basket next door and leave it on her next-door neighbor, Mrs. Finn's, porch. As she moved around her kitchen, she paid attention to the birds outside, searing the memory in her brain. Moving was the right thing to do, and she was absolutely ready to set up house with Brian, but she didn't want to forget her time in this home. As she arranged the veggies and herbs in the basket, she paid silent homage to the tears of joy and pain and the memories of Denny as a child.

All right. Enough nostalgia. Grabbing one card from her stationery box, she penned a quick note to accompany the vegetables and headed outside to deliver them.

Lucy Waynesbarrow and Olivia first met thirty years ago when their kids were in the same class. Although Lucy had never needed Olivia's services as a family-law attorney, she'd hired Olivia to review contracts a few times over the years. Flamboyant and known for her zany hats, Lucy saw herself as a real-estate matchmaker and had built a reputation for using this romantic sentiment to match families to their forever homes. Olivia had always had a begrudging admiration for Lucy, who could always be counted on to stick up for the underdog.

Today, Lucy wore a bespoke suit in a subtle shade of purple, along with a matching fascinator. She carried a red handbag, finishing the outfit off with a pair of comfy walking shoes.

Olivia walked outside and met Lucy on the street, where the two women hugged and air-kissed each other's cheeks.

"I can't believe you're leaving, but you look happy, Liv. Happier than I've ever seen you." She wove her arm through Olivia's, as the two of them strolled toward the front door.

"I'm going to start skiing again. And my boyfriend, Brian, is dying to buy a fishing boat."

"Ah, boys and their toys."

The smell of garlic, basil, and fresh tomatoes greeted them as they moved into the kitchen. Brian stood at the stove, wearing an apron and stirring a pot of his homemade marinara.

"If I were a buyer, I'd make an offer just by the smell of whatever's in that pot." Lucy held out her hand. "Lucy Waynesbarrow. Nice to meet you, Mr. Vickery."

"Call me Brian."

"You've made my friend very happy, so you're aces in my book."

"What's the process? Do you want to walk the house and property? You haven't been here in ages."

"Sure," Lucy said. "You can give me the tour. Let's start outside. I long for the feel of sunshine on my back."

An hour later, Lucy and Olivia wound up at the dining-room table, each with a cup of coffee in hand as Olivia reviewed the listing contract and made notes about the best way to stage the house.

"I think some brighter paint in the downstairs bedrooms will help. And I hate to do this, but when I start showing the house to potential buyers, you're going to have to remove most of the knickknacks and personal stuff."

"I know. I'm not looking forward to packing all this stuff. Dreading it, actually."

"Oh, but you're starting fresh. A new life in a beautiful town with a hunky man." Lucy leaned close and whispered, "Are you going to marry him?"

"I don't know. We haven't discussed that," Olivia said. "It's so easy between us, Lucy. I am happy as things are."

"Do you ever talk to Richard?"

"Nope. He is in touch with Denny. I think she does a good job of managing granddaughter visitation so we don't run into each other."

"Okay. This is ready for you to review and sign. Once you get the painting done and take care of the issues we discussed, we can start marketing and bringing buyers through. There's no rush here, Olivia. No need to stress. We can show the house after you move, if you'd prefer. It's going to sell fast, of that I am certain."

"Thanks, Lucy. You've made this a lot easier than I thought it would be."

"I've just enjoyed spending a bit of time with you. It seems like yesterday we were doing bake sales, car pools, and the play-dates, doesn't it?"

"It does." Olivia sat back in her chair.

"We've both had good lives, haven't we?"

"We're lucky," Olivia said.

"And we've worked our you-know-whats off."

"True," Olivia said. "I've been happy in this house, but I'm also ready to leave, if that makes sense."

"I understand. This house has good energy."

Olivia picked up her pen and signed her contract with a flourish. She just finished when Brian came into the room, a worried look on his face.

"We have an issue," Brian said.

"What's happened?" Olivia asked.

Lucy, ever tactful, took the hint. "If you'll excuse me. Restroom's down the hall?"

"Yes," Olivia said, not taking her eyes off Brian.

Once they were alone, he said, "Ken's been picked up by the SFPD and taken to 850 Bryant for questioning. Sabine isn't coping. She's asking for you."

After her own arrest last October, the media flocked to her house, waiting like sharks circling blood, ready to pounce. Lucky for the Ridgelands, there were only two news vans and three photographers milling about.

"It's not as bad as I thought it would be," Brian said, as he pulled into the drive and carefully avoided the journalist with a microphone who clamored toward their car.

"No, but it's bad enough to send Sabine into a frenzy," Olivia commented, not bothering to hide the dread in her voice.

They got out of the car and started walking up to the massive front door. "We're not obligated to babysit Sabine Ridgeland," Brian said.

"No, but we're obligated to help Asher."

Lexy Ford opened the door for them.

"Lexy?"

"Asher called me. He needs a friend right now. Come in. They're in the living room."

"This is Olivia Sinclair," Brian said, by way of introduction.

"I know Olivia. I'm an admirer of your work, always have been. That opinion was solidified last October. Nice to meet you."

Olivia shook Lexy's hand, instantly liking the no-nonsense redhead.

"I was Mikala's roommate," Lexy explained as they walked toward the living room. "Asher's a friend. We've been helping each other through this." She lowered her voice, speaking in a whisper. "Sabine is not doing well. See for yourself."

They found Sabine sitting on the sofa, staring straight in front of her. Asher was fussing with a throw, trying to make it stay around her shoulders. When that failed, he placed it on her lap.

"Olivia and Brian are here, Mother," Asher whispered. "You've got a lot of people supporting you."

In a frenetic rush of energy, Sabine pushed the throw off her lap and turned her eyes toward Olivia and Brian. "You need to represent Ken, Olivia. You're the only one who can make all this go away. You've got clout, and you're the best lawyer for the job. I'm begging you. My family needs you."

"Mom," Asher said.

"This is your fault, Asher. You betrayed me, your father, and this family when you talked to the police."

Olivia watched Asher's face mottle as he got his anger under control.

"This isn't my fault. This is dad's fault for lying to us, blackmailing his doctor friends, and murdering my girlfriend. Olivia is retired, Mother. She's here because she's assisting Mr. Vickery, who is working for me."

175

Sabine snorted and dismissed Asher with a wave before she tried to stand up. Wobbly on her feet, she sat back down again.

"All right, Olivia. You know all about this kind of situation. What should we do?"

"First of all, you need to get Ken a lawyer. I know three good ones off the top of my head. In a perfect world, you'd interview each one, but you don't have that kind of time. You need someone to get to the jail now, to make sure Ken isn't talking."

"What about the mob outside?"

"Well, it's not a mob—"

Sabine interrupted, "It's not yet, but it will be. My family is influential. The press will be all over this."

Asher, who stood well away from Sabine now, rolled his eyes.

Sitting down next to Sabine, Olivia took out her cell phone. "Sabine, listen to me. You're the backbone of this family." At these words, Sabine straightened her spine and lifted her chin. "You can deal with this. You'll get Ken the best lawyer. I'll walk you through what's going to happen, okay?"

"I want you, Olivia."

"You don't. I'm not a criminal defense attorney. You need someone who knows how to play this game. Let's make some calls, okay?"

Sabine took Olivia's hand. "Thank you, Olivia."

Two hours later, Olivia and Brian drove away from Sabine's house. Brian had arranged for security, unnecessary in his mind, but the effort had assuaged Sabine. Olivia had arranged an attorney.

"That was intense," Brian said.

"And it's going to get worse." Olivia sunk deeper into the seat of the car. "This is totally off topic, but I'm actually hungry."

"Yes. I'm ready to be home."

"A nice glass of red wouldn't go amiss."

"True."

176

Chapter 20

Captain Wasniki, Inspector Lambada, and a young woman with angular cheekbones, a serious expression on her face, and a brief-case chock-full of documents stood in front of the two-way mirror in the interrogation room. Ellie stepped between Lambada and Captain Wasniki, and watched Ken Ridgeland, who was staring at his hands.

"I find it odd that a man gets arrested and is so calm that he can sit and push back his cuticles. He's a little too relaxed about this," the woman said before she turned to Ellie and held out her hands. "ADA Michaels. We haven't met."

Ellie shook the assistant district attorney's hand.

"What are we waiting for?" Ellie asked.

"You," Captain Wasniki said. "We all agree that having a woman do the interrogation might be the best way to throw him off his game."

Ellie's heart thrummed in her chest. She could feel Lambada's energy rolling off him in waves, wound up, eager to go head-to-head with Ken Ridgeland.

"Are you up for this, Inspector?" ADA Michaels asked.

"Yes," Ellie said without hesitation. She turned to Wasniki and asked, "What's my angle here?"

"We're good to go on the blackmail charges. I'd like you to bring up the murder if possible, just to see if you can get him talking. The only thing we have to go on with the murder is that the money was transferred into his account from Mikala's account."

"What about the tie?" Ellie countered. "Mikala was strangled with a hand-painted tie owned by Ken Ridgeland. I've got the pictures from Ken's social media account to prove it."

"I get that," ADA Michaels said, "but the picture you found on social is ten years old."

"But it was his," Ellie snapped, looking to Captain Wasniki for support.

"I acknowledge that, but we need to be able to prove that he was in possession of the tie at the time of the murder."

She nodded at the two-way glass. "We also need to have solid proof that Ken Ridgeland was the actual person who did the transferring. Listen, we all know that this guy is going to get the best attorney money can buy. I don't want to lose this one."

"We'll get you your evidence, counselor," Lambada said, in a surprise show of support.

ADA Michaels sighed and faced Ellie. "Don't give too much away about the murder. Try to use the blackmail for leverage."

"Can I mention all the victims we've discovered? I've got at least ten other people that he and Mikala went after. I was going to surprise him with that info and see if it rattles him."

"That's fine," Michaels said. "Just don't say too much about the murder. If he cries lawyer, we'll have a uniform in to arrest him for blackmail. We can add the murder charge when we're ready."

She turned to face Wasniki and Lambada. "And before you say anything, Lambada, I would ask if you and your team could find me some evidence that Ken Ridgeland actually transferred the money himself, or that he spent it. For all we know he might not even know the money is in his account. And if you could find evidence that he wore that tie within the last – I don't know – year or so, that would be great."

Lambada made some smartass comment under his breath. Ellie tuned it out. Clutching her notepad to her chest, she took a deep breath and stepped into the interrogation room.

"You're the person they chose to interrogate me?" Ken chuckled. "Wonder why they chose you?"

"Because I'm smarter than you." Ellie sat down and arranged her notepad and the stack of evidence folders on the table before her.

"I can tell you this little fiasco is going to be a colossal waste of time. I'll have a team of lawyers here in about thirty minutes. They'll make mincemeat of you and then they will sue the department. Kiss your badge goodbye, young lady. I'm not saying a word until my lawyer gets here."

"No problem. How about I do the talking and you just listen."

"Who's behind that two-way mirror?"

Ellie ignored him. "We know about the blackmail scheme you and Mikala were running. We know you paid a year's rent on her apartment." Ellie took four statements and laid them out like playing cards on the table in front of Dr. Ridgeland. "I'm assuming she coerced you to do that?"

At least Ken was looking at Ellie now, his expression guarded. Good. She had his attention.

"We've got Harry George. He's made a statement and is willing to testify at trial. We know that he called your bluff. Bet you didn't count on him telling his wife about his affair with Mikala. Lucky for him, she stood by him. You must have been so shocked to discover that Harry recorded you asking him for more money." Ellie didn't have to look at Ken Ridgeland to know that he was feeling the pressure. She could smell his anger. "Anyway, as I was saying, we've got Dr. George's testimony. He was more than happy to cooperate. We also have Linda Wesley. That was quite a coup for you and Mikala, wasn't it? Catching a socialite who worries about appearances and has unlimited funds."

"Linda Wesley? That woman's a drunk. She'll make a crappy witness."

"We disagree. We have proof that she made large withdrawals from her bank, half of which was deposited into Mikala's bank account and your account the next day. You and Mikala were splitting the takings." Ellie put another witness statement in front of Ken Ridgeland. "Lance Endicott. You've got him on a payment plan, right – $20,000 a month? No more. And, finally, we've got Bruce Fleishman, who died of a heart attack over the stress of your con. His wife wants to sue you.

"That's four counts of extortion, each carrying a four-year prison term. Sixteen years."

Ken Ridgeland smirked at her. For a brief second, his confidence made Ellie wonder if he had something up his sleeve, something that would exonerate him. "You're going to prison, Mr. Ridgeland." She emphasized the *mister* and plowed on. "But let's move on. Why did you kill Mikala?"

Ellie knew Ken Ridgeland wouldn't take the bait, but she didn't expect him to tip his head back and laugh. When he wiped his fake tears and met Ellie's gaze, he said, "You'll never make a murder charge stick. As we speak, my wife is finding the best lawyer money can buy. I'll fight the blackmail, and I'll win. But you won't charge me with murder. You can't prove it."

"I can."

Ellie didn't flinch when Ken slammed his hand on the table. "You can't, and you won't. If what you say is true, that Mikala and I were running a blackmail scheme together, why would I kill her? If this operation were real, Mikala would be the honey trap. Without her, there's no mark. Without a mark, there's no money. Ergo, I have zero motive to kill her."

"Nice try." Ellie smiled as she spoke. "I'm thinking Mikala didn't pay you, so you killed her. Once she was dead, you accessed her bank account and transferred funds in the amount of—" Ellie made a show of looking through her paperwork, even though she knew the amount of money transferred to the penny "—four hundred sixty-two thousand dollars, give or take, into your personal account."

Startled, Ken looked up but quickly composed himself.

He doesn't know about the transfer. The thought popped into Ellie's mind.

"That makes no sense. I don't have access to Mikala's bank account. Why would you think I transferred money?"

Ellie put another sheet of paper in front of Ken. "That's the transfer confirmation from your bank. It shows the deposit amount. See that number right there? That's Mikala's bank account number. How do you explain that?"

"I didn't kill Mikala. I didn't transfer money out of her account."

"The evidence says otherwise." Ellie pushed the bank statement and the transfer paperwork across the table.

Confident now, Ken Ridgeland studied the bank record that Ellie offered him. "I see that this transfer was completed, but I didn't do it. I don't bank electronically. Never have. Never will. Listen, Inspector whatever-your-name-is, I didn't do anything here. I didn't blackmail anyone. I didn't take any money. Nothing. You have no case, and you know it. But I will tell you this. My wife hated Mikala. Hated the idea of her dating Asher. Have you looked into my wife's bank records and my wife's cell phone records? Ah, I can see by the expression on your face that you haven't." Ken pushed all the papers back to Ellie's side of the table, crossed his arms, and closed his eyes. "I'm finished talking. My lawyer should be here any minute. Why don't you do your job and find someone else to pick on."

Inspector Lambada and a uniformed officer entered the room. "Stand up, Dr. Ridgeland."

"I'm waiting for my lawyer."

"I know. We'll let you see him after you're processed. Stand up."

Ken Ridgeland stood. Lambada read him his rights, while the uniformed officer cuffed him.

"Officer Simms will take you for processing. When your lawyer gets here, we'll send him that way."

Ken didn't fight the handcuffs. Before Officer Sims led him out, he turned and said to Ellie. "Inspector Standish, right?"

"Right," Ellie said.

"I'm coming for your badge."

"Do your best," Ellie said.

Lambada turned off the video recorder and took the chair that Ken Ridgeland had been sitting in.

"You don't think he did it, do you?" Lambada asked.

"I'm not sure," Ellie said. "I like it when I'm absolutely positive, with all the evidence to back me up."

"Well, I'm not sure either. This was all too easy. And I believed Ridgeland when he said he doesn't bank electronically. His history proves that. All of his deposits are made in the branch. He doesn't even have an ATM card. He cashes a check for one thousand dollars every Monday."

"That's a lot of spending money," Ellie said.

"Not to Sabine Ridgeland," Lambada said.

Chapter 21

"I have a bad feeling about this," Brian said. He put his arm on Olivia's to stop her forward motion just as she was about to open the door to Dan Winter's law office. It had rained during the night, leaving the cold morning air redolent with the smell of damp vegetation. "Let's just leave. You and Dan can talk on the phone, right? You're not obligated to go in there."

Olivia faced Brian, scrutinizing his face, surprised at the concern she saw there. "What's going on? I've never seen you this worried before."

Brian shook his head. "I don't like it, Liv. A Sunday afternoon phone call for an urgent Monday morning meeting? What kind of a lawyer does that? I think Mark Bledsoe forced all of this." Brian waved his hand in an expansive gesture. "He's up to something. I can feel it in my bones. I feel like we're being manipulated, like we're the stars of Mark Bledsoe's dog and pony show. While I'm at it, I'll go on the record saying that I'm suspicious of the sudden cooperation on Bledsoe's part, especially the agreement by Mark to set Ava up for life. It stinks. I don't like it. Not one bit."

"Why didn't you tell me this yesterday?"

"You were so relieved after Dan called, so eager to have this case put behind you, that I didn't have the heart to speak up."

183

"Do you think we're in danger?"

"I don't know. But Scott will be here, so at last we've got backup." As if on cue, Scott pulled into the parking lot, taking the spot next to Brian's car. "There's always the chance that Mark Bledsoe has found Lauren's beach hideout."

Olivia sobered. "So soon? Do you think that's possible?"

"I do. It's not wrong to turn around and leave. There's no shame in picking your battles. You're not obligated to go in there, Olivia."

Inside the office, their presence had been noted through the glass side panels on the entrance. Out of the corner of her eye, Olivia saw Dan Winters step up to the reception desk, and look their way when the receptionist pointed at them. She stepped close to Brian and spoke softly. "I've already picked this battle. I need to see it through to the end."

"Then let's go. I've got you." Brian placed a gentle hand on the small of Olivia's back, the heat of his touch penetrating her blazer and instantly grounding her.

"Battle stations," Olivia said, forcing a smile as she pushed open the office door and stepped into Dan Winter's reception area, Brian at her heels.

"Good morning," Dan Winters said, moving toward Olivia, a fake smile on his face, hand outstretched. Dan shook Brian's hand briefly. "Mr. Vickery can't be in with us when we discuss settlement. Surely you understand—"

"Mr. Vickery is my investigator, and, as such, my agent. He most definitely will be in with us when we discuss this case."

"Olivia—"

"Stop it, Dan. I've every right to have Brian with me, and you know it."

"Very well. Let's move into my office." With a nod to the receptionist, Dan Winters led Olivia and Brian down the hallway and into a large office, austerely furnished with a sleek, uncluttered desk, a round glass table large enough to hold six chairs, and an expansive view of Mt. Tamalpais.

Mark Bledsoe sat at the table, pretending to be engrossed in a document. At the sight of him, the bitter taste of fear blossomed in Olivia's mouth as her heart pounded against her ribs. Dan stepped into the room, taking a seat near his legal pad and Montblanc Meisterstück pencil.

When Mark Bledsoe finally looked up, his eyes registered Olivia's fear. "What's the matter, Mrs. Sinclair – aren't you happy to see me?"

"You mean after you threatened my daughter in the grocery store?" When it came to sarcasm, Olivia could give as good as she could get. "Sure, Mr. Bledsoe, I'm just full of goodwill and bonhomie toward you." She and Brian exchanged a smile as Olivia sat down. Brian chose to remain standing.

"Is your guard dog going to sit?" Mark asked.

Olivia ignored him. "So, Dan, let's have a look at your settlement agreement."

"Where's Ava?" Mark Bledsoe directed his question at Olivia before he turned his gaze on Dan Winters. "You said Ava would be here."

"I said no such thing, Mark. Don't try to put words in my mouth. You called this meeting – quoting you verbatim now – in a good-faith effort to bring this case to a close."

Mark Bledsoe seemed to diminish right before their eyes. His shoulders slumped. The hard clench of his jaw softened. When he looked at Olivia, his icy blue eyes seemed to swim with tears.

Faker. Olivia thought. She didn't buy it. Not for one minute.

"I've made a mess of everything. I love Ava. Always have. Always will. I know I was cruel to her, and I'm ashamed." Olivia didn't respond to the beseeching look he gave her. "On my honor, I swear that I have never physically hurt her. I just want to see her, want to tell her how sorry I am. Will you at least ask her if she'll meet with me?"

Olivia couldn't believe what she was hearing. Mark's pleas were so outlandish, Olivia nearly laughed out loud. "I've already asked her that, Mr. Bledsoe. She's not willing to be anywhere near you. She's afraid you'll make good on your promise and kill her."

Before Mark Bledsoe could respond, Dan jumped in. "Let's stay focused on the paperwork, shall we?" He pushed two property settlement agreements toward Olivia. "Here are two agreements. Both have Mr. Bledsoe's notarized signature. One of them provides for a generous lump-sum payout in exchange for a face-to-face conversation between the parties. The other allows Ava to keep the money in her possession. No face-to-face meeting, no lump-sum payment."

Olivia took her time reviewing the documents. The language contained in them was as promised, without ambiguity and within the parameters as set out in the statute. She pushed the agreement that provided for a meeting between the parties back to Dan Winters.

"Thanks, Dan. These are both in order. My client has no interest in seeing or speaking to Mr. Bledsoe." Olivia turned, facing Mr. Bledsoe directly. When their gazes connected, she didn't look away. "You have physically abused and emotionally terrorized my client during the entire time you were married to her."

"That is not true."

"It is true," Olivia continued. "You broke your wife's clavicle; you broke her jaw. You poisoned yourself with ethylene glycol and tried to tell the police—"

Mark Bledsoe said, "You can't prove any of that."

"Olivia, cool it with the accusations," Dan said.

Ignoring him, Olivia plowed on. "I can prove all that, along with all the other instances of domestic violence perpetrated by you over the years. I've got medical records from more doctor visits and hospitalizations than I care to name, along with a handful of policemen who aren't afraid to take the stand and testify against you."

"Those were accidents. People do have accidents, Mrs. Sinclair. If I was so abusive, why didn't my wife leave?"

"It's called coercive control," Olivia said.

"That's absurd."

Olivia was furious all of a sudden, angry with all the abusive men who had sent women like Ava through her doors over the years. She was tired of the bullies, the abusers, and all the men who treated their wives and daughters like chattel. "There will be no meeting with Ava. You may as well resign yourself to the fact that you will never see your ex-wife again."

A tsunami of anger washed over Mark Bledsoe. Red-faced, eyes blazing with fury, he pushed away from the table, knocking his chair over in the process, and glared at Olivia like a snorting bull ready to charge. Brian countered this by stepping further into the door and pulling back his sport coat to reveal his holstered gun. When Mark Bledsoe saw it, he moved to the window, where he stood with his back to them, his shoulders heaving as he breathed through his nostrils.

Meanwhile, Dan Winters who had been watching the entire scenario with a wide-eyed look of shock, stood. "All right. Let's stand down, shall we? Message received. There will be no more violent outbursts." Dan waited a beat. "Mark? Come on. Sit back down. Let's wrap this up."

After Mark Bledsoe grunted and returned to his seat, looking at Olivia as though he wished he could hit her, Dan wheeled on Olivia. "I don't appreciate being blindsided, Olivia. Having Brian armed? Isn't that a bit over the top?"

"I don't think so. I don't feel safe around your client." Brian still stood in the doorway, blocking Mark's exit. He'd taken off his sports coat and tossed it over one of the chairs that were tucked around the conference room table, leaving his holstered Glock on display for all to see.

"Your client took a baseball bat to my process server's car after he was served with divorce papers. I don't like being bullied. Even more than that, I don't like having to bring someone with a gun to my meetings. But here we are."

"All right," Dan Winters said. "When can we get the signed paperwork—"

"I'm leaving." Mark Bledsoe stood and moved toward the door. Brian stepped out of the way. They all sat in silence as Mark paraded past them and walked out of the office, leaving a vacuum behind him.

"Jesus," Dan said, his voice tremulous.

Olivia scooped up the proffered paperwork and shoved it in her briefcase. "I'll get this signed. Do you want to file the final paperwork, or do you want me to do it?"

"I'll do it. I am not ashamed to say that Mark Bledsoe is a terrifying human being. Get the documents back to me, and I'll hand-deliver them to the judge for signature."

Brian held the front door open for Olivia. Before she stepped outside, she turned to Dan and said, "Be careful."

"You too."

Brian and Olivia didn't speak as they got in Brian's car and strapped on their seatbelts. As they pulled away, Olivia said, "Nearly there."

"Yep. With any luck, this time next month, we'll be packing your house up."

Chapter 22

Asher's car, along with the thousands of others who commuted into the city each day, crept toward the Golden Gate Bridge at a snail's pace. At this rate, he reckoned it would take them two hours to travel the 17.3 miles from his mother's house to the criminal court. Sabine sat next to him, her hands folded on her lap. As usual, she had taken care with her appearance, but the face makeup, blush, and garish red lipstick made her seem a caricature of herself.

"If you keep chewing your lip like that, it will bleed," his mother said. She put a hand on his arm, in an attempt to be comforting. He brushed it off.

"I expected press. Odd they left us alone. God knows they'd do anything to get salacious pictures of us. Do you think they'll be in the courtroom at Ken's bail hearing?" His mother's voice, usually soft and melodic, was tight and strained.

"I don't know. If they are, at least there won't be cameras."

"No cameras?"

"They're not allowed in the courtroom."

"This will all be over soon. We can get on with our lives and put this sordid mess behind us."

"He killed her, Mother. How can you not see that? How can you let him come into your home after all he's put you through?"

"Your father didn't kill your girlfriend. He's too much of a coward to do anything so bold."

"How is killing Mikala bold?" He was itching for a fight, but now wasn't the time. All he had to do this morning was get through the bail hearing, which should take two hours, tops. Deliberately softening his voice when he spoke, Asher said, "The evidence points to the contrary, Mother. You need to prepare yourself for the worst-case scenario. The incriminating evidence is there. It's irrefutable."

"We'll see about that. There was incriminating, irrefutable evidence against Olivia Sinclair, too. But she never even went to trial."

"That's because she didn't do it – never mind."

"I didn't mean to upset you. I'm just saying that I know how you feel right now. Guilty for allowing this woman to come into our lives—"

"Wrong, Mother. I feel no guilt. Zero. Dad's the one who brought her into our lives. He knew her before I did."

"She was a fling to him. If you hadn't fallen for her, she wouldn't have come into our day-to-day lives, wouldn't have sat at our table, wouldn't have had this effect on us."

"The blackmail scheme she was running with Dad brought her into our lives. Look, let's not talk about this, okay? Let's get through this hearing."

"Is there a chance you've changed your mind? I know your father would be grateful to have your support. Say you'll come home with us after your father is released on bail."

There is no guarantee he will be released on bail! Asher wanted to shout. Instead he bit his tongue so hard, he nearly drew blood.

"I'm sorry, but I can't. I've arranged a car service to drive you home. A limo. With a chauffeur who knows how to navigate the press. Brian's security is still in place. You'll be fine."

"I don't understand your way of thinking."

"I know. I just can't be around him."

"Asher—"

"Can you please respect my wishes here, and not bring this up again?"

Sabine sighed. "What's that term? Scared straight? Something tells me when this is over, your father will turn his life around. Maybe he'll realize what he has: a wife who loyally stood by his side and a son who he harmed."

"People like Dad don't change. He'll find some other con to work, find another girlfriend, and, once again, leave you to clean up after him. As for your loyalty, the only people who appreciate loyalty are those who are loyal themselves, a quality that my father – your husband – singularly lacks."

Asher pulled up to the curb in front of 850 Bryant Street. Sabine clung to her purse and started to get out of the car.

"I'll park and see you in there."

Sabine shut the door and walked toward the queue that had formed near the metal detectors and the security checkpoint she would have to pass through to gain entrance to the courthouse.

The only parking Asher could find was three blocks away from the courthouse. By the time he arrived, out of breath and sweating, his father and his attorney were standing before the judge. Sabine was seated in the first row behind him, her back rigid and her shoulders tense. Two rows behind her were Inspector Standish and her partner.

A group of people – likely attorneys, based on the business suits, briefcases, and the harried look on all their faces – milled in the back of the courtroom. Some sat on an uncomfortable-looking bench that rested against the back wall, reading paperwork and making notes. Others milled together. Using the group as a buffer between himself and his family, Asher remained in the back, out of the way.

The sight of his father in the standard-issue orange jumpsuit pleased Asher. When the judge said, "Plea, Mr. Ridgeland?" his father's voice was confident and sure.

"Absolutely not guilty. Not guilty at all."

"So noted, Mr. Ridgeland. You may be seated."

"Let's hear from the people on bail."

The assistant district attorney, a young woman with a no-nonsense blond bob and angular cheekbones stood. "We request remand, Your Honor. Dr. Ridgeland and the deceased were running a blackmail scheme. He dosed her and her boyfriend, the defendant's own son, with Rohypnol, waited until both parties were unconscious and then strangled her with his tie. While his girlfriend lay dead and his son lay passed out next to her, Mr. Ridgeland used the decedent's computer to transfer money from the decedent's account into his own. The officers who searched the defendant's apartment found Rohypnol, syringes, and a quantity of opioids, repackaged for sale on the street."

"These are allegations, Your Honor. Nothing more. My client contends those items were planted. We will prove that at trial."

The ADA plowed on. "Furthermore, Mr. Ridgeland's family has the means and the wherewithal for Mr. Ridgeland to run. He's a doctor who has lost his medical license, and has a slew of other legal troubles. He's a prime candidate to flee. Again, we request remand."

"Mr. Vine," the judge said.

"The people have a series of allegations, none of which have been proven. However, Mr. Ridgeland would be willing to post any bond the court would require, along with surrendering his passport, in exchange for home detention and monitoring with an electronic device. As Ms. Livingston mentioned, there are a rather comprehensive set of charges against Mr. Ridgeland. None of them are true. I need him home, so I can adequately prepare for trial."

Keep him in jail. Keep him in jail. Asher ran the silent mantra round and round in his head.

"Bail is set at five million dollars. Mr. Ridgeland will surrender his passport and wear an electronic device. He is not allowed to

192

travel more than ten miles away from his home, with the exception of his court appearances. Mr. Ridgeland, if you violate this order, you'll be immediately remanded. Do I make myself clear?"

"Yes," Ken said.

"We'll have a status conference in two weeks to set a trial date. Next case."

Moving with care, trying to avoid his mother by staying behind the clusters of people who clogged the corridors, Asher slipped out of the courtroom. Once in the corridor, he stayed tucked out of the way as Sabine and his father's attorney went to the processing desk and stood in line to fill out the paperwork to post his father's bond.

Soon his father came out of a side door, dressed in the navy-blue suit and red power tie Sabine had brought for him. Although Ken looked a little worse for wear, his commanding presence and the indignant expression on his face proved Ken Ridgeland's night in jail had done nothing to diminish his raging ego. When Sabine moved down a corridor, following the signs that led to the restrooms, Asher stepped away, turned his back on his family, and headed out into the cold San Francisco morning.

Chapter 23

Tuesday morning broke with the promise of sunshine and the last kiss of summer. Since Ken Ridgeland's arrest, Brian's work for Asher had come to a screeching halt. Or at least that's what Brian had told Olivia. On more than one occasion she'd caught him engrossed on the computer, only to shut the screen. He was up to something, and he didn't want her to know what it was. The Bledsoe divorce still hung over their heads, a ticking time bomb ready to reduce their carefully constructed happiness to ruins. Neither of them were sleeping well. Brian, usually so sweetly disposed and unflappable, had become irritable, while Olivia went through her day-to-day tasks on pins and needles. One multi-step task remained: getting the divorce decree signed by Ava, returned to Dan Winters, and then filed with the court.

Olivia and Brian sat at the table pretending to eat breakfast, until Olivia, who was well aware they were both pushing food around with their forks, said, "What's going on, Brian? Something's bothering you. What is it? Is it Asher?"

Not meeting Olivia's eyes, Brian pushed away from the table and topped off their mugs of coffee. He took his time about it. Olivia waited. "I'm nervous about taking the settlement agreement to Ava," Brian admitted.

"Me too," Olivia admitted. "This whole thing just seems a bit too easy."

"Agreed. Why would Bledsoe – who takes so much pleasure in terrorizing others – suddenly capitulate?"

"I'm worried that he's found Lauren's beach house," Olivia said. "I just have a bad feeling about this, as though there's something we're not seeing."

"Me too."

"I don't mean to pry, Brian. What aren't you telling me about Asher?"

"It's nothing. I just want to do a little more digging."

"But I thought Asher asked you to stop investigating?"

"He did. I have. Stopped, that is. It's just an old habit. I need to finish things, carry it through before I close a case. I think it's just that I don't trust my judgment anymore."

When Brian met Olivia's gaze, she was surprised at the worry – no, vulnerability – she saw there. "What happened with Leanne wasn't your fault. Look what Richard did to me."

"That's not the same thing," Brian said. "I'm a retired cop. I should have seen the red flags, seen that she was running a con. I'm ashamed that I fell for her, allowed my loneliness to be exploited."

"Brian, don't be so hard on yourself." Olivia stood, pulled Brian up with her. When they were both standing, she wrapped her arms around his neck. "We're all vulnerable, Brian. That's what makes us human. You don't have to tell me what's worrying you, but one incident of bad judgment shouldn't make you disregard a lifetime of intuition." Olivia pointed to the kitchen counter and the sealed envelope with Ava's name emblazoned across the front. "Am I going to have to worry about Mark Bledsoe for the rest of my life?"

"You know you're safe with me."

"I'm always safe with you. Will I ever feel safe with just me again? How long am I going to need bodyguards to go to the grocery store? Do you think he's going to stop terrorizing us after his divorce is final, after Ava has fled to safety? Because I don't."

"I've put a lot of horrible people – people like Mark Bledsoe, even worse – in jail. I always have to look over my shoulder. I thought you understood that about me."

"I did. I do. But we've been together for nearly a year now, and I've never seen you like this. You're . . ." Olivia hesitated ". . . hypervigilant. Uber focused. On our surroundings and on me. It's like your hackles are always up, and I fear it's starting to wear on you. What can we do to make it stop?"

"We need to be patient and wait and trust this will sort itself out."

"That's not good enough. Way too passive for me," Olivia said. "I feel like a prisoner, waiting for Mark Bledsoe to make whatever the hell move he's going to make."

Brian cradled his coffee mug in his hands. "I don't think Mark will continue to hassle us after Ava is gone."

"How can you be sure?"

"Ava is the one he had control over. Let's not forget that Mark has a public persona to maintain. Given his position, his employer may even be investigating the divorce as we speak. I have a feeling that rather than risk his lucrative job, the respect of his peers, and his reputation, Mark Bledsoe will turn his attention to something else."

"And what if he doesn't? What if he continues to harass us?"

Brian shrugged. His nonchalance irritated Olivia. "We'll deal with it. More importantly, worrying isn't going to help us. We'll be careful, continue to be careful. And we're moving. Soon we'll be off Mark Bledsoe's radar."

They were interrupted by the ring of the doorbell. Olivia's heart pounded as she moved to the kitchen window and peered out to see who was standing at her front door.

"Are you expecting someone?" Brian stood.

Olivia whispered, "It's Sabine."

"Why are we whispering?"

"I don't want to deal with her. Let's pretend we aren't home."

"If we pretend we're not home, she'll just come back later. Talk to Sabine. Get it over with. If she gets too long-winded, I'll pretend we have some important appointment to get to."

Olivia pushed away from Brian and headed to the front door. "Coming," she called, as she gave Brian a wry smile.

Sabine, who would never drop in on a friend unannounced, stood at the door. She'd missed a button on her silk blouse and a spot of pink lipstick was on her front tooth. Her bespoke cashmere jacket hung on her frame, and her eyes had the haunted look of stress-filled exhaustion.

"Sabine?"

"I'm so sorry to drop in on you, but I have something that needs to be taken care of, and I didn't want to discuss it over the phone." Sabine stepped around Olivia and made her way into the living room, where she marched to Olivia's picture window, came to a stop, and stood with her back to them. "I've forgotten what a stunning view you have. I heard you were selling."

Not wanting to embark on a lengthy conversation about her plans, Olivia hesitated for just a second. "How are things moving along with Ken's case?"

"We're happy with Stephen Vine. He's a good fit for Ken; strong-willed with a spine of steel. Ken's acting like he loathes me. My son has sworn that he will never be in the same room with his father again."

"I wish there was something I could do for you."

"There is, actually. That's why I stopped by."

Although she had no idea what Sabine was going to ask her, the first word that came into Olivia's mind was an emphatic *no*. The emotion must have showed on Olivia's face because Sabine immediately smiled and said, "It's an easy thing. I just need to reconfigure my will and tweak my trust a little bit. And since you're retiring, I'm wondering if you would provide my new attorney – if you don't want to do this for me, which is totally fine – the computerized version of the typed documents, so I don't have to start all over."

Olivia's relief was tangible. Sabine noticed it.

"It should be pretty straightforward, correct?"

"Yes. It's just a matter of pulling up the documents and making the changes. I can do this for you, no problem. Do you have an idea of what you'd like me to do?"

Sabine dug into her capacious bag and pulled out an envelope. "I want to put Asher in charge of my money, all of it. I've made minimal provisions for Ken, but as you'll see, I've decided to—" Sabine gave a tactful cough "—shorten his leash, for lack of a better word. I've made notes on the original document. Can you work off that?"

"Probably. Does Asher know of your plans to do this? There are a lot of responsibilities with managing your affairs."

"I know that. But I've got my trusted accountants. They will give Asher the guidance he needs. Mostly, Olivia, I want to make sure that if anything happens to Asher, anything at all, Ken will still only receive that minimal stipend."

Olivia opened the envelope Sabine handed her and quickly read through the new provisions. Sabine wasn't exactly cutting Ken off. He would still have a generous annual allowance that he could live on if he were careful. Olivia folded up the notes and placed them back in the envelope.

"You're playing with fire, Sabine. Ken is not going to be happy when he discovers you've done this."

Sabine was once again staring out Olivia's window, a dreamy look in her eyes. The sudden wave of calm and equanimity seemed strange, an incongruity in the face of Ken's arrest, and the murder of Asher's girlfriend. On guard now, Olivia said, "Are you sure this is what you want to do? Maybe you should think—"

"I'm sure. And all of these funds are my inheritance, not a community asset. I've been very careful not to mingle my inheritance with our household funds, just like you advised me years ago."

"I'm more worried about Asher," Olivia said. "What if Ken pressures him for control."

"Asher's a grown man. He'll have to stand up to Ken."

A frisson of doubt crept up the back of her spine. Asher would never be able to stand up to his arrogant, overconfident, and domineering father.

As if reading her mind, Sabine said, "Don't underestimate my son, Olivia. He's a far stronger man than Ken. Emotionally, at least, and that's what matters most." She stood. "I'd like you to prepare the documents, then Asher can meet with my accountant."

"Okay," Olivia said. "This will be my last bit of work as a lawyer."

Sabine stuck out her hand. "Thanks, Liv. When will I hear from you?"

"Give me a week at the most. I'll call you when everything's ready. Do you want me to messenger you a rough draft?"

"No. You can email me."

"Email? Sabine Ridgeland." Olivia smiled. "You've got email now?"

Sabine gave Olivia a sardonic grin. "I'm on a mission to join the twenty-first century. Not so sure I like it here."

Olivia wound her arm through Sabine's as they walked slowly toward Olivia's front door. "The world is a different place, isn't it? Remember when we used carbon paper?"

"You're talking to the woman who still has her Underwood typewriter on her desk." She stopped and pulled an Hermès scarf out of her purse. As she tied it over her hair, she said, "I suppose being nostalgic is not the best use of time. But I do long for the *good old days*. Don't you?"

Not at all. Olivia didn't express her disagreement out loud. Instead she gave Sabine a quick hug and said, "I'll be in touch."

"Thank you, Olivia. I appreciate it."

Olivia waited while Sabine, so slight and frail, walked to the Mercedes sedan she'd parked on the street. Change was afoot for the Ridgelands. The only thing to do was prepare the documents and see how things unfolded.

Chapter 24

"Sabine's not coping with Ken's arrest," Olivia said.

"Really? She seemed fine to me." Brian expertly navigated the twisty, two-laned road that arched over Mt. Tamalpais toward the coast. Often called Kamikaze Highway and flagged as one of the most treacherous stretches of road in California, the two-mile trek consisted of blind curves, steep drops, almost no shoulder area, and no guardrails. While the drive in and of itself was terrifying, the payoff for the danger was the expansive and dramatic view of the San Francisco Bay. On a clear day, the passengers on this drive – the driver couldn't afford to take her eyes off the road – had a sweeping view of the San Francisco Bay and the Farallon Islands. Although Olivia had driven this road thousands of times, the first glimpse from the top of the mountain never failed to take her breath away.

"What does Sabine want you to do for her?"

"She wants me to change her will."

"Disinheriting the husband, I imagine," Brian said. He slowed the car as they passed the Mountain Home Inn, the most dangerous spot on the drive. "God, I hate this road."

Olivia put a hand on his leg. "Not quite disinheriting, but greatly cutting his benefits. Ken Ridgeland's life is about to change."

"Especially if he goes to prison," Brian said. "What makes you think Sabine's not doing well?"

"First of all, she showed up at my house with lipstick on her teeth and her blouse misbuttoned. She's struggling mightily, as if she's holding it all in, trying to put a brave face forward."

"You need to let your worry for her go, Liv. We have our own problems to deal with."

"I know. And maybe I'm misinterpreting." Olivia pressed her forehead against the cold glass window, taking in the swirling bank of fog as it made its way across the bay toward San Francisco. "She's worried about Asher, and she's trying to protect her family's reputation. I know that so much concern over what people think seems shallow, but Sabine sets great store by it. You're right. I can't take on her problems, nor do I want to. I'll do this final thing for her, then I'm finished."

"And we'll be busy packing and moving," Brian said. "Do you have cell service?"

Olivia pulled her cell phone out of her purse. "Yes. I'll try Lauren again." She punched in Lauren's number. No answer.

"Can you try Scott or Ian? Use my phone if you want."

Olivia tried Lauren one more time. When she answered, she put the call on speaker.

"Hey, Liv."

"Oh, I'm so relieved to hear your voice," Olivia said. "I've been trying to call. You had us worried."

"No need to worry. The ever-handsome Scott has arrived on scene. Blake and Ian just left. We're safe. Ava is loading her suitcases in my car as we speak. We're all ready to leave, I think. Scott said he's going to ride with us to the airport, and then stay with me until we're sure Mark's not a threat. Did Brian arrange that?"

"I did," Brian piped in. "Just want to make sure the threat is behind us before I pull security. This is standard operating procedure. We have no reason to think that Mark will harass you after Ava is gone."

"Thanks, Brian. Honestly, I'm feeling a little cooped up here. I'm ready to go home."

"You mean you want to leave your hippie pad?" Olivia piped in.

"Don't tease, Olivia. I know that you love this place as much as I do. Although poor Ava isn't used to such shabby living. I'm sure she's ready to get away from here. Where are you?"

"We're about thirty minutes away."

"Okay. See you soon."

Despite Olivia's unconditional trust in Brian's driving, she breathed a sigh of relief when they reached the bottom of the Panoramic Highway and turned right onto Highway 1, where the road was perfectly flat without any precipitous drops into jagged rocks.

"There goes the sun," Brian said.

Olivia drank in the view as the sun dipped into the western sky in a blazing riot of purple and orange. Neither one of them spoke as they drove past Stinson Beach State Park, finally taking the hard-to-find dirt road that wove toward Lauren's small neighborhood.

"She really is secluded out here," Brian said.

"You know how Lauren likes her privacy. It's secluded for now, anyway. A developer has purchased the forty acres that adjoins this area. New houses will probably go up within the next few years."

"Shame," Brian said.

"I know."

When Lauren purchased the beach house in 1985, she was looking for a place to escape when she wasn't touring with her band. Being a rock star had its downside, namely an utter lack of privacy. Although Lauren engaged with fans with ease and grace, she needed a secluded place to get away from it all. The house, a ramshackle shack with faded yellow shingled siding and a myriad of windows, captivated Lauren at first sight. Inside, the floor was made of a jumble of red brick and flagstone, with knotty pine walls. The bathroom had a small sink and a ceramic tub. Other than fill the house with thick rugs when the hard floors started to hurt Lauren's aging back, and replace the funky furniture with two comfortable couches, Lauren had left things as they were.

Olivia leaned forward. "Slow down. The drive is just here, past that oak tree."

They turned into a long winding dirt road that wove through dense woods, each side bordered by a thick hedge.

"Lots of places to hide out here," Brian said.

"True, but also difficult to find," Olivia said. Brian had just rounded the final bend in the drive, and the house came into view. He stopped the car for a moment, taking in the aged shingled siding that had been replaced and repaired as necessary. Lauren's old Volvo station wagon was parked out front, along with Scott's pickup truck.

"This is Lauren's beach house?"

"You don't have to sound so incredulous," Olivia said. "It's nice on the inside."

Brian gave Olivia a look that said he wasn't buying it. At all. He turned off the headlights and pulled his car over to the side of the road, near one of the overgrown hedges.

"What's wrong?"

"Not sure," Brian whispered. He turned off the engine, pulled out his cell and sent a text to Scott. "We'll just wait to hear from someone." Seconds ticked by. Brian stared at his phone. No response.

"The service out here is spotty. Let's go in." Olivia opened her door and started to get out of the car.

"Just wait a second, okay? Can you shut the car door, please?" When Olivia hesitated, Brian explained, "The overhead light."

"Why are you worried?"

"There are no lights on in the house. I'm assuming Lauren has electricity?"

"Of course she does. But she uses candles when she's here."

Brian reached across Olivia, took his gun out of the glove compartment, and holstered it discreetly under his jacket.

"I'm going in. Wait here, okay?"

"Not a chance."

"Olivia, I can't cover you and—"

"I'm not waiting in the car by myself, Brian. I'll be careful." Olivia gently shut the car door and followed Brian up the sandy path toward Lauren's house, their footsteps silent in the growing darkness.

"Hang on a second," Brian whispered, pulling Olivia to a stop next to him. "Just stay behind me, okay? If the door is unlocked, I'm going to slip in. I know I can't ask you to stay out here, but if things aren't right, I want you to look for a way to take Lauren and Ava and go. Do you understand?" He handed Olivia the car keys. "Don't be a hero. Don't try to save me. I can't handle Mark Bledsoe and protect you at the same time. Get yourself, Lauren, and Ava to safety. That's all you need to do." Putting a hand on her shoulder, he forced her to look him directly in the eyes. "Will you do that?"

"Yes." Olivia took the keys as Brian opened the front door of Lauren's beach house and slipped inside. The breeze from the open front door caused the curtains to undulate. Other than that, the house was dark, quiet, and unusually still. Brian stood still, gun in hand, as he and Olivia waited for their eyes to adjust.

"Do you know where the light is?" Brian whispered.

"Yes. It's right by me," Olivia whispered back.

"Flip it on," Brian said.

Olivia did as he asked, throwing the living room into bright light from the overhead fluorescent light fixture. The scene before them spoke of frenzied violence. Two overstuffed club chairs had been turned over, the down cushions on the couch had been slashed, leaving feathers strewn everywhere. Broken ceramic and glass lay all over the floor, derived from Lauren's china cabinet – a heavy relic that came with the house and was too big to be removed. It had been pushed over with such force that all the dishes inside had smashed to the ground, leaving a wreckage of shattered glass and porcelain.

"Lauren?" Olivia called, her voice filled with panic.

"Back here," Lauren called out.

"She's in the back room, down that corridor," Olivia said.

Brian put his finger over his lips and motioned Olivia to stay behind him. She nodded, heart pounding, as they crept down the long dark hall, toward the back room. The door to the room was open. Brian paused before stepping inside. Olivia felt the tension coming off his body in waves. There were no curtains on the windows in this room, but the waxing crescent moon provided enough light for Olivia to see Mark Bledsoe, sitting next to Ava on the couch. Brian and Olivia stepped into the room. When Brian turned on the lights, Olivia saw Lauren sitting on the couch, looking furious, while Ava sat on her husband's lap, trapped. Mark Bledsoe had one hand wrapped around Ava's waist, holding her tight against his body, while the other hand grasped Ava's hair.

Brian pointed his gun at Mark and moved into the room.

"Took you long enough to get here," Mark said. "You may as well put that gun away. You don't have the stones to shoot me. Plus, you might miss and hit my lovely wife." Mark yanked Ava's hair, forcing her head to tip back, revealing her long white throat. Mark let go of his wife's waist and grasped her around the throat. Ava, wide-eyed with terror, whimpered. "I could just press my fingers into her throat and squeeze, couldn't I?"

"What a chickenshit," Lauren said. Mark Bledsoe ignored her.

Brian was calm and still as he stood with his gun trained on Mark. "Liv, you remember what I said?"

Adrenaline pumping, Olivia eyed the room, took in Lauren's car keys, which rested in a brass dish by the back door. "Yes."

Without warning, Brian fired. Ava screamed. Olivia pulled her away from Mark and shouted to Lauren. "Come on." Olivia's eyes connected with Lauren's. She shouted, "Grab your keys!" Lauren, who had the presence of mind to also grab the two purses that sat on the floor, snatched up the car keys, and grabbed Ava's other arm.

"Get out of here, Olivia," Brian said.

The force of the bullet had knocked Mark Bledsoe off the chair, but he had somehow managed to pull himself into a sitting position. He leaned against the wall. His face was white and covered in a sheen of sweat. A red peony of blood bloomed on his shoulder. His eyes blazed with fury as he touched his wound and looked at the blood on his hand.

"You shot me." He sounded incredulous.

"Go, Olivia," Brian said.

Olivia burst out of the house, running on pure adrenaline. Ava and Lauren stood outside, huddled together. Ava watched Olivia approach, a look of terror in her eyes, while Lauren stood with her fists clenched, as though she were ready for a fight.

"Do you think there's a chance anyone heard the gunshot and will call the police?" Olivia asked.

"I don't think so. I'm pretty secluded out here," Lauren said.

"What happened? Where's Scott?" Olivia asked.

"Mark ambushed us," Lauren said, her voice full of anger. "I can't believe I let that happen. He just came in the house. Snuck up behind Scott, and put a rag over his face. Scott collapsed."

"*Where* is Scott?" Olivia insisted. "Did you see where he took him?"

"I think he dragged him to the back bedroom," Lauren said.

"How can I get in there?"

"You'll have to break the window," Lauren said.

"No. I left it unlocked. I was opening it when Mark came in," Ava said. She'd started to sob. When Lauren moved to comfort her, she held up a hand. "No. This isn't the time. We need to leave. Now."

"Was Mark alone?"

"Yes," Ava said. "We really need to leave."

"Agreed. Can you take her to the airport, Lauren?"

"And leave you here? I don't think so."

"Just take Ava to the airport."

"Should I call the police?"

"Yes, once Ava is safely away."

"What do I tell them?"

"Everything. The truth."

"I'm going to come to your house after the airport, okay? I'll wait for you there. Text me when it's over, please," Lauren said.

"I'll contact you the minute I'm able." Olivia moved to Ava. The two women hugged. "Good luck, Ava."

"Thank you, Olivia, for everything." Ava turned and hurried off at a clip toward Lauren's car. With a final glance filled with worry and doubt from Lauren, Olivia turned her back on the women before she hurried back to the beach house, doing her best to stay in the shadows.

Once she was alone, her instincts took over and she was filled with a surprising sense of calm and purpose. *Stay smart, stay calm, and get Brian and Scott out of here.* Slipping behind the hedge that surrounded Lauren's house, Olivia stayed hidden as she crept toward the house and the unlocked window. Toward Brian.

Chapter 25

Olivia climbed in the guest-room window. Once inside, she held her breath and listened for an indication of who was where and what was happening. Try as she might, the only sound she heard was the hammering of her heart against her ribs and the slow repetitive refrain of the waves pounding on the beach. Using the flashlight function on her cell phone, she headed toward the back room, where Brian had shot Mark Bledsoe. The room was empty. She checked around, looking for any sign of Scott. Nothing. A grunt and a thump stopped Olivia in her tracks. It came from the living room.

"I'm going to teach you a lesson," Mark Bledsoe said, his voice full of anger. "You and that bitch girlfriend of yours hid my wife, kept her from me. Now you're helping her get away. You'll pay for that."

The sound of fist on skin told Olivia that someone had thrown a punch, likely Mark Bledsoe with Brian on the receiving end.

"Cheap shot," Brian said, his voice sounded unfazed. "Should have known you'd take the coward's way. You're nothing but a bully. Beating on women. Shame on you." Olivia was shocked to hear Brian taunt Mark Bledsoe.

She checked her cell phone, just in case by some miracle she now had service. Nothing. The grunts and sound of fists connecting with skin grew faster and louder. As she passed the built-in book-case, she saw a life-sized raven made of solid bronze. Olivia grabbed it and held it fast as she stepped into the living room to find Mark Bledsoe and Brian engaged in a full-on street fight.

Blood ran down Mark's arm from the gunshot wound to his shoulder. Brian's nose gushed blood and seemed to swell before Olivia's eyes. His gun lay in the doorway to the bathroom, forgotten. Neither man noticed Olivia standing there, so intent were they on each other.

Not sure what she could do, Olivia stood frozen while the two men went after each other with all they had. Mark, red-faced and grunting like a barnyard beast, charged Brian, using his shoulders to ram him against the wall. Olivia thought about grabbing the gun but didn't see a way she could navigate around the men to retrieve it. Using his bulk to pin Brian against the wall, Mark landed a punch. When his fist connected with Brian's cheek, Olivia cried out. Still, they didn't notice her. She needed to do something. Fast. The back of Mark Bledsoe's head was within reach. One strike should bring him down. She hoisted the statue and moved toward them, just as Brian headbutted Mark Bledsoe, sending the big man reeling backwards. Olivia stepped out of the way as Mark struggled to remain standing. "This is finished," Brian said, as he punched Mark in the shoulder where he'd been shot. With a bellow of pain, Mark Bledsoe went down on his knees and fell to his side, limp and unconscious.

"I'm way too old for this." Brian moved to Mark. He stood over him, his breath coming in gasps, blood dripping out of his nose and onto the floor.

Olivia took in the destruction around her, the damage to Brian, and had a moment of true empathy for the hell Ava had endured at the hands of her abuser. She tasted salt and was surprised to find she had been crying.

"Liv." Brian stood over Mark Bledsoe, panting, drenched in sweat. "I thought I told you to leave."

"I'm never going to leave you in a dangerous position. I just won't do it."

Brian came over to Olivia and took the raven statute from her, and asked, "What were you going to do with this?"

When Olivia spoke, her voice was tremulous and weak. "I was going to hit him on the back of the head. He had you pinned, I thought – I didn't know – I've never experienced—"

"Are you two going to stand there like that all night, or do we want to figure out what to do with him?" Scott stood in the entry of the living room, pale-faced, leaning against the wall. "I know, I look like hell. Your buddy there . . ." Scott nodded at the figure on the floor ". . . gave me a healthy dose of chloroform."

"Come and sit down, Scott. We need to find a way to call the police," Brian said.

"I'm seeing double," Scott said, as he moved to the sofa, his gait unsteady.

Brian pulled Olivia away from Mark Bledsoe's body and whispered in her ear. "Did they get away?"

Olivia nodded.

Relief washed over Brian. "Let's get you out of here. You can drive Scott back to our house. Once Ava is on that plane, Lauren can come and stay with us. How does that sound?"

"No," Olivia said. "I'm not leaving you here. We need to stay together."

"Olivia, I need to deal with this mess. The sheriff needs to come out. We're going to have to give statements; it's going to be a nightmare. Best if I handle this alone."

"He's right, Liv," Scott said. "They're going to want to talk to me, and I need to sleep for an hour or three before they do. I don't feel good at all. If we wait with Brian, they'll take all of us to the Civic Center for questioning, leaving us in an interrogation room to stew for hours. Ava's situation will need to be explained. The best person to do that is Brian," Scott said.

"Shouldn't we tie him up or something?"

Brian picked up his gun, and stuck it in the holster under his jacket. "That's a good idea." Brian stepped close to Mark and went down on one knee.

Olivia saw Scott's eyes widen. He shouted, "Look out!" Just as Mark grabbed Brian's wrist and tried to pull him off balance. Mark reached for Brian's gun. Lightning quick, Brian knocked Mark's hand away, causing the gun to go skittering across the floor. The two men were standing now, facing off against each other, once again circling. Out of the corner of her eye, Olivia saw Scott try to approach the two men, but he wasn't steady enough to do anything useful.

Mark Bledsoe threw the first punch, which landed squarely on Brian's shoulder. She looked for the statue of the raven, ready to come up swinging, just as Mark pushed Brian hard, knocking him off balance and leaving him sprawled on the floor. Once Brian was out of the way, Mark, unsteady on his feet, stumbled toward the entrance to the bathroom, where the gun lay in the doorway. Without thinking, Olivia followed him. When he bent over to pick up the gun, she put her foot on his butt and pushed with all her might until he went sprawling into the bathroom.

Lucky for Olivia, the bathroom, which had once been a supply closet, had a door that opened outward. Olivia slammed the door, locked it, and managed to wedge a heavy oak chair underneath the doorknob, locking Mark Bledsoe inside.

"He'll be able to smash that door in a matter of seconds. Let's get out of here." Brian put an arm around Scott, and the three of them fled the house. Olivia ran ahead, unlocked the car and started the engine. Once Scott and Brian were in, Olivia peeled out of the drive, just as Mark appeared in Lauren's doorway, the light from the house flooding out behind him, the gun trained on the car.

"Punch it!" Scott cried out as he ducked.

Olivia punched the gas and went skidding around the bend, putting them safely out of danger.

"He's going to follow us," Brian said, as he gave Olivia a sideways glance and fastened his seatbelt.

"And he's got my gun," Brian said.

"Get us out of here, Olivia," Scott said from the back seat.

Chapter 26

They drove in silence as Olivia sped up Highway 1, driving as fast as she could on the narrow road, hoping a random sheriff would pull her over for speeding before she headed up the mountain. No such luck.

"It wouldn't hurt for you to put the pedal to the metal, Olivia," Scott said.

"Maybe we could pull into a side road and wait until he passes?" Olivia asked.

"And risk Bledsoe seeing us? We'd be sitting ducks. Bad idea," Scott said. "Most definitely a bad idea."

"Or keep going," Brian said. "We have a solid lead."

Olivia clenched the steering wheel so hard the joints in her knuckles hurt. They *did* have a solid lead, so all she had to do was stay calm and steady and drive over the Panoramic Highway. Once they were in Mill Valley, they could get to safety. Holding on to that thought, Olivia took a deep breath, forced herself to relax, and focused on the road. "If I can get us into Mill Valley, I can drive us right to the police station." She glanced at Brian. "We should have phone service soon. Maybe we could call the police and tell them we're coming?"

"Good idea."

"I don't have service yet," Scott piped in from the back.

Brian checked his phone. "Me neither."

Olivia took the curves as fast as she dared. As the minutes ticked by, Olivia fell into the routine of the drive, braking gently as she approached a turn and accelerating out of it. Seconds turned into minutes. The tension eased. Brian sat stone-faced, staring ahead, while Scott had positioned himself sideways across the back seat, keeping a vigil out the back window.

Stay calm. Stay calm. Olivia repeated the words and focused on her breathing. They were going to make it.

"Someone's behind us."

Olivia checked the rearview mirror. "I don't see anything."

"That's because he has his headlights turned off. He's taking the corners way too fast. God, he's on a suicide mission." Scott turned around, placing his hands on the seat in front of him, as though bracing himself. "Olivia, you need to speed up."

Brian winced as he turned around to look out the back window.

"Olivia, you need to hold it together, okay? He's behind us." Brian's voice was calm and reassuring.

"We could have her pull over, Brian. Then you and I could deal with Bledsoe."

"He's got my gun," Brian said.

"I've got an extra you can use."

"I don't think a gun fight is the answer." He turned to Olivia. "You're doing great, Liv. Just keep going, okay?"

Olivia tuned out Brian's gentle encouragement and Scott's edgy one-liners as she took the corners. They were almost to the top of the mountain, the most dangerous place on the entire drive. If she could evade Mark Bledsoe until they passed the Mountain Home Inn, she could get them to safety. She sped up a little, surprised at how smoothly Brian's car handled the hairpin turns. Forcing herself not to think about the steep drop, the lack of guardrails, and the fact that there was no room for error, Olivia pressed the accelerator.

"What's his endgame, Brian—"

Suddenly halogen headlights flooded the car with light as Mark Bledsoe bumped her car, causing it to lose traction for a split second. At the last second, Olivia veered into the other lane, missing the cliff wall by inches. Olivia stayed in the lane closest to the cliff wall, risking a head-on collision with oncoming traffic. At least she was away from the precipice. Bledsoe took this opportunity to get beside them. His tank of a car couldn't take the turns as fast as Brian's. Olivia used this to her advantage, inching ahead of Bledsoe's car. Two more turns, and they would be at Mountain Home Inn, the top of the mountain, the most dangerous part.

"You've got this, Liv," Brian soothed.

"Speed the hell up," Scott called in the back.

As Olivia entered the short, straight stretch before the last corner, she came up with a plan. If Mark didn't know the mountain, it would work. She hit the brakes, slowing down deliberately.

"What are you doing?" Scott asked.

She uttered a silent thank you as Mark slowed down and tried to pull up beside her. As she reached the final hairpin turn, the spot in the road where dozens of cars had plunged into the steep ravine, Olivia floored it.

Scott screamed. Olivia slammed on the brakes as the car skidded toward the cliff. Brian shouted her name. The brakes got traction. As Brian's car skidded to a stop, Mark Bledsoe's car passed them. As if in slow motion, Mark Bledsoe's car flew by them, until it launched into the air. For a second, the car seemed to climb skyward, as though it were going to fly. And then it dropped out of sight. Olivia, Scott, and Brian sat in the car, silent, as if mute. Seconds later, a loud boom shook the night, followed by a burst of orange that lit the sky.

"Olivia?" Brian's voice was tentative as he placed a hand on Olivia's arm. "Are you okay?"

"I think so."

"Scott?" Brian asked.

"Other than nearly soiling myself, I'm just fine," Scott said. "That was some mighty fine driving, Olivia. I didn't know you had it in you."

Without speaking, they unbuckled their seatbelts and stepped out into the still night. They wove their arms together, with Olivia in the middle, as they walked toward the edge of the cliff, careful not to get too close. Below them, the fire raged.

Scott untangled himself, checked his phone, and dialed.

"Nine-one-one. What's your emergency?"

"I've just seen an accident off the Panoramic Highway," Scott said. "It looks like someone drove off the cliff near the Mountain Home Inn."

"That accident has already been reported. First responders are on their way."

"Thanks." Scott hung up. "Can we please get out of here?"

They filed back to the car, silent and somber. Olivia put the car in drive and headed into Mill Valley, driving as slow as she dared. When a car approached, Olivia pulled into the layby and let them go around her.

"It's over," Brian said.

"Ava's safe now," Olivia said.

"We all are," Brian said.

Chapter 27

They decided to drop Olivia off at home, so Brian and Scott could drive to the Marin County Sheriff's office and give a detailed statement of everything that went down at Lauren's beach house. When they pulled up to the house, a figure sat on the front step, head resting in hands, a backpack next to her.

"It's Lauren," Olivia said, turning off the headlights.

"We should circle the property and make sure the perimeter is safe," Brian said.

"It's safe, Brian. Mark Bledsoe's dead. I'm safe."

"You'll have to go it alone," Scott said from the back seat. "I'm feeling like crap. Probably should save what energy I have for the sheriff."

As Olivia got out of the car, she heard Brian say, "Let me take you to the hospital—"

She ignored them, as she approached Lauren. "Hey." Tension radiated off Lauren in waves. Olivia kept her voice soft, holding out her hand.

"Ava's safe," Lauren said as Olivia hoisted her to her feet. "She sent me a text when she was on the plane. They wouldn't let me go to the gate with her. But I don't think we were followed. What happened? Where's Bledsoe?"

"It's over."

"Over?"

"Bledsoe went over at Mountain Home Inn."

Relief washed over Lauren. Her whole body shifted, as though her muscles and skin were now connected and in sync with her bones. She wiped her eyes with the back of her hand. "Are you sure, Liv? Because the way I see it, the only way this thing can be over is if Mark Bledsoe's dead. He definitely holds a grudge; are you saying – is he – are you sure?"

"There's no way he could have survived. He's gone. Let's go in and I'll tell you everything."

Olivia was pouring two glasses of red wine when Brian joined them ten minutes later. "Hi, Lauren."

"What's happened to your face?" Lauren asked. "Did Mark Bledsoe do that to you?"

"He did. Oliva will tell you everything. I need to go talk to the sheriff."

"I never called them. I started to dial, twice, but I had no idea what to say." Lauren's eyes darted from Olivia to Brian. "I hope I didn't make matters worse."

"You didn't. I'll explain your involvement, tell the police that you're traumatized. They're probably going to want a statement. When you talk to them, just tell them the truth." Brian kissed Olivia on the cheek. "You sure you're okay?"

"I am," Olivia said.

"Good. Because I need to go to the sheriff before they discover my involvement and come looking for me. I have a lot of explaining to do. The appearance of cooperation will go a long way." When he put his warm, steadying hand on Olivia's back between her shoulder blades, she leaned into it, as if to draw strength. "The house is secure. I'll turn the alarm on."

"I'll wait up," Olivia said.

"Please don't," Brian said. "You need to rest. I'll be fine."

Olivia didn't tell Brian there was no way she could sleep without

219

him next to her. Not now. Not after what she'd been through. By the time Brian kissed Olivia's forehead and left them, Lauren had finished her wine. Olivia refilled her glass. "Are you okay?"

Lauren shook her head. "No. No, I'm not okay." Her voice cracked as tears spilled down her cheeks. She took a breath that sounded like a gasp. "I'm terrified."

"It'll pass," Olivia promised.

"How can you say that?" Lauren snapped. "This won't just *pass*. Don't be so dismissive, Liv. It's patronizing. I don't know how Brian does this, lives in this world, among this type of drama. Because you know what, Liv? I'm scared to go to my own freaking house. And I love my house." Lauren blew her nose and wiped her eyes. "So, pardon me if I don't agree with your *this will pass* comment."

Olivia closed her eyes, wanting to fall apart, but knowing that she needed to hold it together for her friend.

Lauren took a respectable drink of wine and looked at Olivia with bleary eyes. "What happened?"

"Short version?"

"The least dramatic version would be appreciated."

"Fighting ensued. Brian got punched in the face more than once by Mark Bledsoe, who ultimately went into your bathroom for the gun, which had skittered across the floor. When he went in there, I pushed him. He went sprawling, we locked him in, got in the car and sped off. I'm afraid there's damage to your beach house . . ."

Lauren waved Olivia's concerns away. "Aren't you glad I didn't change the door? If it had closed from the inside—"

"I'd be telling a completely different story, I suspect. He chased us over the mountain." Olivia's voice shook as she explained how close they'd come to going over the edge of the cliff, how she'd slowed down and Mark Bledsoe had blown past her, missed the turn, and had flown off the cliff. "He went off the road near Mountain Home Inn."

They sat quietly for a few minutes, lost in their own thoughts until Lauren finally broke the silence. "This is a turning point for me. My life will forever be divided into two eras, the before times and the after times."

"Like me before I was arrested for murder," Olivia said.

Lauren divvied up the rest of the wine. "We're getting old, Liv."

"Tell me about it."

"I was in my kitchen making a cup of tea when Mark came in," Lauren said. "One minute I'm pouring half-and-half out of the mouth of that stupid cow-shaped creamer. The next minute, Mark Bledsoe is standing in front of my fridge. His energy was so full of menace. It was tangible. One look at him, and I thought, *So this is how I'm going to die.* I shouted for Ava to run, but she didn't. She'd come into the kitchen. When she saw him standing there, she froze, wouldn't move. I'll never forget the feeling of helplessness, of being trapped." Lauren drained her wine glass. "It's going to take a long time for me to recover from this. I'll have to resign myself to that."

Me too, Olivia thought.

"You're not going to change your mind about retirement this time?"

"No. I'm finished."

Lauren went to the kitchen sink, rinsed her wine glass, and filled it with water. "I'm leaving for a while. I need to get my bearings."

"Leaving? Where are you going?"

"France," Lauren said. "I got invited to participate in a music mentoring program. The offer came months ago. I sent them an email accepting yesterday. It's sudden, I know, but I need to recover myself. I can't stop looking over my shoulder. I haven't slept since Ava came back into my life. Not to mention that I feel utterly guilty for subjecting you to all of this."

"When do you leave?"

"Tomorrow morning. I have a taxi to the airport picking me up here at 5:00 a.m. You don't care if I crash on your couch tonight, do you?"

"But where's your suitcase?" Olivia noticed for the first time that Lauren wasn't dressed in her usual tie-dyed, flowing hippie style. She had on jeans, a long-sleeved sweater. Her backpack was in the corner, a down jacket draped over the top of it.

"I'm not bringing one. I have the basics in my backpack. I'll buy what I need there. Swear to God, Liv, I'm about to go out of my skin. If I don't get out of here, I'm going to fall apart completely."

"I feel the same way."

"Brian does too. I can tell by the look in his eyes. Big changes ahead for all of us." Lauren wrapped her arm around Olivia.

"I'll miss you."

"I'm sorry I won't be here to help you move, but I'll be at your house for Thanksgiving." Lauren let her guard down, and for the first time in their decades-long friendship, Olivia sensed Lauren's vulnerability. "Everything's going to be okay, isn't it?"

"I think so. With time," Olivia said.

"Well, if I can't summon the courage to stay in my house again, I'll just move to Tahoe."

"I'd love that. So would Denny and Brian." Olivia smiled and grabbed Lauren's hand.

Chapter 28

It was 10:00 a.m. on the dot when Ellie packed up the last of Mikala Glascott's bank statements, wrote the contents of the box on a label, and sealed the whole thing off with packing tape.

"That's it?" Lambada asked, as he lifted the box and stacked it up with the others.

"I hate this part," Ellie said, "giving away our hard work, not seeing it through."

"I know, but it's the job." Lambada picked up an insulated cup of water and took a big drink. "At least we don't have to work with the lawyers. I'd last five minutes there."

"You'd be fine, Lambada."

"But then I wouldn't get to work with you," Lambada said.

Ellie, who had been avoiding Lambada's gaze by tidying her desk, faced him now. "Are you going to ask Wasniki to assign you another partner?"

"No," Lambada said instantly. "Why would I do that?"

"Because of what happened to Sharon."

"Sorry, Standish, but I'm not tracking."

"Forget it," Ellie said.

"No, no way. You don't get to do that. Tell me what you mean."

"I've just had the impression that people avoided me because of what happened. Sharon and I violated policy and protocol by splitting up while we were investigating. I should have gone with her to the boat in Sausalito. She should have never gone off to find a suspect or question a witness without backup. We did something that we weren't supposed to do, and Sharon almost died. It should never have happened. If I had been with her—"

"You think you're the only cop who bends the rules a little bit? We all do that. Regularly. You cannot operate within finite boundaries in this job. None of us can. If we did, we'd never make an arrest. Predictability is not a good thing in people chasing criminals. We need to adapt. You and Sharon adapted, probably to save time. You thought your decision to separate was harmless, something without consequence. You misjudged. It happens. It will probably happen again. You need to get over it, Standish. Forgive yourself. Focus on the job."

"I feel responsible for Sharon. She's such a good cop—"

"Did I hear my name mentioned?"

Startled, Ellie look up to find Sharon standing in the doorway. She looked well rested. Her cheeks had good color, and she didn't look as though she were ready to jump out of her skin, like she had when they had met for dinner.

"Hey, Sharon." In two short strides, Lambada reached Sharon and pulled her into a bear hug. Ellie was surprised at the affection between the two of them.

When Sharon and Lambada finally disentangled themselves, Sharon said, "What were you two saying about me?"

When Lambada piped in, Ellie felt her face go hot with shame. Why couldn't he just keep his mouth shut? "I was just saying how the thing that happened with you – getting thrown in the bay – wasn't anyone's fault. It was an unfortunate event. Standish blames herself. I was just telling her she doesn't need to do that."

Sharon looked at Ellie, her eyes full of understanding. "It's time to move on from all of that. You'll both be pleased to know that

I walked on the Marina Green today. Granted I didn't look at the water, but I didn't run home and lock myself inside."

"That's good, right?" Lambada said.

"It is."

Ellie felt like she should say something, but she didn't know what that should be. Instead, she just stood there, mute.

"You know what my mom would say?"

"Do I even want to know?" Sharon teased.

"You should just go swimming." The words hung in the air, as Sharon froze and Ellie held her breath.

"Lambada, can't you just stop talking for once?" Ellie snapped.

"Hey, I didn't mean—"

"It's okay," Sharon said. "You know, Lambada, you might be onto something."

"I'll go with you," Ellie said. "We could get wetsuits and swim to the place where you went overboard."

"Let me think about it," Sharon said. "I need to talk to Captain Wasniki. Signing off on my disability."

"So you're really not coming back?"

"I'm not," Sharon said. "And before you ask, I don't know what I'm going to do. Honestly, I'm not worried about it."

"That's good," Lambada said.

"I'll see you both, okay?" With a wave, she was gone.

After she was gone, Ellie said, "Do you think she'll do it?"

"Confront her fears? Go swimming? Maybe. I've known Sharon Bailey for a long time. I am certain that she will do whatever it takes to get herself right again." Lambada picked up his backpack. "Now that we're officially partners, we should start our own traditions."

"What did you have in mind?"

"You buy me pancakes today, and I'll buy you pancakes tomorrow."

Ellie laughed. "You're on."

Chapter 29

Ken heard them in the kitchen, Asher and Sabine, talking to each other in a soft murmur. Careful not to make any noise, he crept down the hall to Asher's room, pausing before he tried the door. Upstairs he heard Asher's voice, the sound of the oven opening and shutting. Pulling out the unbent paperclip, Ken used it to unlock the ineffective lock. Voilà. He was in. The room was dark and cold. His feet sank into the thick padding under the white wool carpet – ever impractical, especially for a growing boy. Careful not to make any noise as he pulled out the computer chair, Ken then sat down at the laptop computer that was propped open on the desk. He'd memorized the instructions, reading them over and over until they were etched in his brain.

Once the computer was turned on and asking for a password, Ken slipped the jump drive into one of the slots. The computer came alive. Soon he was directed to another screen and asked for a password. Using two fingers, Ken entered the configuration of letters, numbers, and symbols. Once that was finished, the computer did its thing, whatever that was. All he had to do was sit and wait.

He'd never understood technology, and had always preferred doing things the old-fashioned way. He preferred cash to credit, hearing someone's voice rather sending a text. But times had changed. As the computer did whatever it was supposed to do, Ken thought of his family and of the son he failed to connect with. When Asher was a baby, he was too busy and exhausted from his residency and subsequently his grueling surgery rotation to do the things fathers were supposed to do. He'd missed the growing-up years, trusted that Sabine would be a good mother, would hold a place for him in the constellation of their small family.

Of course, she hadn't. Instead she'd corrupted their only child – of that Ken was certain. One day, he found himself alone with his young son and realized that Asher had, for all intents and purposes, taken on the personality of his mother. Just as the computer finished, Ken came to the realization that the time for regret had come and gone. When the computer shut itself down, Ken removed the tiny jump drive and stuck it in his pocket. He stood in the middle of his son's room and sent a quick text. *It's done.* The response was immediate. *We're in. You have a deal.*

"What are you doing in here?" Asher stood in the doorway, a look of suspicion on his face as his eyes swept the room, taking in the computer, the desk, the cell phone, and finally his father. "Well?" Asher demanded.

"Looking for a phone charger," Ken said. "Sorry to invade your privacy. I haven't been able to find mine since I got out—" He let the words hang between them, not wanting to say, *since I made bail.*

Asher softened. "We have different phones. My charger won't work for yours."

"Okay," Ken said, swallowing the massive sigh of relief. "If you'll excuse me. Your mother has issued a command for my presence."

Ken swore he caught a wry smile on Asher's face as he let himself out of the room.

Ken sat in his wife's opulently furnished living room, wishing he were anywhere else. Even his tiny urine-smelling prison cell was better than being in the sphere of his wife's insanity. A look of disgust flitted across his face as he took in the opulent furnishings, the uncomfortable seating with its pretentious silk upholstery, the wool carpets, every stick of furniture, every stupid knickknack worth a small fortune. Their home was a mid-century modern, built in the 1950s, all angles and edges, cleverly designed to blend in with the wooded landscape of their property. His wife had decorated the interior as though it were a Gothic castle. He'd had nothing to say about it, of course. Sabine had quickly made it clear at the beginning of their marriage that the house was her domain. Her trust fund had purchased it, and her trust fund had provided the means for the ludicrous furnishings.

When they'd first met, courted, and married, he'd found Sabine's old-world mannerisms and style charming, a breath of fresh air from the unrepressed freedom of California. Yes, he begrudgingly admitted to himself, he'd been drawn to her wealth. She had enough money to buy a small country. And even though the bulk of it was tied up in family trust funds, properties in Europe, and legacies over which Sabine had little control, she came with her own sizeable chunk of disposable income. Lucky for him, she'd been generous and hadn't hesitated sharing. But time had cast its patina over their marriage, and Sabine's attitude toward Ken had changed. As had his toward her.

Over the past thirty-five years, forks in the road had presented themselves to him. Seduce the new nurse or go home to his wife? Have another line of coke in the executive lounge of the club, or go home to his wife and newborn baby? Drop another five hundred dollars on a lap dance, or call it a night? Pop another pain pill or go through the excruciating process of detoxing? Although he'd kicked the hard stuff – anything that required a needle – Ken had always had a proclivity for the hedonistic path. He'd never apologized or hidden the fact that he wanted – no, needed – pleasures of the flesh. He needed sex. Regularly. Sabine knew this, and over the years she had turned her head.

Now his life was a hot steaming pile of legal and financial troubles. Never mind that he'd never practice medicine again, at least not in the United States. He had his blackmail proceeds, well hidden and safe in an account in the Cayman Islands. There wasn't much there, not by his current standard of living. But he could cash out and move to Mexico. Get a shack on the beach, maybe open a bar. Spend his days in shorts and Hawaiian shirts, surrounded by nubile young women in bikinis. One thing Ken knew for certain: he'd be fine. He would always land on his feet. He trusted the best course of action would reveal itself. All he needed to do now was ride out the next few days.

Ken stepped into the living room just as Sabine came in, carrying a tray of coffee cups. By Ken's count there were twelve cups and saucers on the tray.

"Are we having company?"

"No. Of course not. I'm just restocking the coffee area." She stopped and stared at Ken. "What's the matter with you? You've got a funny expression on your face."

"I'm going back downstairs. I'll take my coffee down there."

"You will not." Sabine spoke in a voice that conveyed her expectation of obedience.

Ken stopped and checked himself. Did he really want to do battle this morning? Did he want to risk sending Sabine over the edge? His hand slipped to the jump drive in his pocket, his fingers ran across the surface, its presence giving him comfort.

"Please sit back down, Ken. I'll just get the coffee and we'll proceed."

"It's eight o'clock in the morning. What, exactly, are we proceeding with? If you don't mind telling me."

"We're discussing our family strategy."

For a moment, Ken thought about telling Sabine exactly what she could do with her *family strategy*, but years of marriage had taught him the best way to deal with Sabine was to capitulate, or at least pretend to do so. He sat, resigned and defeated as Sabine

229

excused herself, finally returning with the stupid tea trolley. A full breakfast buffet was laid out on the top. There were eggs, bacon, fruit salad, biscuits, pancakes, and a selection of gourmet jams and jellies. Ken's stomach roiled at the smell of it.

"I don't want any food."

"Then let's begin." Sabine took out a sheaf of papers from a manila envelope. "First of all, Ken, with regard to your criminal matter. The evidence against you for the blackmail scheme is solid. We do not want to take this matter to trial."

"Have you been meeting with my attorney without me knowing?"

"No, of course not. I tried, but Mr. Vine told me that he couldn't discuss the case without your permission."

"Thank God," Ken whispered.

"Need I remind you, darling, that I'm paying for all of this, that *my* money allowed you to get the best attorney money could buy?"

"No need. You've been reminding me at least three times a day."

"Don't get sharp. I did some research. You could go to prison for over twenty years," Sabine said. "I think you should take a plea, maybe get Mr. Vine to negotiate five to seven years in prison. That way you can spare us the embarrassment of a long, drawn-out trial." Sabine sipped her coffee, her pinkie sticking out.

"No," Ken said.

"What do you mean, no?" Sabine countered.

"I'm going to fight the charges. My lawyer and I have a plan. I'm officially asking you to stay out of my legal case. Thank you for paying my fees. But I'll be making decisions on how *my* legal matters are handled. From this moment forward, I'll thank you to not overstep."

Flustered, Sabine set her tray down. "I am only trying to hold this family together, Ken. Why are you – I don't understand—"

"You should know that once my legal affairs are handled, I'm leaving. I'll be seeking a divorce."

"No. You will be seeking nothing. You will stay a part of this family. You do not get to drag us down and then abandon us."

"Abandon? What are you talking about? You and I have been living separate lives for decades. Asher and I can't stand the sight of each other – don't recoil and act surprised. You know as well as I do that we have no relationship. While I admit that I'm partly to blame for the demise of our marriage, you know it's over as well as I do." Ken waited for the dramatic scene to begin. He expected it, and had planned to do his wife the favor of letting her vent her anger, before he left. Instead, she pinched her mouth together, set her teacup down, stood up, and said, "If you'll excuse me." And walked out of the room.

Relieved to have dropped his bombshell, Ken poured himself a cup of coffee and sat back down to wait. When the text message came through, Ken would walk out the door of this house for the last time.

Chapter 30

Brian and Lauren were both gone when Olivia made her way into the kitchen for a cup of desperately needed coffee. She'd slept the deep sleep of the emotionally exhausted, but she still felt drained, wrung out like a wet towel. Out of habit, she turned on the news as she settled into her usual chair in the kitchen. Mark Bledsoe's death had made the national headlines. The media – and some hired PR guru, Olivia imagined – portrayed Mr. Bledsoe as a titan of the financial world, whose intelligence, foresight, and generosity to various charities would be sorely missed. Olivia marveled at the artful way Bledsoe's violent and controlling nature had been sanitized. At least Ava had arrived home safely. Too bad she'd likely have to turn around and come back to deal with all of the issues surrounding her husband's death.

She'd just stepped out of the shower when her cell phone rang. Sabine. For a minute, Olivia thought about not answering the call and going back to her coffee, but knowing how persistent Sabine could be, she decided to answer.

"Olivia? You need to come."

"Sabine?"

"Ken and Asher are fighting." Olivia heard a crashing sound in the background.

"Call the police," Olivia shouted as she scrambled for her car keys.

"I will. Just come. Please, Olivia. I'm scared."

"On my way," Olivia said.

Sabine was waiting outside for Olivia. Her face was devoid of color, deep worry lines etched on the sides of her mouth. When Olivia got out of the car, Sabine ran up to her.

"Ken is going after Asher. I'm afraid he's going to kill him."

"Are the police sending someone?" Olivia stopped, listening for sirens. She heard nothing. No sirens. No traffic. Nothing, except the occasional shout in the house.

"I'll just call them and find out when they are getting here. First rule of domestic squabbles, let the police handle—"

Olivia pulled out her phone, but Sabine snatched it out of her hand. "No police."

"I came here because you told me you would call the police." Olivia didn't bother to hide the edge in her voice. She'd allowed herself to be manipulated by Sabine and wondered what other secrets Sabine was keeping from her.

"You better tell me exactly what happened, right now, or I'm leaving."

Sabine held up her hands in surrender. "Okay. I'll tell you. Please, just hear me out."

Olivia waited.

"I think Ken did something to Asher's computer. I don't know. Ken's about as computer literate as I am. Asher got so mad. And Ken didn't back down. Asher threw a vase at him. I ran outside and called you."

"And?"

"And that's it. I swear on my life," Sabine said, crossing her heart like a schoolgirl.

Olivia held her hand out for her phone. "I'm texting Brian." When Sabine hesitated, she said, "I contact Brian, or I get in my car and leave. What's it going to be?"

Sabine reluctantly handed over the phone. Olivia dialed Brian's number. He answered on the first ring.

"I'm at the Ridgelands."

"Why?" Brian asked, his tone irritated. "Haven't we had enough—"

Olivia interrupted. "Ken and Asher are fighting. Sabine called me and is insisting that we don't call the police."

"Are you telling me to call the police?" Brian said, picking up on Olivia's cue.

You brilliant, lovely man. "That's exactly what I'm trying to tell you."

"I'll call on my way," Brian said. "Just stay away from them until I get there."

Olivia tucked her phone in her back pocket.

"Let's go in," Olivia said. Sabine hesitated. Olivia ignored her and headed toward the house, Sabine on her heels. As she approached the wide-open front door, the heavy silence enveloped her. The house was too quiet. Olivia's heart pounded as though it were about to burst. Taking a deep breath, she stepped into the hallway and crept toward the kitchen. All the curtains had been drawn, casting the interior of the house into a foreboding gloom. She sensed Sabine slip away, but wasn't sure where she went. As Olivia stood still waiting for her eyes to adjust, she heard voices.

"What, are you going to strangle me like you did Mikala?" Olivia recognized Ken's voice.

"She had it coming."

The voice that answered sounded like Asher, but the force of it, the pitch and cadence was wrong somehow. And why would Asher say his girlfriend deserved to be murdered? She inched closer to the kitchen.

"I have to admit, Asher, when the FBI told me that you have been under investigation for four years for cybercrimes, I was skeptical. But then an agent approached me, after the blackmail scheme came to light and made me an offer I couldn't refuse."

"What did you put on my computer?" Asher asked, his voice full of hatred.

"I have no idea," Ken said. "Something to capture and transfer activity, passwords and the like. It was easy. I'm pretty sure I just gave the FBI all the evidence of your crimes, your passwords, the bank accounts, the web of lies, all of it has been turned over. You're done."

Olivia forced herself to calm her breath.

She didn't see the picture frame on the wall as it snagged on her sweater. She didn't mean for it to come crashing down in a cascade of splintering glass. Olivia covered her head with her arms, not seeing Asher, who grabbed her arm with surprising strength, dragged her into the living room and pushed her on the floor, where she landed with a thud, her shoulder hitting the corner of a massive bookcase. Shooting pain rocketed through her shoulder and down her arm, so intense she cried out.

"What are you doing here, Olivia?"

For a few seconds, stars danced in Olivia's eyes, white bits of light. She clenched them shut and focused on her breathing.

"Get over it, Olivia. We both know that didn't hurt."

Olivia opened her eyes and looked at Asher. He stood in front of the living-room window, a gun in hand. At the moment, it was trained on Ken, who had sat down on the sofa. Ken held his hands up. "Just don't shoot anyone, Asher. So what if I gave your computer to the FBI. It's going to take them a while to figure out how to get past your firewall – whatever. It would be stupid to shoot us. Just run."

"Don't tell me what to do," Asher said, his voice calm, as though he hadn't a care in the world. "You've got no idea what you've put yourself into."

"You're a two-bit punk who's wet behind the ears. Don't presume to lecture—"

"I don't work alone, *Dad*." Asher's voice was venomous. "I know I can get away. Right now. And be sipping a drink with an umbrella on a beach by this time tomorrow night. But you won't be safe now. You know that, right? They'll come for you. And they'll kill you. Probably torture you first."

The color washed out of Ken Ridgeland's face.

"Don't believe him," Olivia said.

"Shut up, Olivia," Asher said. "You've no standing here."

"I've got more criminal experience than both of you."

"My son's a cybercriminal. He's been wanted by the FBI for years. Because of his stupidity, I've got leverage for my own legal issues." Ken smirked at Asher. "Does that about sum it up?"

"I don't believe you," Olivia lied, her eyes darting between Asher and Ken. The tension between them was palpable.

Ken continued.

"What happened, Asher?" Ken continued. "Did Mikala find out about your scheme and want a piece of the action?"

"She wanted half," Asher said, as though he were discussing the weather. "If she hadn't been screwing you, I would have shared with her. If she'd been faithful to me, I wouldn't have had to kill her. But she was a slut. So she had to die, and you will go to prison for that."

"I won't," Ken said. "I'm going to testify against you at trial."

"And what are you going to tell them? You're the one who received the money from Mikala's account. You're the one whose tie was used to strangle her. What can you possibly tell them about me?"

Ken smirked. "The FBI found the dealer who sold you roofies. There's other evidence too, but they wouldn't tell me what it is. There are cameras all over Mikala's building."

Ken's words hit home. Fear flashed in Asher's eyes.

"I didn't believe it at first. My son, my gullible mama's boy son, a cybercriminal who's stolen millions of dollars from banks and businesses."

Olivia felt her throat go dry as Ken turned to face her. "Can you believe that, Olivia? Asher, a brilliant criminal mastermind?

Well, not anymore. His girlfriend tried to blackmail him. When he wouldn't share, she went to the FBI."

"She didn't go to the FBI."

"Yes, she did. How do you think they found me? Mikala told them about our little scheme. She told the whole story in exchange for a walk, complete immunity, plus a reward. Asher is part of a gang of international hackers. He steals from banks and treasuries. Hard to believe my stupid son is wanted by Interpol, the FBI, the CIA, Scotland Yard, basically every law enforcement agency in the industrialized world."

Olivia's mind reeled, as she took it all in.

Asher pointed the gun at his father and released the safety.

Stalling for time, Olivia said, "Why did you hire Brian? I don't understand."

"Because he's connected. He could keep me informed about the investigation, make sure all the evidence I planted was being processed."

"You can still get away. Go. Get out of here," Olivia pleaded.

"No. I have to see this through." Asher pointed the gun at his father. "He can't testify if he's dead."

"But you're not a murderer," Olivia said, desperately trying to stall for time.

Asher sighed. "Yes, I am. Killing Mikala was one of the most difficult things I've ever done, but now that first one is under my belt, I won't have any trouble killing my father. Or you, for that matter."

"You're not going to kill me," Olivia said, with more confidence than she felt. *Keep him talking.* She cast her mind back to the scant information Brian had given her. "How did you drug yourself with Rohypnol? You could have died."

"I practiced, Olivia. I dosed myself until I knew just how much I could take. It was rather scientific."

"Don't be so pleased with yourself," Olivia said. "You're clearly not getting away with this. Even if you kill us both and manage to run away – which is highly unlikely – you think Brian will let this go? He'll hunt you to the ends of the earth. You'll be the prey, and he'll be the predator."

"I don't think so. I've got more money than him, and he will never find me."

"Asher, wait. Please."

"No. No waiting." Asher pointed at Ken. "Good bye, Father."

Ken charged. He bent over and ran toward Asher, throwing himself on his son with all his might. Both men crashed into the wall, but Ken was bigger, and by brute force, he pinned Asher down until he was straddling his chest, while Asher wriggled underneath him, until Ken pinned his arms still with his knees. Olivia watched, helpless, as Ken wrapped his hands around Asher's throat and started to throttle him.

"Ken, don't. You'll kill him. You'll spend the rest of your life in jail," Olivia shouted. "Think about what you're doing."

He ignored her.

Next to her, Olivia sensed Sabine before she saw her, standing in the doorway, a resolute look in her eyes, as she pointed a gun at Ken. "Look at me, Ken," Sabine hissed.

Something in the tone of her voice caught her husband's attention. Ken turned to face her. When he saw the gun, he smirked. "You're not going to shoot me."

Ken hoisted Asher, who was now gasping for breath, to his feet. "I'm going to give you the beating I should have given you years ago."

"Mommy," Asher cried, his voice high and shrill like a child's. "Make him stop."

Sabine fired.

Chaos ensued.

Chapter 31

Olivia couldn't hear. She slunk to the ground, unable to stand or move, her eyes squeezed shut, her arms wrapped around her knees, as what seemed like a million FBI agents swarmed the house. She watched as Ken was taken away in an ambulance. Sabine's bullet had hit him in the knee. From what she could sense, Ken would survive. The FBI took Asher away in handcuffs. Four agents were circling Sabine, who had dropped the gun, when an agent who looked too fresh-faced and young to work for the FBI approached Olivia. He mouthed his name, but she couldn't make out his words. He had a no-nonsense way about him. Olivia allowed him to help her off the ground and lead her outside, where she saw Brian. When he saw her come out of the house he ran to her as though he were going to wrap his arms around her, but came to a skidding stop when he noticed the look of pain on her face and the way she cradled her right arm with her left, trying to immobilize it.

"Are you hurt?" Away from the cacophony of the house, Olivia was just able to make out Brian's words.

"My shoulder," she said. "Asher pushed me into a bookcase."

Brian led her over to an ambulance and sat with Olivia while the paramedic put her arm in a sling and suggested she go to the hospital immediately. "Your shoulder is dislocated." The young man turned to Brian. "Can you take her to the emergency room?"

"We'll go right now," Brian said.

Olivia felt numb, as though she were underwater and couldn't put her thoughts together. She rambled about Asher being part of an international hacking ring, wanted by Interpol, the CIA, Scotland Yard, and everyone else. Brian just listened. He didn't ask questions, didn't make her explain anything, he just let her be.

Chapter 32

Olivia ended up being admitted to the hospital. She needed to have anesthesia in order for her shoulder to be reset. At 3:30 a.m., a nurse found Brian asleep in the chair next to Olivia's bed. She gently shook him awake and asked that he follow her out into the corridor. She was in her fifties, with thick blond hair streaked with gray, and eyes that had seen too much trauma and suffering. She had a knowing look in her eyes that all nurses had.

"Mr. Vickery? I hope you don't think me too forward, but in my professional opinion you should really go home, get some sleep, change your clothes, and come back tomorrow refreshed and ready to take Ms. Sinclair home. She's going to need your support for the seventy-two hours after her surgery. You being tired because you didn't want to leave her side isn't going to do you any good. Go home. I'll call you the minute anything happens."

She was right. In the end, Brian capitulated. Once he was home, he fell into bed and didn't wake up until his phone rang at 9:15 the next morning.

"Mr. Vickery? Mrs. Sinclair is being prepped for surgery. Come down whenever you're ready. Go to the outpatient surgical center. I'll have a pass waiting for you."

"Thank you," Brian said.

He'd just showered and made himself a cup of coffee when there was a knock on the door. Dennis Culligan. Shaven, shorn, dressed in a suit and tie.

"Sorry, Agent Culligan. My girlfriend just had surgery, and I'm about to go get her."

"I know. I just wanted to talk to you for a minute. I'll need to take her statement, but I can put that off for a day or two." He hesitated. "Can I come in?"

Brian stepped aside. "Coffee?"

"No, thanks. Listen, Vickery, you did us a solid not meddling in our investigation. I feel like I owe you a bit of an explanation."

"About Asher Ridgeland?"

"I've been chasing him for years. He's got many aliases; he's stolen millions of dollars. And he's involved with some horrible people."

"What horrible people?"

"Russian mafia, mostly. Guys in his job don't usually make it to old bones, if you get my meaning. He was working for a Russian oligarch, hacking and stealing. But he kept a lot of the money for himself. He was a marked man."

"And now he'll go to prison."

"Prison won't protect him," Agent Culligan said. "We'll try to keep him separated, keep him safe. But he's in bed with some bad guys. I fear it won't end well."

Stoic now, Brian refilled his coffee.

"I just felt you were owed an explanation. Best if you don't involve yourself further."

"Got it," Brian said. "Now, let me show you out."

"Call me on my cell phone, and I'll come take Mrs. Sinclair's statement." Agent Culligan handed Brian his card.

"She's going to need a couple of days," Brian said.

"Understood." With a wave, Agent Culligan walked back to the tan Crown Vic parked across the street.

* * *

"How long had you known about Asher?" Olivia asked, her voice still groggy from surgery, as Brian drove up the twisty hill to their house.

"I had my suspicions," Brian said.

"So did I," Olivia said. "Asher told me he hired you, so you could keep him informed regarding the investigation."

"That's a very industrious way to take advantage of my trusting nature," Brian said.

"This isn't your fault, Brian. Asher lost his way a long time ago. Is he really involved with the Russian mob?"

"Looks like it," Brian said.

"I can't believe he almost got his father to take the fall for Mikala's murder. Quit worrying about me, Brian. I'm not worried about talking to Agent Culligan. It will be fine. And as much as I could cry over Asher's situation, I'm not going to. I'm numb. I'm ready to retire, walk away from it. God, I'm so tired."

As they approached the house, Brian said, "I have a surprise for you."

"What is it?"

"Something that we both will enjoy."

As they turned into the driveway, Olivia saw Denny sitting on the porch, holding Carly, rocking her in her arms. When she saw the car, she stood and walked to meet them.

"Denny!" Olivia turned to Brian. "You called her and asked her to come?"

"No," Brian said as he parked the car. "I called her and told her what's been happening. When I got to the part about Asher, she said she was on her way and hung up on me."

Denny had reached the car. She opened the passenger door and Olivia got out, grabbed her daughter, and pulled her close.

"Watch the baby, Mom."

"I'm so glad to see you," Olivia said. The words caught in her throat.

"I had no idea how dangerous things were, Mom. Brian told me everything that's happened. Asher Ridgeland an international criminal? Who would have thought."

"There's more, honey."

"About Asher?" Denny said.

"He confessed to killing his girlfriend."

Denny's eyes filled with tears. She wiped them with the back of her hand. "Right now, I'm just glad to see you. Can we talk about this later?"

"Yes, we can. How long are you staying?"

"Oh, I'm not leaving until this house is sold and I've got you two safely tucked away in Lake Tahoe." Denny handed Carly to Olivia, so she could help Brian carry in her luggage. When Brian met her eyes, Olivia mouthed, *Thank you.*

I love you, Brian mouthed back.

Olivia pressed her nose into Carly's soft downy hair and felt the stress of the past few days fade away. The release of it took her breath away. Her eyes filled with tears, and she let them flow. The baby stirred in her arms. For now, all she wanted to do was hold her granddaughter and recover. After that, she and Brian would worry about packing and moving. And buying a fishing boat.

Chapter 33

The foghorn sounded in the distance as Sharon and Ellie stood on the beach near the dock in Sausalito. The morning was still, the light flat, and the water smooth as glass. Sharon's face had turned an alarming shade of gray and – unless Ellie's eyes deceived her – her knees were a bit wobbly. Neither one of them spoke as they wriggled into the wetsuits that Ellie had borrowed from her little brother, a surfing fanatic who spent every free minute at the beach, surfing in the frigid Pacific Ocean.

"You sure you're up for this?" Ellie asked. She wouldn't mind if Sharon backed out.

"Honestly, I'm not sure of anything." Sharon pulled the wetsuit over her lean body and zipped it resolutely. "But I'm going to do this."

"Okay. Don't mean to sound bossy, but I think we should face each other and swim side stroke. That's the best way I can make sure you're safe." Ellie was singularly uncomfortable giving orders to Sharon. "If that's okay," she added, so as not to sound bossy.

"You can be as bossy as you want, El. I owe you big time for this one. So yes, we'll swim side stroke. If I pass out, I'm counting on you to get me to shore." Sharon gave Ellie a smile that didn't quite reach her eyes.

The two women stood on the shore, staring past the docks. Ellie didn't have to look at Sharon to know her eyes were riveted to the buoy just past the last berth. "That's the spot, right?"

"Yep."

Ellie followed Sharon as she walked into the water until she was waist-deep, then dove under. Ellie followed. The water was cold for a few seconds, until the wetsuit did its job. As long as Ellie kept her head above water, she was fine. Soon she caught up with Sharon, who was treading water, waiting for her. Both of them were physically fit and strong swimmers. They side-stroked toward the buoy, as Ellie suggested. Sharon's eyes were riveted on Ellie.

"I've got ya," Ellie reassured her.

"I know. I wouldn't be doing this, if it weren't for you. None of this would have happened if we had gone to the boat together. I shouldn't have come here without backup. I didn't follow policy and set a bad example for you, Ellie. I'm sorry for all the grief this has caused you. I know you've had a difficult time."

"I'm fine. And it's over, right? I mean, here we are, with you in water."

The water clung to Sharon's eyelashes as she smiled at Ellie, the frantic, haunted look that had alarmed Ellie over the past months diminishing ever so slightly.

As they approached the buoy, Sharon said, "I know that people talk, especially the boy cliques at the SFPD. They gossip like a sewing circle." They stopped and treaded water.

"*Boy cliques?* I like that," Ellie said.

"Don't be afraid to stand up for yourself. If anyone gives you any trouble, tell them to stay in their own lane and keep their nose out of your business. If they push back, and believe me, they will, don't back down." Sharon smiled. "Pro tip for dealing with male colleagues. You can quote me on that." When she dunked under water, Ellie started to panic, until Sharon resurfaced, her blond hair slicked back. "This actually feels good."

246

In tandem, they turned to face the shore. Two figures stood on the beach, watching them from a distance.

"Is that Olivia and Brian?" Ellie asked.

"It is. I hope you don't mind. But I thought Brian should be here."

"Are you glad you did this? Do you think it helped?"

Sharon splashed water at Ellie. "Race you back?" And she took off swimming.

When they arrived back at the shore, Brian and Olivia were waiting for them, each holding a thick beach towel.

Once Ellie and Sharon slipped out of their wetsuits and dressed in their warm clothes, Brian poured them each a large cup of coffee from a Thermos. "There's a little Irish in there. No offense, but you both look like you could use it."

Sharon turned toward Ellie. "Do you realize how terrified I was out there?"

"Could have fooled me," Ellie said.

"Since I'm among friends," Sharon said, "I'm going on the record saying that I will never, and I mean *never*, do that again."

"I take it the demons are sufficiently slayed?" Brian asked.

"I'm here, at the beach. I swam out to that menacing buoy and survived to tell the tale. My heart's not pounding and I'm not vomiting. So, yea, I'll clock that up as a win."

"I'll drink to that," Ellie said, holding up her coffee.

"I'm starving," Brian said. "Can I buy you two breakfast at the Lighthouse Café? I hear the waffles are the best."

When they all headed toward the parking lot, Brian held Ellie back so Olivia and Sharon could walk ahead of them.

"Let's leave them to it," Brian said. "They need to talk."

Ellie put her hands in her pockets, as she turned to face the bay. "You know what, Vickery? You're a good partner. You and Sharon, gold standard for sure."

"Having the right partner makes the job a whole lot better," Brian said. "But when Sharon and I first were forced together

– the brass at the SFPD puts the outliers together – we didn't get on well."

"Really?"

"Really. But we grew close, came to trust each other."

"Are you telling me I should give Lambada a chance?"

"I'm telling you that I think you are both good cops who have different strengths that have the potential to be strong together." As if reading Ellie's mind, Brian continued. "His ego is something else. Don't take it too seriously."

"Thanks, Brian."

"I think we're okay to join them." Brian nodded at the parking lot, where Olivia and Sharon were hugging each other.

"Looks like a happy ending."

"Sure does," Brian said.

Epilogue

Olivia and Lauren sat in Adirondack chairs on Olivia's back deck. The fire crackled in the pit, piled high with logs. The night sky, cold and vast and full of stars, shone above them. Denny and Carly had headed up to bed while Brian bustled inside the kitchen. They were bundled for the cold, their bellies full from their Thanksgiving feast. Neither of them spoke. The silence between them was comfortable, that of old friends, who had been together through life's joys and troubles.

The events with Ava Bledsoe had changed Lauren. Gone were the long curls and the flowy dresses, replaced now with a short edgy haircut, jeans and boots. She'd started wearing glasses, heavy-looking with dark rims. Olivia reasoned that Lauren's new look was a protective mechanism, a way to blend in with the crowd, remain anonymous. Her dear friend had battened down the emotional hatches.

"I had no idea Brian was so domestic."

"He's changed since we moved here," Olivia said. "He's become passionate about cooking."

"That's your thing, I thought," Lauren said.

"I've changed too."

"Understandable. Mark Bledsoe was bad enough, but Asher

Ridgeland . . . I can't even wrap my mind around that. It's funny how there hasn't been much coverage in the papers about Asher. You think catching an international cybercriminal would warrant some serious press."

"They are trying to find the rest of his gang, I think," Olivia said.

"I'm just glad we're all away from it," Lauren said.

Olivia's eyes swept over Lauren. Her voice laced with concern, she asked, "How are you doing, Lauren? Really?"

"I'm struggling, Liv. Can't shake what happened with Ava. I'll never forget the look in Mark Bledsoe's eyes— I've never been scared of anything. Now I'm scared of my own shadow. But that night – I haven't had a good night's sleep since then. Sleeping pills don't help. I'm constantly looking over my shoulder, and I am terrified to go out after dark." The place I stayed in France was heaven on earth. Isolated, but within walking distance of a bakery, an old church, and a beautiful town square. It was as safe as could be. No one ever recognized me. Yet by the time the sun went down, my house was locked down like a fortress, and I was holed up in my room, jumping at the slightest sound. The idea of going out at night terrifies me. Hand shaking, Lauren took off her glasses and dabbed her eyes."

Olivia waited, knowing her friend had more to say. "I'm moving to England. I'm going to travel for a while, and maybe buy a secluded cottage in a quaint village. But I need to get away, far away. If I stay in one place for too long, I panic. I am desperate to fix myself, but I have no idea how."

"I'm sorry, Lauren."

"There's no need for apologies, Olivia. I brought this on. I never should have allowed you to get involved with Ava, especially before you were set to retire. I'll have to live with that." Lauren grabbed Olivia's hand and squeezed it. "I'll miss you."

"It isn't forever," Lauren said. "Just for now."

Lauren grabbed her hand and squeezed it.

Olivia saw Brian through the window, carrying a tray with

dessert. She let go of Lauren's hand and stood up to help him. "Here's Brian."

Lauren stood. "Thanks, Brian. You're spoiling us."

"Glad to do it."

Soon the three of them were sitting together around the fire, with Lauren regaling Brian with stories of her antics from the old days. They laughed and cried and reminisced about old times. Later, when Olivia and Brian finally snuggled under the duvet, Brian said, "Is she going to be all right?"

"I think so." The day had been long and busy. Lauren, Denny, Carly, and Olivia had spent time playing games and walking on the trails that were dusted with snow, while Brian worked in the kitchen. Exhausted and heart full, Olivia switched off the bedside lamp. Brian scooted close to her, melding with her body like spoons in a drawer, while the wind whipped outside. She had so much to be grateful for. She and Brian were together. Those they loved were safe, and their entire future lay before them, like a promise.

The Betrayal

Attorney Olivia Sinclair is shocked when she receives an anonymous video showing her husband Richard sleeping with someone else. After years of handling other people's divorces, she thought she could recognise a marriage in trouble.

She angrily throws Richard out of the home they share. But days later she's arrested – for the murder of his mistress.

Olivia knows she's innocent but, with all the evidence pointing at her and an obvious motive, she must find the real killer to clear her name.

She may be used to dealing with messy divorces, but this one will be her most difficult case yet. Olivia's husband has already betrayed her – but would he set her up for murder?

Keep reading for an extract from *The Betrayal* . . .

Chapter 1

Friday, October 10

Olivia Sinclair's life fell apart on the day of her sixty-second birthday. The morning started with promise. She and Richard lay entangled in the sheets, their limbs intertwined and glistening with sweat. Olivia marveled – as she often did – at the way their passion had withstood decades of marriage. Somehow, she and Richard had managed to keep passion alive.

"Happy birthday, beautiful." Richard ran his fingers along her side, taking his time at the curve of her hip. "I've got something for you."

Olivia watched her husband, his body still athletic and strong as he moved to the dresser and opened the top drawer. When he turned to face her, he held a familiar blue Tiffany box.

"This is for you, for your birthday and your retirement, a celebration of your accomplishments, if you will. I don't tell you this enough, but I'm proud of you, Liv." Richard always gave Olivia jewelry from Tiffany's at birthdays and Christmas. This year's gift was a platinum necklace, the pendant an antique skeleton key studded with diamonds.

"It's beautiful," Olivia said. She held up the platinum key to the morning light, the sunbeams making the diamonds dazzle.

Richard took it from her. "Let me help you put that on." He hooked the clasp and kissed the back of her neck. "When do you and Claire sign your paperwork?"

"She's coming in today. I'm going to ask for all the changes you suggested. Assuming she agrees, we'll wrap things up.

"She's got the capital?"

"She does. I think she's probably borrowing the money, but she'll be fine."

Richard ran his fingers through Olivia's thick hair. "I hear she's a go-getter. Are you okay with walking away from all that success, the notoriety?"

"Notoriety? That's your department. You're the television legal guru. I just help beleaguered women get their fair share."

Richard laughed.

"At least we can travel now, or at least I can come with you when you go away for weeks on end for depositions and trials," Olivia said.

"That's great, honey."

"We need to talk about your plans, Richard. Do you have any idea when you might walk away from Rincon Sinclair?"

Richard turned to Olivia. "I'm not ready, Liv. Not now. Maybe a year or two?"

"That long?"

"We'll talk about it later, okay?"

Olivia recognized this ploy. *We'll talk about it later* meant they wouldn't talk about it again until Richard was good and ready. She was about to push him, wrangle a commitment to retire out of him, when the alarm by his side of the bed started blaring the morning news.

"You shower first. I'll make the coffee." Richard tied his bathrobe around his waist and turned off the radio. "Are you sure you don't mind cooking tonight? It's your birthday."

"I'm sure," Olivia said. "I want to cook dinner for my family."

"Maybe you can strike a truce with our son-in-law," Richard said.

Olivia held her hand over her heart. "I swear, I'll try."

As she headed into the shower, she thought of the promise of freedom, and the time she would have to garden, travel with Richard, and tackle her toppling To-Be-Read pile of books.

After Richard left, she took her time over the morning paper and was going over her calendar when the front door opened and Denny called out, "Hello? Anyone here?"

"In the kitchen," Olivia said.

Her daughter stepped into the kitchen, a sweet smile on her face, her golden hair cascading around her shoulders, a huge bouquet of flowers in her hand.

"Happy birthday, Mom." Denny kissed Olivia's cheek before pouring herself a cup of coffee.

"Thanks, honey." Olivia watched her daughter over the rim of her cup, trying to ignore the dark circles under Denny's eyes and the tight lines around her mouth.

"How's David?"

Denny smiled to take the edge off her words. "Come on, Mom. We both know you don't care a bit about my husband. But he's fine, thank you very much."

She set her coffee cup on the table and pulled her hair back into a ponytail, a gesture that reminded Olivia of Denny when she was an outspoken, opinionated little girl. Richard and Denny would debate at the dinner table, Richard subtly teaching his daughter to argue like a pro. Olivia suspected that those arguments were Richard's attempt to get Denny interested in the law.

Olivia loved that irreverent spark in her daughter and had been dismayed to see it diminish when David Grayson came into her life. Now Denny watched what she said, and if David was around, she would cast anxious glances his way, worried – to Olivia's mind – that what she was doing would make David angry. Denny never argued, never expressed an opinion these days. That impulsive, no-filter child had married a man hell-bent on putting out her fire.

"Honestly, Mom, I don't mean to sound harsh, but I wish you

two could spend some time together. If you got to know David, you'd come to realize what a good man he is. You're just not used to his traditional values. You're a modern woman, Mom. I'm not."

Olivia longed to ask her daughter about her marriage, to make sure she was okay, but she was afraid that her inquiry would be seen as an intrusion, which would push Denny even further away, so she let it go. For now. "Honey, I'm never going to believe that women need to be told what to do by their husbands or boyfriends. Marriage should—"

"—be a partnership." Denny laughed as she finished the sentence. "You look nice. Court today?"

"Very tactfully done, Den. I see how you changed the subject. No court today. I'm meeting with Claire Montreaux about selling my practice."

"Somehow I can't see you retiring, Mom. Are you sure you're ready?"

Was she ready? Her small practice was nothing compared to Richard's illustrious career, but Olivia and Richard had planned it that way. Olivia's office was close to home, so she had been able to care for Denny, freeing up Richard whose relentless litigation schedule kept him away from home. While Denny was young, Olivia had attended her plays, piano recitals, and pageants. As Denny got older and became more independent, Olivia turned her attention to the vast sloping hillside behind her house, turning the wild grassy area into a terraced garden. She did all the backbreaking work herself and soon had fruit trees, a large plot dedicated to vegetables, and a vast picking garden, which kept Olivia and her friends in fresh flowers all summer long.

Olivia had spent a lot of time alone in her marriage. Even though she kept herself busy, she missed her husband and looked forward to spending more time with him, even if that time was spent traveling for his work.

"So to answer your question, yes, I'm ready. I can travel with your father now."

"I don't see Dad retiring anytime soon. He likes the limelight. I honestly don't think Dad would know what to do with himself if he retired."

And therein lies the problem.

Richard worked long hours and each week spent a night or two in their condo in the city, with its galley kitchen and an even smaller bathroom. Nestled on the top of California Street, the condo had a beautiful view of San Francisco, and since it was the first place they had purchased – mortgaging their souls after Richard passed the bar – they kept it out of sentimentality. That was thirty-two years ago. Olivia consoled herself with the knowledge that after all these years, despite him sometimes seeming married to his career, she and Richard still loved each other. *Thank goodness for that*, Olivia thought.

"I'm hoping I can get him to slow down a little bit. As for me, I'm happy in the garden. Maybe I'll take up painting or something." Olivia sipped her coffee. "Den, tell me the truth. Did your father plan a surprise party for me?"

"Of course not," Denny said. "You made it perfectly clear you absolutely didn't want one."

Olivia sighed with relief. She was looking forward to an intimate family gathering. Maybe tonight she would come to see her son-in-law in a new light. For Denny's sake she would try.

"Are you having your birthday lunch with Lauren today?"

"I am," Olivia said.

"Tell her I said hello. Maybe the three of us could meet for lunch sometime?"

"That would be great," Olivia said. "I know Lauren would love to see you." This wasn't the first time Denny had mentioned lunch with Olivia and Lauren, but despite half a dozen invitations, Denny always had some excuse.

"Are you sure you don't want me to bring anything besides the cake? It doesn't seem like much of a birthday with you slaving away in the kitchen."

"It's not slaving when you enjoy the labor. Anyway, I've got it all under control. Shopping's complete, most of the prep is already finished. I'll come home early and get the lasagna in the oven. Want to come and keep me company while I throw things together?"

"Can't. We're going to struggle to get here by 7:30 as it is. David's busy at work right now." Denny hoisted her purse onto her shoulder and kissed Olivia's cheek. "Love you."

Her conversation with Denny left her troubled. Olivia had meddled in Denny's life behind the scenes, hiring an investigator to follow Denny's husband. The investigator had reported back, worried that David had spotted him. Of course, Olivia had terminated the relationship, but it left her unsettled. If Denny knew what she had done, she'd feel so betrayed, and David wouldn't miss an opportunity to exploit Denny's anger. After all, Olivia had no concrete evidence that David was having an affair, but her years as a family law attorney had honed her intuition to a sharp edge. She knew a cheater when she saw one. David Grayson was a cheater.

"Love you, honey," Olivia said. She walked Denny to the door and stood for a moment in the cold October sun, watching the daughter she loved with her heart and soul drive away.

The Witness

HE SAW WHAT YOU DID . . .

Teenager **Ebby Engstrom** witnesses a murder – and then passes out. The next morning, he wakes in his bed with no memory of how he got there, and is told his mother was stabbed to death the previous night.

Thirty years later, the case has gone cold, with numerous suspects but no new clues – until Ebby starts having uncontrollable flashbacks to that night. As repressed memories surface, he questions his own role in the murder, leading to a dramatic confession and Ebby's arrest.

Family friend and attorney **Olivia Sinclair** is convinced of Ebby's innocence, but the only way to clear his name is to find the real killer herself. And it seems almost everyone connected to the Engstrom family had a reason to want Cynthia dead . . .

Acknowledgements

So many hands have touched *The Suspect* and have helped me turn this rough diamond into the book it is now. First and foremost, big thanks to Helen Williams, who helped me mold and shape and tweak this book from its inception to its completion. Her editorial suggestions were spot on. They not only improved the story, but they also helped me grow as a writer. Helena Newton's copyediting and fact checking caught the loose ends that needed attention. Audrey Linton kept all of us organized and moving forward. Conventional wisdom says you shouldn't judge a book by its cover, but I disagree with that ethos, especially regarding the Olivia Sinclair series. *The Betrayal*, *The Witness*, and *The Suspect* have captivating covers that portray the mood of the series brilliantly. Kudos to the entire team at HQ Digital. Your professionalism shines through in every published book.

My beta readers make the world go round. Angela Baxter, Gloria Rowland, Jennifer Young, and Gina Lackey Thompson read my book with tender consideration. Special shout out to Kim Laird, who has beta read all my books, and read this one twice.

The Sunday morning Zoom group, Marti Dumas, Samantha Downing, and Rebecca Vonier helped me through the intense scenes that are hard to write but so very important. Thanks, you three, for pushing me to make those parts of the book real and edgy.

Big thanks to my writer buddies Andie Newton, Jo Allen, Kris Waldherr, Kath McGurl, and Susan Buchanan for walking this crazy artsy road with me, for knowing what to say when I doubted myself, and for helping me keep my feet on the ground as I wrote.

Finally, a million thanks to my readers. When I sit down to a blank page and start writing a book, when I craft scenes, cut characters, and struggle to make my prose just right, I do so with you in mind. Thank you for spending your precious time with my stories. I truly appreciate you.

#ReaderLove

Dear Reader,

We hope you enjoyed reading this book. If you did, we'd be so appreciative if you left a review. It really helps us and the author to bring more books like this to you.

Here at HQ Digital we are dedicated to publishing fiction that will keep you turning the pages into the early hours. Don't want to miss a thing? To find out more about our books, promotions, discover exclusive content and enter competitions you can keep in touch in the following ways:

JOIN OUR COMMUNITY:

Sign up to our new email newsletter: http://smarturl.it/SignUpHQ

Read our new blog www.hqstories.co.uk

🐦 https://twitter.com/HQStories

f www.facebook.com/HQStories

BUDDING WRITER?

We're also looking for authors to join the HQ Digital family!
Find out more here:

https://www.hqstories.co.uk/want-to-write-for-us/

Thanks for reading, from the HQ Digital team